MW00641571

WAYNE STINNETT

RISING WARRIOR

A JESSE MCDERMITT NOVEL

◆ ◆ ◆ ◆

Caribbean Adventure Series
Volume 18

2020

Copyright © 2020
Published by DOWN ISLAND PRESS, LLC, 2020
Beaufort, SC

Copyright © 2020 by Wayne Stinnett

Library of Congress cataloging-in-publication Data
    Stinnett, Wayne
    Rising Warrior/Wayne Stinnett
    p. cm. - (A Jesse McDermitt novel)

ISBN: 978-1-7339351-8-0 (print)

Cover photograph by Surakit Sawangchit
Graphics by Wicked Good Book Covers
Edited by The Write Touch
Final Proofreading by Donna Rich
Interior Design by Ampersand Book Designs

This is a work of fiction. Names, characters, and incidents are either
the product of the author's imagination or are used fictitiously. Any
resemblance to actual persons, living or dead, businesses, companies,
events, or locales is entirely coincidental. Many real people are used
fictitiously in this work, with their permission. Most of the locations
herein are also fictional or are used fictitiously. However, the author
takes great pains to depict the location and description of the many
well-known islands, locales, beaches, reefs, bars, and restaurants
throughout the Florida Keys and the Caribbean to the best of his ability.

Dedicated to my grandchildren, Kira, Lexi, Emily, and Jack. May your lives be as full of adventure and love as Pappy's has been.

"If your work is deathwork, one weapon is not enough, just as a plumber would not answer an urgent service call with a single wrench."

–Dean Koontz

If you'd like to receive my newsletter,
please sign up on my website:

WWW.WAYNESTINNETT.COM.

Every two weeks, I'll bring you insights into my
private life and writing habits, with updates on
what I'm working on, special deals I hear about,
and new books by other authors that I'm reading.

The Charity Styles Caribbean Thriller Series

Merciless Charity
Ruthless Charity
Reckless Charity
Enduring Charity
Vigilant Charity

The Jesse McDermitt Caribbean Adventure Series

Fallen Out	*Rising Storm*
Fallen Palm	*Rising Fury*
Fallen Hunter	*Rising Force*
Fallen Pride	*Rising Charity*
Fallen Mangrove	*Rising Water*
Fallen King	*Rising Spirit*
Fallen Honor	*Rising Thunder*
Fallen Tide	*Rising Warrior*
Fallen Angel	*Rising Moon*
Fallen Hero	

THE GASPAR'S REVENGE SHIP'S STORE IS OPEN.

There, you can purchase all kinds of swag related to my books. You can find it at

WWW.GASPARS-REVENGE.COM

MAPS

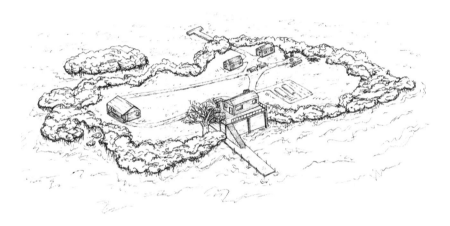

Jesse's Island

Southwest Florida

CHAPTER
ONE

September 1968
Collier County, Florida

T he two-lane road was dark and ran straight as an arrow through the swamp. The headlights from a lone pickup pierced the darkness, showing two elongated, yellow pools of light on the broken pavement.

The truck slowed, and the headlights splashed across a trailer on the corner as the truck turned off the main road and pointed toward the end of the abandoned trailer park.

No lights burned in any of the trailers' windows. The deteriorating hulks were mere shadows in the moonlight, some not sitting quite level, as the elements continued to take their toll on them.

The previous two summers had been dry, and farming had suffered greatly. Each was followed by the normal dry season—the winter months up north—and water levels dropped further. Most of the water had been diverted to the big sugar plantations to the east.

Many of the residents had simply given up, not having enough food or water to survive the harsh climate. The trailer park was a failed development, built to house migrant workers. It now lay abandoned in the swamp.

Finally, the summer storms did come, but by the spring of 1968, few people remained in the area. Hurricane Abby had made landfall just ninety miles to the north in early June, bringing much-needed rain to the parched southern half of the state. But the soil had been so dry for so long, and the storm had moved so quickly inland, that very little of the precious rainwater had seeped into the aquifer. It simply ran off, causing flash floods in many areas.

The sun had blazed for two weeks after Abby, turning Southwest Florida into a sauna, and baking the soil to a dry crust once again.

Abby had been a tease.

Then Tropical Storm Brenda landed just twenty miles to the south of Chokoloskee, bringing more rain to the arid soil, now rutted with dried-up runoff creeks that in no way resembled the regimented furrows of the small farms on the mainland.

And that was it.

A total of nearly twenty inches of rain fell in two short periods during early June, and nearly all of it had just run down to the Gulf.

For the rest of June, July, and on into August, the sun had beaten down without mercy, scorching the coast of Southwest Florida beyond endurance.

Wells dried up and more people left, until only the hardiest remained.

What nobody knew was that some of that rainwater hadn't run off. It had pooled around anything that stuck up out of the earth and then leached down alongside it, softening the soil. All through the summer, whenever the wind blew, if you looked closely at the base of a power pole, you might have seen that it was moving.

But nobody looked. Most had left, given up, beaten, and defeated.

It wasn't just the power poles, either. The water had seeped around concrete bridge abutments, fence posts, water towers, buildings, cracks in the roads, and anything else that was built into or on the ground.

Water was the great equalizer, and Southwest Florida was rife for disaster.

And then disaster came.

Not in the form of a massive hurricane, nor even a named storm, but in the guise of a very slow-moving tropical depression that arrived in late August. The storm had formed in the Gulf of Mexico and moved northeast toward the coast far to the north. It was broad, and rain bands reached the small communities to the south days before the storm made landfall.

When it had first reached the coast near Clearwater, it suddenly turned south and reemerged into the Gulf.

Tropical systems rarely moved southward and this one moved very slowly, not developing in strength. But its counterclockwise rotation brought heavy rain, wind gusts, and pounding surf to the south of its loosely organized center. The storm—later called Tropical Depression Eleven—made two more landfalls; one in Holmes Beach and another near Venice, before turning to the north and setting its sights on Jacksonville.

The eight-day heavy rain, dumping fifteen inches in some places, had been all that was needed. Water filled the now widened cracks again, and the wind gusts used the force of the water like a hydraulic ram, pushing out more soil from around the bases of everything manmade.

The combination of wind and rain brought down the power grid, but that was just the beginning. The storm surge and wind-driven waves as high as ten feet flooded out bridges and undermined roads, as well as water towers and other structures, which toppled in comedic slow motion. Many buildings were left damaged to the extent they might as well have been destroyed, as foundations settled, and walls cracked.

Many homes became uninhabitable, because the pilings they were built on sank at different rates, fracturing floors, walls, and ceilings.

So, the trailer park was empty.

All the former residents were gone, and the developer had been left with cracked roads, damaged trailers that were sinking into the mud, no electricity or water, and no means to make repairs or pull the trailers out to sell elsewhere. The wooden bridge to the island the trailer park was built on was barely passable, and impossible to cross while pulling a heavy trailer. After the storm, the developer had just pulled up stakes and left, leaving the trailers to the elements.

The same had happened to scores of other would-be settlers throughout Florida's history. The beautiful beaches and waterways were enticing, but the climate was too severe for all but the heartiest.

The truck moved slowly along the road. It was a Power Wagon built in the 1950s. It came to a stop, its brakes squeaking. The headlights went off and the engine stopped, then the single working brake light also flicked off. The driver opened the door and got out, looking all around as he waited for his eyes to adjust to the darkness.

He'd been to this little island many times in the past, but back then, he'd used his small bateau to cross over from the mainland. Or simply walked through the swamps and tidal creeks.

The storm that had destroyed the electrical grid and finally ruined the lives of so many in the area had only happened two weeks before, but it was doubtful much of the area would ever recover.

The man standing by the truck had visited this trailer park twice since the storm to confirm that it was abandoned, both times on a Monday, just like tonight. The trailer park was north of Goodland on the main road to Marco Island and just a little past the swing bridge.

Nobody was around and it was deathly quiet.

He was a slight man, gaunt, with a raw, bony face that was showing signs of a man half again his thirty-eight years. He and his kin were some of the hardier ones—people at one with the swamp. Once he was certain he was alone, he walked to the back of the truck and unhooked the chains, dropping the tailgate.

He was glad the island was once more abandoned. The man considered it his own and knew every inch of it. Or he had, before the trailers were brought over the bridge that connected the island to the main road.

There was a squeal from the bed of the Dodge.

"Well, hey there, Miss Twenty-four," the man said, as he moved some cinder blocks off a tarp. He threw the canvas to the front of the bed and looked down at his prize.

A girl lay tied hand and foot, moving a little against her bonds.

The man smacked her on the ass. "Girl, you'd best move a bit more'n that onced I git yo' purty little ass inside."

He grabbed the knots that bound her feet and dragged her roughly to the end of the truck's bed, causing the hem of her dress to ride up. Then he paused and pulled a silver flask from the back pocket of his dirty overalls. His eyes filled with lust just looking at her thighs.

The girl squirmed and looked up at him, panic in her eyes.

"Hang on there, Twenty-four. Imma need a snort before I tote'cha up them steps."

He took a long pull from the flask, then his lips pulled back as he closed his eyes tightly and grimaced. "Hoo wee, that's some good mash."

The girl tried to scream, but only a muffled sound came from the dirty rag that was tied securely in her mouth.

"Ya know," he said, as he put the flask away and leaned closer to her face, "it was a good bit of luck, I come up on ya when I did. We probly never woulda met, if'n you had'na had that flat tire on yo car."

Twenty-three girls before her had come out of whatever store or bar they'd been in, only to find their car had a flat. And twenty-three times, the wiry little man had "come up" on them. The last two times, he'd brought them to this same trailer, which had nothing but swamp for a backyard. With the gators so close at hand, he hadn't had to dig a hole.

He grabbed the girl by the rope at her wrists and pulled her closer to the end of the bed, then took her hair in one hand and forced her to her feet.

His eyes roamed up and down Twenty-four's body. Her dress was dirty from bouncing around in the back of the truck. One of the shoulder straps was torn, exposing her bra strap, and there was a ripped seam at the side of her waist from his rough handling. She'd realized her mistake minutes after she'd accepted his offer of a ride and gotten into the truck with him.

She was as tall as him, but at five foot six, that wasn't saying a whole lot. His wife, Bertha was taller. And after six kids in ten years of wedded bliss, she was nearly as big around.

"Ain't you a purty thang," he said, as he bent and lifted the woman easily to one shoulder. She was tall, but no heavier than a dressed-out doe carcass.

He carried her to the trailer and mounted the steps. He knew the door wouldn't be locked. He doubted anyone had been there since he'd brought Twenty-three way out to the trailer park a week ago. Crossing the creaky bridge was scary enough. Balancing the girl, he pulled open the door and stepped inside.

The man's need came more often of late. Other things had occupied his time and his mind when he was younger. It'd taken ten years for the first ten girls and only five years since then.

When he'd brought Twenty-three to the trailer park, he'd pulled a stained mattress from one of the back rooms and put it on the living room floor, pushing the rest of the tattered furniture out of the way.

He dropped Twenty-four on the mattress and stared down at her. The pretty summer dress she'd worn when she'd come out of the bar in Coral Gables, now torn and stained, had ridden up, exposing her right hip.

Moonlight streamed through a busted-out back window, falling across her legs and waist. "Yessiree," he said, as he looked down at her, "me and you gonna have us a fine time tonight."

The girl rolled onto her side and looked up at him with tears streaming from her eyes.

"Cryin' ain't gonna do ya no good," the man said, dropping to his knees. "But you jest go ahead and boo-hoo. I like it."

He reached for the neckline of the girl's dress, intending to rip it right down the middle seam. "Now, let's have a look at them goodies."

Suddenly, he heard the sound of a car turning the corner, its tires protesting on the rough road.

"Shit!"

Rising quickly, he pulled a snub-nosed revolver from his pocket and went to the door. He looked out, ready to make a run for it if he had to.

The truck was stolen, and nothing in it belonged to him. If it was the cops, he'd simply disappear into the swamp and be gone.

The man's family had lived in the area since his great-granddaddy had fought in the Civil War. They'd reproduced faster than most families, blurring the lines between kin and outsiders when it came to taking a mate. There just weren't that many people around in those days for a man to be choosy. He had four brothers and three sisters in the area, along with dozens of cousins, nieces, and nephews. All were a hard- scrabble bunch of cutthroats, thieves, and rumrunners. Before he'd taken her for his bride, Bertha had been his second cousin, once removed.

"Dammit," the man cursed under his breath. "What the hell's that fool woman doing out here?"

He shoved the pistol into his pocket and went outside.

The door to the 1964 Ford Galaxie opened and the springs creaked as his wife climbed out.

"C. Roy!" she yelled across the yard at him. "I know what you're up to in there."

"Bertie, what in the Sam Hill are you doing out here?"

She stomped toward him. "I come to snatch you bald-headed, C. Roy Blanc. That's what I'm a doin'."

"It ain't what yer thinkin', Bertie," C. Roy began, holding up both hands as his mind raced to come up with something. Anything. "Jest give me a minute to explain."

"You're a cheatin', lyin' son-of-a-bitch, C. Roy." Bertha stopped right in front of him. "I know you got another woman holed up in here."

She pushed past him and swung the door wide open. The girl on the mattress looked up at her, a newfound expression of hope on her face.

"It ain't what it looks like, Bertie! Honest to God."

Bertha Blanc turned to her husband, a fat finger pointing down at the girl. "What the hell is that?"

C. Roy's face fell and his shoulders slumped. There was no way he could talk his way out of this one. Bertie was way too smart, and he'd always known it. She'd finished junior high before the summer when C. Roy had knocked her up. She was supposed to be his third victim, but she'd kicked him in the balls and taken his knife. Then she'd forced him at knife point to have sex with her, which he found a lot less appealing than sex with him holding the knife.

Bertha Blanc had been a big girl all her life. And she'd had an attitude to match. She'd been fourteen when C. Roy had pulled that knife, but already a grown woman and a regular at several bars of ill repute. The fact that they shared the same last name didn't mean anything to her. Half the county did.

"You tole me you was done with all this ten years ago!" she yelled at C. Roy. "Once we started having babies, you promised no more."

Bertha stomped across the room and back, pacing and flapping her arms as she cursed him and his whole lineage.

"I read the papers, C. Roy. I know the "flat tire killer" has still been at it all these years. And he ain't never been caught. Now I know."

"It ain't cheatin'!" he yelled back, unable to come up with anything else.

"Just what in the fuck was you plannin' to do to that?" she roared, spittle flying from her mouth as she again pointed a finger at the young woman on the mattress.

C. Roy had never seen her so angry. "I wasn't—"

"Don't you bullshit me, mister," Bertha yelled. "Take her out back."

"Why?"

"So's you can finish what you brung her here for, ya simple-minded fool."

With that, Bertha bent and grabbed one of the woman's arms and pulled her to her feet, holding her upright with a firm hand on the woman's elbow.

"Go," she said, pointing to the back door.

C. Roy moved that way and pushed the door open, stepping out onto the small, raised back porch.

There was a scurrying sound and then a splash as a small gator or croc was startled. He couldn't tell which in the dark.

When he reached the bottom of the steps he turned around. Just as he was about to say something, Bertha pushed the woman off the steps.

With her ankles tied, the young brunette couldn't control her fall and she toppled into C. Roy, knocking him to the ground and landing on top of him.

The sudden closeness of all that firm flesh excited him.

"Untie her feet," Bertha ordered, as C. Roy struggled to get out from under the bound woman.

He did as he was told, then stood up, leaving the woman on the ground, hands still tied behind her back.

"Hand me that rope and bring her 'round to the side of the porch rail."

Again, C. Roy did as his wife demanded.

"Back her up, right here," Bertha said, grinning now.

When he did, Bertha looped the rope around her neck and tied it tightly to the rail, leaving her barely enough slack to breathe.

"Now hand me your gun," Bertha said.

"I ain't got no—"

"I done tole you not to lie to me, C. Roy! Now hand it over."

Once more, he did as his wife ordered. C. Roy was under no illusion. Even if he was inclined to shoot her, she'd get hold of him before he could get a second shot off, and a woman like her would take a lot of killin'.

Bertha looked behind her and saw an old lawn chair, which she sat down in very carefully in case it collapsed under her weight.

"What now?" C. Roy asked.

Bertha's eyes locked on his in the moonlight and she smiled. "Do her. Right now. Fuck that skinny little white trash whore while I watch you do it. Get it all outta your system. Right here and right now."

A slow realization came to C. Roy's alcohol-soaked brain. An instant fantasy developed in his mind. With Bertie's help he could continue what he'd been doing since he'd left the army after Korea. Young girls would be even more inclined to accept his offer of a ride with his wife right beside him.

His offer of a ride had been turned down ten times as often as it was accepted. He'd let the air out of many a tire, only to have the woman he'd followed decline the ride and go back inside to call someone. With Bertie along, he was bound to be more successful.

He'd learned in Korea that he liked killing. He'd killed some people who weren't soldiers and enjoyed the feeling of power it gave him. Bertha had killed a man before, he knew that. But it'd been in self-defense. Not like this.

Had she enjoyed it just the same? The idea excited him more.

He began to paw and tear at the woman's clothes, ripping her dress open to the waist and tearing her bra and underwear loose. Finally, he unzipped his fly and moved closer to the girl. His excitement was fueled by the look of terror in her eyes.

It wasn't gentle. He started rough and only got rougher as muffled screams escaped the gag with each thrust of his hips. He grabbed the lower rail for leverage, his face just inches in front of and slightly below hers, as Bertha urged him on, shouting at him to go faster and harder.

He did. His mouth twisted into a grotesque, lustful grin as he grunted with each thrust. His eyes burned with rage as he looked up at the girl's tear-filled eyes, just inches above his own.

C. Roy felt it building in his loins. He was just seconds from release when a loud boom split the humid night air.

Blood and parts of the woman's brains hit him in the face, and he stumbled back, spitting, and wiping his eyes.

"You crazy bitch!" he shouted at his wife, as he wiped more goop from his eyes.

Bertie stood above Twenty-four's corpse, the gun barrel still smoking above where the top of the pretty young woman's head used to be. The body now dangled by the rope around its neck. Blood, brain tissue, and skull fragments now stained the shoulders of her pretty white dress. The oozing mass dripped from her breasts.

"You just remember this, next time you wanna get yo' pecker wet."

Bertha untied the rope holding the corpse and it collapsed to the ground.

"Roll that thing over by the water," she said. "Let's get out of here."

After pushing the body out into the swamp, the husband and wife got into separate vehicles. C. Roy followed Bertha to a sulfur pit road, where he abandoned the truck and got in with her. The whole ride home, he wondered if she'd been as thrilled at the killing as he was.

The fact that he didn't finish didn't matter a whole lot. To him, it was all about the control and the actual moment he ended a life. Sometimes it was after he finished, and sometimes it was before.

But Bertie had stolen that control from him, too.

Once home, they went inside. The house wasn't much to speak of, just five rooms under a tin roof, and set far back in the swamp. But it had been built from sturdy Dade County pine by C. Roy's grandfather way back in 1903 and it sat on five hundred dry acres that were owned free and clear. Dry ground was hard to find.

It was late and the younger kids were in bed. But the two oldest, Jubal and Marley, were still up, watching TV. They looked up as their parents walked in.

"Where ya been, Momma?" the girl asked.

"Hadda drag Pop's sorry ass outta the bar again," Jubal said to his sister.

Bertha smacked the thirteen-year-old in the head. "Watch yer mouth, boy. His sorry ass weren't in no bar."

Jubal turned suddenly, the fire of puberty bringing defiance to his eyes. Then he saw the blood.

"What happened, Pop?"

"Y'all git to bed," C. Roy ordered.

The two looked up at their mother, but she put a hand up. "They can stay up a bit longer," she said, then turned toward C. Roy. "Want me to heat up some leftovers while you get cleaned up? There's still water in the tub."

"What's on the stove?" C. Roy asked.

"We had spicy gator steaks."

"Yeah," he said, puffing up a little. "I think I'd like that a lot."

C. Roy strutted toward the back of the house, full of himself once more. He got his other pair of overalls from the bedroom closet, then went into the single bathroom. He stripped down and eased himself into the tub's nearly cold, mostly dirty water. He scrubbed the blood off as best he could, dressed, and returned to the living room.

Bertie saw him and motioned toward his Sears and Roebuck lounge chair.

She might let the damned kids get away with shit, he thought. But she knew that C. Roy Blanc was a deadly man. She knew her place. She was gonna serve him food, and later he'd serve himself up some of what he hadn't finished. *Yeah*, he thought, *I'll show ya who wears the britches, bitch.*

The TV was tuned to the only channel they could get from the antenna mounted high above the house, the NBC station up in Tampa.

Dean Martin and his Golddiggers.

The sound was turned way down, but it didn't matter to C. Roy and he wasn't interested in Dean Martin. He had to admit, the man did have the perfect life. Sit down and tell a joke or sing a song and have a dozen pretty girls hanging all over him, looking at him with puppy eyes.

He watched as the Golddiggers, all dressed in short skirts, stepped up onto the bleachers Dean was sitting on and arranged themselves all around him, being sure to show a lot of leg.

C. Roy was mesmerized.

"Here," Bertha said, handing him a plate, and interrupting his fantasy.

He sniffed it. "Smells like almonds."

"Yeah, well, I thought you might like it with some crushed almonds sprinkled on, to stifle them hot peppers. Jubal was complainin' it was too hot. Go on, you earned it."

Too hot? C. Roy thought, looking over at his oldest son. *The boy's a panty-waist and ain't never gonna 'mount to shit.*

Balancing the plate on his knees, C. Roy dug in with his knife and fork, cutting out a big bite of the gator tail steak. It was a little pink in the middle, just the way he liked it, and the peppers sure gave it some fire. Bertie must have toasted the almonds or something. They tasted kind of like lye soap.

C. Roy didn't care. He swallowed and began to cut another piece. Then his knees began to tremble as he felt a twisting pain in his gut.

"Marley," Bertha said, taking the knife and fork from C. Roy's hands, as they, too, began to shake uncontrollably. "I want you to pay close account here. You too, Jubal."

Both kids turned to look at C. Roy. His plate fell to the floor as his body began to spasm uncontrollably.

"Marley, don't you ever let a man hit ya or cheat on ya. If he does, kill his ass, and find you another one. And Jubal, this sorry fucker ya see before ya? He's you if ya ever cheat on yer woman. You two unnerstan' what I'm a sayin'?"

Both nodded as bubbly pink foam dribbled from C. Roy's mouth.

Bertha bent close to her husband's face and spat on him. "You was a cheater when I met yer lazy ass, and you was a cheater all this time, but ya ain't gonna cheat no more, C. Roy. I done poisoned yo sorry ass."

C. Roy's body jerked twice more, then fell limp, eyes vacant, pink froth at the corner of his mouth.

Bertha looked over at her oldest son. "Go dig a hole, Jubal."

CHAPTER TWO

After the rain stopped, the heat and humidity became oppressive, as it always did. But I savored it. Some prefer milder climates or to stay indoors in air-conditioned comfort when it gets hot. But that's not how the human animal was intended to live.

We evolved from lesser creatures who figured out how to endure the elements. In many harsh environments, only the strongest survived and contributed their DNA to the gene pool. The advent of electricity and conditioned air in the home happened a mere instant ago in the evolutionary timeline of man. And in that instant, mankind had made itself vulnerable. There were now people living in South Florida who couldn't survive outdoors for two days.

I'd grown up living with my grandparents, not five miles from where I was now. Mam and Pap didn't have air-conditioning in their home. Not because they couldn't afford it; they just didn't need it. Pap was an architect and he'd designed his home to take advantage of the cooling Gulf breezes in summer.

I couldn't remember ever being hot as a kid and later, as a Marine, we'd trained in every clime and place, just as our hymn said. At the time, it was thought that the next big land battle would be in Russia, so we'd trained a lot in cold weather.

And that was the primary reason I lived in the Florida Keys. When I retired from the Corps after twenty years, I never wanted to see ice and snow again.

There had already been a lot of rain, and thunderheads could be seen building to the south. The air was loaded with moisture. But for the time being, it was clear, hot, and humid on the upper Caloosahatchee River. The perfect day. At least in my book.

Salt air isn't thin; it sticks to your skin and the heaviness pushes down on you like a pressure cooker, making the air feel even hotter. It was a labor just to draw the humid air into your lungs and expel it.

There was a slight stirring to the super-heated air around me. Nothing you could call a breeze, and certainly not wind. Just the feeblest attempt at movement; perhaps less than a person's skin would feel at a slow walk in dead air.

"South Florida ain't for sissies," my old friend Billy Rainwater used to say. "It's the last place a man could truly live."

I know it made *me* feel alive.

It's the nature of the beast in South Florida in late August. You either got used to it or you didn't. Those who didn't led a shut-in life, venturing out only to get into their SUV or minivan. They used remote start, so it would already be cooled off before they got in. Or they went back up north to what they deemed a more hospitable climate.

Personally, I'd take the near-triple digit temperature and humidity numbers, along with the sweat, over the below-freezing and windchill factors, with the accompanying shivers of a northern winter.

Any day of the week, and twice on Tuesday.

Stripped down to nothing but a pair of khaki cargo shorts—which had definitely seen better days—I continued my work. I wore a mask to keep the dust out of my eyes and nose. Not some high-tech respirator thing, but an old M1A1 gas mask, which was irritatingly uncomfortable and hot. Pulling air through its filters doubled the required effort, but those filters could stop CS or mustard gas, so paint dust was nothing.

I'd been working since dawn, stopping only to guzzle a bottle of water every fifteen minutes or so. Sweat poured from my body, my hair was matted to the back of my neck, and my Dockers were long since drenched and sagging low on my hips.

The sander was loud and the dust heavy, sticking to my sweaty body like a wetsuit. I could feel the vibration all the way into my shoulders as I moved it back and forth across the surface in long, slow sweeps.

With so much dust in the air, I worked more by the sound and feel of the rough sandpaper against the hull, rather than by sight.

Something cold touched my arm and startled me. I switched off the sander, and the loud buzzing gave way instantly to the sound of cicadas in the mangroves and my radio up in the cockpit.

An island tune by Jim Morris wafted down. He sang about sunny skies and standing knee-deep in the Gulf with a cooler full of beer floating beside him.

That sounded pretty good to me.

"I think you oughta call it a day," Savannah said, stepping back from the dust cloud hanging around me. "You've been at it non-stop since sunrise."

I'd worked on the port side all morning, and when there'd been no more shade there, I'd stopped for a quick lunch, then moved around to starboard, stripping the old anti-fouling paint from *Salty Dog's* hull. The last bottom job had been more than three years ago, and she was past due.

I pulled my mask off and grinned. "Got something fun in mind?"

She laughed. "Oh, yeah, sure. You look really sexy, covered in an inch of blue dust with a red ring around your face."

I glanced down at my chest and belly. "What? You don't like oversized Smurfs?"

Savannah covered her mouth and laughed again. "Hefty Smurf *was* my favorite."

"It's just dust," I said, still grinning. "It'll wash right off."

"*With* a hose pipe," she said, pointing toward the metal boat house. "You're not coming aboard *Sea Biscuit* like that. Dinner will be ready in half an hour. Flo's cooking."

24

I looked up at her as I unplugged the sander and put it in the big boat box I'd brought up from my island in the Keys.

I nodded agreement. "We need to do something to get her out of that funk."

Our daughter, Florence, had applied for admission to University of Florida and been accepted. After two laps in their competition pool, arranged in early March by a friend of a friend, Florence had been offered a full athletic scholarship and a spot on their swim team. She'd turned down the scholarship but accepted the position.

It was the only logical thing to do. I'd already set aside money for her education years ago, in a special college tuition account, and that was the only thing the funds could be used for.

Florence had insisted that the scholarship be offered to someone else who'd been homeschooled, or boatschooled, as we called it.

She'd met with a friend of Charity Styles last winter in the Cayman Islands, an Olympic trainer and NCAA advisor. Mick Davis thought Florence showed great promise and set up a meeting with the UF swim coach. He'd even scheduled her for an Olympic tryout in early April.

But then another deadly virus had erupted out of China, and the Tokyo games had been postponed for a year.

Florence had taken it in stride, as she did everything, with the knowledge that she'd never really competed. And it would give her a year in NCAA competition to build on before shooting for the Olympics.

I had to admire her attitude. I continue to have great hopes for the generation born at the turn of the century. America had been attacked by terrorists when these young people were infants, or not yet born. They'd grown up not knowing peace and facing an uncertain and chaotic world. They'd watched those before them go off to fight against ideological hate thousands of miles away. Some didn't come home. Through the summer, there had been protests and riots over police brutality in black communities. Florence's generation had taken it all in stride and constantly adapted to an ever-changing world.

Then, at the peak of their game, with commencement ceremonies planned, the virus canceled everything. In certain circles, I called it the Chicom virus. The Chinese communist government had tried to cover it up and fudged the numbers, which resulted in the shutdown of the planet and thousands of needless deaths.

No senior proms or graduations, no baseball or track, no final spring break before stepping into the big, bold, adult world. That transition happened quietly at home for many of those young people, quarantined against an unseen enemy.

Florence's generation had learned to adapt to a fast-changing world. Still, I felt bad for all the kids who were cheated out of a moment that is for many their crowning achievement in education, with memories of it still vivid in the minds of many geriatrics.

Some may think my notions are not "politically correct," and that the term Chicom is a hateful, racist thing. To which I say, I'm a Marine; we're immune to *that* silly disease. Not the virus, but the PC affliction that seems to pervade all of society today. The term Chicom has to do with a certain country's political system, nothing more. I have nothing against the Chinese people or their beautiful country. It's the hardline Chinese communist regime, with its boot on the neck of the people it enslaves that I don't like. Call me old-fashioned. I detest bullies.

But I called the Covid-19 virus by that term only in my own circle, or occasionally through a slip of a tongue, which usually got me an elbow in the ribs from Savannah.

No, I'm not politically correct, whatever that means.

"We could go down to Marco," Savannah suggested, handing me a cold beer. "She really needs to update her wardrobe before school starts next week."

My eyes snapped to *Salty Dog*, her full keel resting on blocks of wood, propped up by a dozen jack stands. No boat owner likes to see their boat on the hard for any length of time.

"You could've hired someone to do this, Jesse."

I took a long pull from the stubby brown bottle. "Yeah, I know. But I enjoy the work."

"I know you do," she said, smiling, then nodding toward the docks. "Come on. Flo's making spaghetti. We're out of fish."

"Give me a minute to hose off," I replied. "Then a quick shower."

"Make it snappy," Savannah said, blowing a kiss over her shoulder as she turned toward the docks.

Out of fish? Maybe a run down to Marco Island in Savannah's trawler wasn't such a bad idea. Forty miles of the trip would be offshore, running eight knots for five hours each way. I could restock the freezer.

My eyes followed after Savannah. She still had the same mesmerizing stride that had first caught my attention so long ago. Just as she'd done then, she turned her head, tossing her blond hair over her shoulder and looking back at me with a smile, confident that I was watching.

We'd sailed up to Fort Myers two weeks ago from my home in the Middle Keys. We'd spent a week there, recovering from a long cruise.

Savannah had had a lot of work done on her boat while we'd cruised the Western Caribbean, from the Yucatan to Belize to the Cayman Islands and back. That adventure had started eight months ago, but our journey together had started long before that.

Salty Dog had been out of the water for ten days, also having extensive work done at the boathouse next to the marina. The owner of the boat-storage building and expansive boat yard allowed work to be done by private boat owners or contractors. He also had one of the few mobile boat lifts in the area big enough to handle *Sea Biscuit*.

The new bottom paint was the last step. Among other things, we'd added more solar panels, a wind generator, and had all of the manual winches replaced with electric ones that could be controlled by an onboard computer like Charity had on her boat, *Wind Dancer*.

I'd also had a foul weather helm installed in the upper salon, with new fly-by-wire technology. The upper salon had once been a pilothouse, but a previous owner had removed the helm, opting for a galley-up layout, and he'd converted the lower galley and dinette into a salon, or entertainment area. The two kind of flowed one into the other, so I just called them the upper and lower salons.

But now the upper salon was once more a pilothouse.

In the galley.

Or maybe the galley was in the pilothouse.

The new inside helm station wasn't ideal—I couldn't see over the bow at all—but in a big blow, far out at sea, it would certainly be a more comfortable watch. And with the big twelve-inch multi-display, you could see anything above or below the water on the combination radar and sonar screen.

We'd hit some storms on the return trip from the Caymans and I'd spent some rough hours at the helm in twenty-foot seas.

I kind of savored that, too.

After walking over to the boathouse, where a hose was hung on the outside wall, I opened the valve and let the hot water pour out before turning the cool water over my head and shoulders, rinsing away the day's work. Then I went back to the boat and climbed the ladder to the *Dog's* aft deck, went forward to the cockpit, then down into the salon.

Fifteen minutes later, I climbed back down the ladder, wearing clean clothes and my new deck shoes.

When I got to *Sea Biscuit*, I boarded from the side and was greeted by Finn and Woden. They both acted as if I'd been gone for a week, wagging their tails, or nub in Woden's case, and nuzzling my hands for an ear scratch.

I stepped into the air-conditioned salon through the starboard hatch, with Woden following behind me.

We'd learned that whenever we were in a busy marina or anchorage, one of the dogs would always stay topside.

"Hey, Dad," Florence said from the galley, just behind the pilothouse. "How much did you get done?"

"More than half," I replied, getting a second beer from the fridge. "A few more hours tomorrow and she'll be ready for paint."

My daughter looked up at me from the spaghetti strainer. "That's a lot. Who was helping?"

"Just me," I replied. "Where's your mom?"

"Aft cabin. She said she needed another shower just going over to the yard to get you."

I sniffed the air. "Smells good."

"Thanks," Savannah said, coming up the steps from the aft stateroom, her hair dark and wet. "She's using *my* sauce recipe, which I got from my grandmother and doctored up just a tad."

As I was about to open the beer, Savannah looked toward the minibar right behind the helm. "I made sundowners."

I should have known better. Savannah liked to experiment with evening cocktails. I put the beer back in the refrigerator and asked what was on the drink menu.

"It's called a sneaky tiki," she replied as she went to the little fridge under the bar and took a pitcher out.

"It's…blue," I said.

She poured the pale blue, frozen concoction into a highball glass, garnished it with a slice of Key lime, and offered it to me. "There's rum in it. And the blue comes from the Blue Curacao."

I accepted the drink and joined her on the sofa in the salon.

"Your dad thought we should go down to Marco and do some shopping," Savannah said to Florence's back.

It hadn't been my suggestion, but I knew better than to say so. By not saying no from the start, it automatically became my idea in Savannah's mind.

"When?" she asked.

Florence was a lot like Savannah in many ways. One of those was that they both enjoyed shopping. Not so much the buying, but just the doing something together. Sometimes they'd shop all day and not buy anything, then talk for days about what they'd seen and should have bought.

"Day after tomorrow," I said, knowing I'd been defeated. "Friday. I'm going to hire someone to do the finish sanding and paint."

Savannah turned to me and smiled.

I was wondering why Florence's excitement meter wasn't pegging.

"If you're not busy," I said.

I wasn't much of a shopper. When I needed something, I went to the store and bought it. Whatever was needed at the time it was needed. But I'd learned that shopping wasn't about *need*.

Florence turned around, setting the strainer in the sink. "Some kids are going kayaking in the Preserve."

By that, she meant that David Stone was going kayaking in Estero Bay Preserve State Park, just south of where the Caloosahatchee River flowed into San Carlos Bay and the Gulf of Mexico. Growing up, I'd canoed every bit of it myself. Sometimes with a girl, but usually alone or with Billy.

I locked eyes with her. "You mean David, right?"

She shrugged. "Yeah, and some other kids. Can I go?"

"Classes start on Monday," Savannah reminded her. "And you need some new clothes."

"Come on, Mom," Florence pleaded. "We bought clothes at every port we stopped in. It's surprising *Salty Dog* got it all home."

"Hey now," I said, grinning, "don't be dissin' the *Dog*."

32

She smiled back at us and Savannah conceded. "Okay, but next weekend, we'll go shopping in Gainesville. Caribbean clothes won't do in the winter."

We ate and talked, and I drank another sneaky tiki. It *was* blue, but it tasted good, and in my book, form followed function.

"So, what time are y'all going?" I asked Florence as we cleaned up. "And when will you be back?"

"We're leaving first thing in the morning," she replied, then paused for a moment. "We'll be back Friday afternoon."

"Overnight?" Savannah said, alarm in her voice.

I looked over at her and shook my head slightly. "She *is* eighteen and starting college."

"We're not sleeping together," Florence said, scrubbing a pot. "We just want to explore the preserve by kayak."

"Bowtie Island?" I asked.

"You've been there?"

"Many times," I replied, thinking back on my youth and the primitive camp sites on the island. "I wonder if it's still the same."

"Can I go?"

Savannah looked at me and I nodded.

"Is there cell reception?" Savannah asked.

"Through most of the park, probably," I said. "Definitely down on Bowtie. It's only a stone's throw from the new tower on Big Hickory Island."

"Okay," Savannah said after a moment's thought. "But you call me at regular intervals."

"Thanks, Mom," Florence said, hugging Savannah.

"Don't thank me," she said. "If it were just me, I'd keep you under my wing till you were forty."

Florence smiled at me. "Thanks, Dad. We'll be fine."

"Has David read the rules for dating a Marine's daughter?"

"He thought some of them were funny," she replied.

"Don't let him make that mistake," I said, looking her straight in the eye. "They're very serious rules."

CHAPTER THREE

Dan Woodbury looked out the trailer window at the rain coming down. He'd been told that the southwest coast of Florida was wet and sweltering and late summer was the worst. The current year's rain totals had been no exception for Collier County. But what they were experiencing was way more than he'd imagined.

August had so far been horrible.

The area had already surpassed the average nine inches of rain for the month, and there were still eleven days left to go. The steady August rains had come after a July that had nearly beaten the July 1995 record of fifteen inches. Once the ground was saturated, all that water had no place to go. It just pooled in low-lying areas.

Places like the new two hundred-lot neighborhood being built by Woodbury Brothers Development on Turtle Island were hard hit. The rains came after they'd cleared the island of nearly all ground cover and brought in thousands of tons of fill from Lake Okeechobee. The intent was to raise the elevation against flooding by the tidal creeks adjacent to the property.

They'd finished the early stages of development, getting the compactable, non-organic fill in the areas where roads were going to be built and bringing the elevation up to FEMA standards. The common areas and yards would be filled with a rich, organic mixture, which was currently piled in mounds in several places on the island. The rain was reducing the size of the mounds and the whole subdivision was a muddy mess.

To make matters worse, the silt nets that bordered the island had been breached by the runoff and the expensive organic fill was now being washed into Marco River.

In the construction trailer, situated just inside what would soon be the gated entrance, Dan was becoming anxious.

He and his brother, Ben, had tired of the long winters in Oswego, New York and had moved their families to Florida as soon as the snow started to melt, sinking their savings into two new homes in Goodland, and buying the island just to the northwest.

The light rain made a constant noise on the roof. It sounded like a million buzzing wasps. It had never rained hard, save for an hour here and there. But it had been relentless for several weeks. Occasionally, the clouds would part and the steam would start to rise from the ooze.

The brothers had been developers up north and had no trouble getting licenses, securing a developer's loan, and renting the necessary equipment. By late spring, they'd started developing the island, plotting out half-acre parcels, half with a water view.

The prime lots along the creek had been selling fast enough to make the loan payments and keep the workers paid.

Until the rain started.

Working the land with heavy equipment was a waste of time and money with this kind of inundation. Ditches for utility services would flood as fast as they could be dug.

As he watched the water run off the property, Dan Woodbury saw dollar signs drifting away in the current.

He sighed, knowing that if the rain didn't stop soon, they'd have to start over completely.

The sound of a diesel pickup outside interrupted his pacing. He looked out the window and saw a white Chevy dually with the Lee County Building Department logo on the door. Dan dropped his head and shook it resignedly.

The driver's door opened, and a man stepped out into the rain. He stood on the truck's running board for a moment and looked all around. He wore orange foul weather garb with the familiar, bright yellow reflective vest over it. Covering his head was a wide-brimmed hard hat, also displaying the building department logo.

The county inspector surveyed the 193-acre island for a moment, now nothing more than a pool of black sludge, only partially held in place by the failing silt netting.

From Dan's higher vantage point, he could see black water flowing into the Marco River from the two major breaches on the south side of the property. The black stream turned and flowed with the outgoing current of the tidal creek.

The flow wasn't too bad, just before and after the high tide. But the inspector had chosen low tide to make an unannounced visit, and the runoff was at its peak, every hour taking with it hundreds of dollars' worth of the expensive, nutrient-rich soil.

Dan's brother, Ben, had told him that they only needed to get through August, that the rain would let up in September and in October, it usually dropped to a third of the average summer rainfall.

"If we can just hold out until the dry season starts," Ben had said, just the previous day, "then investors and buyers would see the work progressing and the money will start rolling again."

Dan headed toward the door, muttering to himself, "October's still five weeks away, little brother."

When Dan opened it, the inspector was stomping mud from his boots on the steps. Then he scraped them through the boot scrubber mounted just outside the door.

"Wet enough for you?" the inspector asked, as he stepped inside.

"Obviously too wet," Dan said, pulling the door closed. "What brings you out? We haven't called for any inspections yet."

"Are you the developer?"

"Yeah. Dan Woodbury," he said, sticking out his hand. "Woodbury Brothers Development."

The inspector shook his hand and handed him a card. "I'm George Wells, Mr. Woodbury. I head the building department's stormwater mitigation section."

Dan glanced out toward the dark water flowing into the turquoise creek. "I guess you're here about the runoff, then. We're just waiting for a break in the weather to repair the netting."

"I'm afraid you don't have that luxury," the inspector said. "You're currently in violation of the Clean Water Act and action needs to be taken immediately. The county requires that any construction site allows only clean water to filter into the surrounding environment."

Dan thought a moment. He and Ben could come up with some fencing or something to stem the flow. "We'll fix the nets tomorrow."

George Wells looked out the window and shook his head. "I'm afraid it's a bigger problem than that. Your soil runoff is too great and might pose a threat to the offshore environment. Netting alone won't keep the runoff to the standards required by the CWA. You're going to need to bring someone in right away to shore up that area along the creek with sand to create a wet retention area that will allow the turbidity to settle out before discharge to the Marco River."

"Sand?"

"Yes, sir," Wells said. "It's a lot more porous and stable than your fill and will filter the runoff before it gets to your silt nets. You should have done that before starting. It's common practice."

Dan didn't like the man's tone. "It might be common practice, but it isn't mandated."

Wells cocked his head with a curious expression on his face. "It's not mandated because it's not the county's money washing away. Developers are free to use whatever method they like to mitigate excess turbidity and possible environmental work stoppage and fines. So long as the discharge is clean water, within the CWA specs, the county doesn't care how you do it. Where are you from?"

"New York," Dan replied. "We don't have rain like this up north. It doesn't go on and on for days, so we do things a little differently."

Wells grinned. "This isn't the north, Mr. Woodbury. You have to adapt to Florida. Florida doesn't need to do things the way New York does."

Woodbury could feel the heat rising. *Who the hell did this yahoo think he was?*

He put aside the slight, whether intended or not. Since arriving in Florida, Dan had dealt with enough "good ole boys" to know what they thought of "how we did things up north." He also knew it was stupid to argue the point.

He looked out the window again. "Sand, huh?"

"They're doing some dredging up in Tampa Bay," Wells offered. "Sand is cheap right now."

The Woodbury brothers had gotten the fill at a discount, too. But it had still been expensive. The Okeechobee Waterway dredging project had started three months ago, and Ben had figured the dredging from the lake itself would bring up some good soil, full of nutrients to make their development green beyond belief.

The trucks had come for weeks on end, one after another. They ran from sunrise to sunset, five days a week. At no point during that time were there fewer than two trucks waiting to dump their loads. Then, Ben and his loader would push the fertile soil out across the island.

All to raise the level of the 193-acre island an average of just two feet. Below the fill was sand for about two more feet down, then it was sandy water beyond that. The tidal marsh was brackish, as was the aquifer, so nothing that rooted deep could live unless they raised the elevation, which they had to do anyway. So, it had made sense to buy the better soil.

Dan turned back to the county inspector. "So, how did you know I had a runoff problem? Somebody report me or something?"

The man grinned again. "No, nothing like that. The soil inspector who did the compaction test in June mentioned that you didn't have any sand. I just figured with the fourteen inches we've had in the last few weeks I'd see just what I'm seeing."

"You waited for it to start raining to bring it to my attention?"

"As you said," Wells agreed, "it's not mandated. You have until the first of the week to correct the problem and curtail the runoff of unclean water. After that, the county will be forced to issue a stop-work order and bring in material, equipment, and labor to rectify the problem.

"And I'll be responsible for the bill?"

"You'll be back charged the expense, yes. You won't be able to close on any of the lots until the back charge is satisfied."

Dan had seen how county crews worked in Florida; ten men leaning on shovels, watching one guy do all the work. And he was acutely aware that he was being shaken down. It was Thursday afternoon. That left Friday and the weekend.

He's got me by the short and curlies, Dan thought.

"We'll get it done," he said, opening the door for the inspector.

Wells nodded. "I'll see you Monday morning."

After he left, Dan called Ben and told him what was going on.

"By Monday?" Ben asked, his voice becoming agitated. "We can't get it done that fast. The loader can't even move in that muck, much less pull it back enough to put sand in."

"We gotta try," Dan said. "You did the survey when we talked about the dock. Remember? We own the seabed out ten feet beyond the mean low tide, right?"

"Yeah, but it's too shallow to build a community dock," Ben replied. "And we can't dredge it. We already agreed that we'd have to go get an exemption to build one thirty feet out to deeper water. Why's that matter?"

"We can't dredge it. But what if we temporarily filled it? We could start dumping loads of sand at one end of the island, *outside* the net, and use the loader to push it along the creek shore. We could build a sand road for the dump trucks all along the creek, where the shallows are now."

"That could work," Ben said. "You're always thinking outside the box, big brother."

"Can it be done?"

"For a temporary fix, yeah, it just might. Later on, we'll have to return the shoreline to original, but once it dries a little, I can use the loader to pull back the good dirt from the edge of the sand, and then pull the sand back into the gap it leaves."

"That's why we're so good together," Dan offered. "You do great inside the box."

"But we better have some big chains ready," Ben warned. "I'll have to pull some of the trucks out when they get stuck. I'll start making calls to line them up for tomorrow. We'll work through the weekend. How's the money?"

The two brothers jointly ran the business. Dan handled the finances, planning, and paperwork, and Ben was in charge of the work crews and usually dealt with the inspectors.

But Dan was no stranger to hard labor. They'd both worked their way up from gofer, to laborer, to foreman in their dad's business before he handed it down to them. He knew this would be an all-hands-on-deck job. If they were to pull it off before the inspector returned, Dan knew he'd have to be out there with Ben.

"Rent another loader," Dan said. "I'll operate one to pull them out, and you can pull them in."

"On it," Ben replied and ended the call.

Dan turned and looked out the window at the money that was just slipping away on the tide. The problem was big, but not insurmountable.

The sand and the extra loader would just about put them in the red. He could go to the bank and probably get a draw against future lot sales, but he didn't want to do that if it wasn't absolutely necessary. Paying twelve percent on a probability wasn't something he took lightly.

Sitting at his desk, he punched in numbers on his calculator from a cost sheet, then compared the total to what funds he knew were available. It was a squeaker, but Dan still had some money left in his personal savings to cover any slight overage. With a little luck, they would remain solvent through the end of the rainy season.

CHAPTER FOUR

"Smedley!" a booming voice called from outside the boat. "You in there?"

Finn barked from the side deck and Woden rose from his spot next to Florence. The big black dog growled, the short hairs on his thick neck bristling.

That voice, I thought. No, it couldn't be.

"Somebody has the wrong boat," Florence said, heading toward the side hatch.

"No," I said, getting up quickly. Too quickly. Florence and Savannah both looked at me, concerned. "I'll get it. I think it's someone I used to know."

"Who is Smedley?" Florence asked.

"That's your father's middle name," Savannah replied.

I didn't remember ever telling Savannah that.

"Smedley?"

Savannah rose and followed me, distractedly telling Florence, "Smedley Butler was a Marine who'd won two Medals of Honor."

"Earned," I corrected her, reaching the hatch, and looking back. "Heroism isn't a contest."

I pulled open the hatch and looked outside. Standing on the finger pier, just abaft the salon hatch, was an overweight, older version of a guy I'd known from my high school football days. He stood solidly on the pier, hands on his hips.

"So," he said, turning toward me, "you did come back."

"Robbins?" I asked, squinting at the man.

He was an inch taller than me when we were in high school and had been a hundred pounds heavier. Now it looked like he was nearly twice my size. There was a scar over his left eye. I knew it had come from our collision. His face guard had broken and torn a gash in his forehead, just missing the eye.

"The big, bad Marine decided to show his face, huh?" Quint Robbins sneered.

Robbins had been a linebacker at another school in the area and had a reputation for never letting a runner get past him. Except once.

In my senior year, our teams had played one another in the division playoffs. I'd scored the go-ahead touchdown late in the fourth quarter but didn't do it by going around Quint Robbins. I'd gone right through him.

And now he was standing right in front of me. Nearly four hundred pounds of him.

Woden was trying to get past me. "*Bleibe,*" I said, ordering him to stay. Finn had stopped barking, but stood at the boarding rail, ears laid back, hackles up, and snarling a low, menacing growl.

"Down, Finn," I ordered.

He immediately sat back on his haunches, but never took his eyes off the large man on the pier.

"Is there something I can do for you?" I asked, stepping up to the side deck and looking down at him.

"Where'd you run off to after you did your four years?"

"Four years?" I asked, puzzled. "If you mean the Marines, I didn't serve four years."

"Couldn't hack it?"

"I retired from the Corps, Robbins." By then, Savannah and Florence had stepped out. "Now just what is it you want?"

His eyes shifted to Savannah, then back to me. "I told you I'd find you one of these days."

What? The guy's held that against me all these years?

I stared down at him, bewildered. "You want to fight me for what happened in *high school?*"

"Jesse, no," Savannah said, taking my arm.

"Jesse, no," Robbins repeated in a high, squeaky voice as he rubbed his eyes like a crying baby.

I grinned and waved a hand toward the dock and shore. "After you, Robbins."

"Dad," Florence whispered, "he's a lot bigger than you. Don't do it."

"I'll just be a few minutes," I said, winking at her as Robbins backed away from the boat. "I promise, nobody will get hurt. At least not physically."

I dropped lightly to the pier and started shuffling slowly toward Robbins. His kind never learned. He'd been a bully then and was probably a bully today. At six feet four inches and, I was guessing, over three hundred and fifty pounds, a bully almost never had to actually fight. They always relied on their size to intimidate. Until the day came when they actually met up with someone who knew how to fight.

"This is gonna be fun," Robbins said, assuming a poor version of a fighting stance. "Right in front of your wife and daughter."

"You can walk away, Robbins. There's no need to rehash something that happened decades ago."

I stood loosely in front of the big man. I presented an easy target, arms at my sides. But if he'd bothered to look closer, he might have seen that my weight was on the balls of my feet, which were shoulder-width apart and staggered. Had he bothered to look up from my stance, he'd have seen that my knees were slightly bent.

"You cost me a scholarship," he growled. "I was on my way to the NFL."

"No, you weren't," I said flatly. "You would have flunked out of college."

He came at me then with an arcing right hand; a widow-maker, meant to end the fight with a single blow. A bully's usual tactic.

Time seemed to slow, my senses acutely aware of speed, trajectory, and distance. I stepped back half a step without raising my hands. His punch went past my face and he nearly stumbled into me.

"I'm serious, Robbins," I said sternly. "Nobody needs to get hurt."

He lurched backward. The exertion had already brought a sheen of sweat to his forehead.

He waved his hands toward himself. "Come on, *Smedley*. Come and get some."

I grinned again, moving toward him.

The next one was a straight punch, which I easily sidestepped and deflected.

"You'll have to do better than that," I taunted him.

He came at me again, swinging wildly, one fist, then the other, like a crazy windmill. I ducked and danced around him, not allowing him to make even the slightest contact. He continued with another flurry of punches, already starting to breathe harder.

He backed off and cracked his neck to one side, his huge chest heaving. "You gonna fight or what?"

"I told you," I said, stepping closer. "I don't want to hurt you."

His last two swings had lacked any energy. He was sapped. It didn't take a lot of physical exertion to wear down an out-of-shape man, especially one his size. His heart and lungs just couldn't match the demand and were quickly overtaxed.

Then he did just what I expected him to do, maybe even wanted. He telegraphed it as his body tilted toward me. His right hand shot out in a straight jab, thinking he'd caught me off guard as I'd leaned in to taunt him.

I caught his fist in my open palm, stopping the punch cold with a loud smack.

"Walk away now," I said quietly, gripping his fist, my eyes fixed on his. "You were out of your league then and even farther out now."

The man was practically wheezing.

"I'm gonna kill you," he roared, his face contorted with rage.

Robbins lunged toward me; arms spread wide to prevent any escape. I ducked low and hammered him twice, just below the sternum, both blows angling up under his ribcage.

I stepped back quickly, out of his reach. But the move wasn't needed. The air whooshed from Robbins's lungs as he dropped to his knees, clutching his midsection.

"Take it easy, now, Robbins," I said, putting a hand on the big man's shoulder and easing him to the ground. "Your diaphragm is going to spasm for a little while and you won't be able to breathe. I know it hurts like all hell, but you're *not* going to die. Just try to relax and let it subside. You probably won't even pass out."

The big man's eyes rolled back and then closed as he lost consciousness.

"Oh, my God," Savannah said, running up to me. "Is he—"

I turned and caught her before she got to close. "Just knocked out due to a lack of oxygen to his brain," I said. "Stay back. He could wake up any minute, and he's going to be madder than a hornet."

Florence ran up to join us, Finn and Woden on either side of her. "Wow, Dad! You only hit him once in the belly."

"Twice. Like you said, he's a big guy."

"Will he be okay?" Florence asked. "Should I call 911?"

"No," I replied. "He'll be okay in a few minutes."

Robbins started to stir. He gasped once, then inhaled a huge lungful of air and began to retch.

The pain from a single blow delivered where I'd hit him is very severe. Some call it the solar plexus, but that bunch of nerve endings is too far below the skin for a punch to reach. But the effect it had, just getting close, fired up all the nerve endings to the abdominal organs at once, including the diaphragm—the large muscle below the lungs that contracts and expands, moving air into and out of the lungs.

Robbins rolled onto his hands and knees, retched again, then vomited on the pavement.

"Easy, big guy," I said. "Just let it out and don't try to rush getting to your feet."

Of course, he ignored my warning and attempted to stand. He promptly toppled and would have fallen into the water if I hadn't caught his shirt.

I turned him toward me. His eyes were glazed. I slapped him on the cheek, not too hard, just enough to bring him out of it.

Robbins stumbled back and stared at me, his eyes menacing.

"Don't get any ideas," I warned him. "I gave you every chance to walk away before you got hurt. But you didn't listen. Come at me again, and I won't be so accommodating."

"What happened?"

"You decided to pick on someone who knows how to fight," I said. "I didn't spend thirty years in the Corps and Homeland Security without learning a thing or two. Are you going to be all right? Need a doctor?"

He was still breathing hard when the dockmaster came running down the dock.

"What's going on out here?" he asked, coming to a stop between me and Robbins.

"Nothing, Trevor," I lied. "Just a misunderstanding. Everything's okay, right Quint?"

Robbins nodded and Trevor looked back at me. "You sure, Jesse?"

"Don't worry about it," I replied. "My friend here was just leaving."

Robbins turned and started to walk away. "This ain't over," he mumbled under his breath.

I grabbed his arm and spun the big man around to face me. He was still an inch taller, but neither that, nor the more than one-hundred-pound weight advantage mattered and he knew it.

I got right up in his face, our noses inches apart, and applied my best Marine drill instructor snarl. "*Yes...it is most definitely over.*"

In his eyes, I saw the feeble thought of trying me again, but it was suddenly replaced with fear and the realization that his size was most assuredly against him, not in his favor.

He turned like a dog that'd been beaten and slinked off with his tail between his legs.

The three of us, along with the two *real* dogs, headed up to *Sea Biscuit's* side deck and into the salon.

"What was that all about?" Savannah asked. "Who was that man?"

"His name's Quint Robbins," I replied. "We played on different high school football teams. He got hurt in the last game of his season."

"And he blames you?"

"He was a big guy then, too—bigger than me—and fast for his size. I'd tried unsuccessfully to get around him on several plays. So, one time, I put a shoulder down and went right at him. He wore a cast for almost two months. The kind that goes over the shoulder and around your middle with a post to hold your arm out like you're leaning on a fence. I broke three bones in his shoulder."

"That out there was because of something that happened when you were in high school?" Florence asked.

"Guess he holds grudges." I said with a shrug.

I rose and moved toward the hatch. "I need to go up to the boathouse and schedule someone to finish up *Salty Dog.*"

"I thought we weren't going to Marco," Savannah said.

I grinned. "I figured maybe while Florence is kayaking, we could head a few miles offshore and restock the freezer."

CHAPTER FIVE

"Your parents seem nice," Jill commented as she and Flo carried a bright yellow kayak out to the small dock behind the country club. Jill was Perry's girlfriend. Flo had met the two of them briefly in Belize. The two girls were dressed similarly; a bikini top with shorts over the bottoms, mostly to provide a pocket for phones and keys.

David and Perry walked behind them, carrying another kayak, loaded with gear.

"Your dad's kinda scary," Perry said. "And those dogs. No offense. How tall is he?"

"Six-three," Flo replied. "Or did you mean how tall were Finn and Woden?"

Jill snickered. "Good one."

"My dad *can* be scary at times," Flo said. "But that's a side you don't want to see. Finn and Woden are just big puppies."

"Big puppies?" Perry persisted. "They moved like they were one, always staying close to you until you left the boat. Then they went to your mom and stood by her. It was like they were daring anyone to try anything."

At the end of the dock, with the sun just risen above the horizon, they put the kayaks in the water next to the two they'd already carried down minutes earlier.

"How long have you lived on a boat?" Jill asked, trying to steer the conversation to a lighter tone as they paddled away from shore.

"All my life," Flo replied. "Mom swears that she made sure to get me aboard the boat before the sun set on my first day."

"How come?" Perry asked. "I mean—why live on a boat? Are they broke or something?"

Flo laughed. "No, nothing like that. We just like it. Dad has an island in the Keys and several other boats. He owns a charter fishing and diving business."

"You mean they *live* on an island in the Keys," Perry corrected her.

"No," she said. "He owns the whole island."

"Really?" Jill asked excitedly, as the four of them paddled along side by side. "You live on your own island? What's it called?"

"It doesn't really have a name," Flo said as she thought for a moment about what she should say. She didn't want to deceive David's friends. "Dad's lived there for a long time."

"Flo's parents reunited after many years apart," David said, coming to her rescue.

"Yeah," she agreed. "It's complicated. I grew up on *Sea Biscuit*. It's the only home I've ever known. We lived on Dad's sailboat this past winter and spring, since just a few weeks before I met y'all. We cruised the Caribbean until June. Our boat was being refitted all that time. In June, we came here to have work done on his boat, *Salty Dog*."

"That's big-time social distancing," Perry said, referencing the health measures taken against the virus that had spread all over the world earlier in the year.

"It was hard at times," she said. "Many of the islands we went to wouldn't grant us permission to enter. We ate a lot of fish, crab, and lobster."

"What about other stuff?" Jill asked. "Vegetables, bread, fruit?"

"Dad has contacts all over the Caribbean," Flo replied. "We anchored in coves and sometimes a friend of his would bring something out. One time, my swim coach air dropped supplies from a helicopter."

"A helicopter?" Perry asked. "Just how rich are your folks?"

The question made Flo uncomfortable. Her mom and dad rarely talked about money with her and she got the idea they *never* talked about it with others. But she knew both of them were very wealthy.

"I'm not sure," she replied honestly.

"Enough of the third degree, Perry," David said.

"I'm just trying to get to know her, bruv."

"Sounds like you're wanting to get to know her folks."

Perry splashed water at David and started paddling away before David could strike back. David immediately dug in with his paddle, giving chase.

"Ignore them," Jill said. "You're a starting freshman, right?"

"Yeah," Flo replied. "And pretty nervous about it. I was boat- schooled."

"Boat-schooled?"

"Like homeschooling," Flo replied and shrugged. "But we live on a boat."

"This will be my sophomore year," Jill said. "I'm majoring in business."

"Me, too," Flo said. "Business, that is."

Jill seemed like a nice girl and was very pretty. Flo wondered how she and the very plain-looking Perry had ever hooked up.

"I don't know if I could have handled being with my mom day and night like that," Jill said. "At least school was a break. You'll be staying in the dorm?"

"For the first year," Flo replied, pondering the comment Jill had made about her mother.

"Then your parents will get you an apartment?"

"We haven't talked about that," Flo replied. "But I'll probably get my own place."

The group had put the kayaks in the water at Forest Country Club, where both David's and Perry's parents were members. From there, it was an eight-mile, half-day paddle down Hendry Creek to the estuary and the beaches at Pelican Landing State Park. They were meeting another couple there.

"How'd you meet Perry?" Flo asked.

"I met him and David last year on a dive trip in the Keys with a friend," she replied. "We started talking and found out we all went to UF. Perry and David have known each other most of their lives."

"Yes, David told me that," Flo said, watching the boys trying to best each other with arcing splashes from their paddles. "He said they'd even gone to preschool together."

Jill pointed with the tip of her paddle. "It doesn't look like they've advanced much beyond that, does it?"

Flo laughed. "Come on," she said, digging harder with her paddle.

David and Perry were both laughing when the girls caught up to them. And they were both soaked. Fortunately, all their stuff was in dry bags lashed to the tops of the kayaks.

"Are you guys done?" Jill asked, as she and Flo paddled past them.

The boys paddled hard and quickly caught up, gliding up silently, then coasting until they'd matched the speed of the girls' kayaks.

David pointed off to the left as Hendry Creek widened into the estuary. "That's Mullock Creek going up that way. About a mile, you go under the Tamiami Trail bridge just before you get to the Pyramids."

"Pyramids?" Flo asked. "Like ancient Seminole burial grounds or something?"

David laughed. "Nothing like that. And this area was the home of the Calusa people. The Pyramids are kind of a middle-aged, hipster vacation resort. It's called that because the rentals are all built like pyramids. Supposed to be therapeutic."

Flo looked around. Aside from a few barrel-tile rooftops sticking up above the mangroves, there was little visible that was man-made. Herons and cranes stalked the shoreline, where turtles lay on logs. White, puffy clouds drifted across a clear blue sky and the water was almost as transparent as in the Bahamas.

"Being out here is therapeutic enough," she said. "You know this area well?"

"Every square inch," David replied. "Perry and I started canoeing out here when we were in like the fifth grade."

"Fourth grade," Perry corrected him. "Well, the summer after that, anyway."

The four spread out, enjoying the paddle and the morning sun. Flo knew that her dad had grown up in this area, too. And he knew the bay and park. Had he canoed here when he was in fourth grade? Paddling along, it somehow felt odd to Flo, knowing that her dad had been here before her and had looked at the same scenery. He'd been about her age when he left the area and joined the Marines.

The man at the docks the previous evening proved that he at least had a past here that he hadn't spoken of. Flo wondered about her dad as a young man.

He'd told her and Mom about growing up with his grandparents from the time he was eight. His father had been killed in Vietnam and his mother had killed herself in grief. Flo thought that so terribly tragic.

Her dad didn't have any siblings and Flo had thought she hadn't, as well. But now she had two half-sisters, and even a niece and nephew. None of them had ever had the chance to meet Dad's parents.

"Your dad grew up here, didn't he?" David asked, almost reading her thoughts.

"Yeah," she replied. "I was just thinking about that."

"Merlin, the mind reader," Perry said. "Trust me. Don't play cards with this guy."

"Dad's parents both died when he was little," Flo said. "So, he went to live with his dad's parents, here in Fort Myers. They've both died, too."

"Her dad's friends with the Rainwater guy," David told Perry. "The Calusa chieftain who owns that 4x4 shop out toward LaBelle."

"Really?" Perry asked. "I coulda guessed that. He's another scary dude."

"Nah," David contradicted. "I worked with Mr. Rainwater and my dad building that playground over in Franklin Park a couple of years ago. And this summer, he hired me to do some computer work on trucks he's building. He doesn't say much, but he's okay."

It felt weird to Flo, hearing them talking about her dad and his friends. She knew that he and Billy Rainwater had been friends since early childhood and that they'd served in the Marines together. But she really didn't know much beyond that. It bothered her that she knew so little about her father's past.

Two hours later, the four of them paddled under the bridge connecting Big Hickory Island and Lovers Key, just to its north. A car passing overhead caused a roaring echo under the bridge.

David checked his watch. "They said they'd meet us at the landing at eleven. We're a little early."

On the west side of the bridge, they turned and paralleled it toward a small beach area. There, Flo could see a sand trail that led up to where several cars were parked.

"There they are," Jill said, pointing at a blue Jeep that had just pulled into the parking area with a kayak on its roof.

"I guess we aren't early after all," Flo said, as they paddled toward the beach.

David landed first and climbed out to greet his friends. Then he turned and said, "Flo, this is JB and Kia."

Flo had not had much opportunity to meet new people in her eighteen years, living with her mom on a boat. But, being a true Carolina girl, Savannah had schooled her daughter well in the intricacies of polite society.

She lifted a hand in greeting to JB and his girlfriend. "Nice to meet you."

"Kia lives over in Cape Coral," David said. "And JB is from up in Georgia, near Savannah."

"*No mas,*" JB said. "I'll be staying right here after graduation."

He was tall, with thick, black hair and a deep tan. Probably a year or two older than the others.

"My mother's from the Lowcountry," Flo said to JB, using the term her mom had taught her, even though she'd only been there a handful of times, herself.

"Where are you from, Flo?" Kia asked.

It was a question often asked in the cruising community. Her mom had always replied in general terms—the U.S., or South Carolina. The home port on *Sea Biscuit's* stern said Beaufort, just a little north of Savannah.

"That's hard to say," she replied. "The same, I guess. Beaufort, South Carolina."

The small, dark-haired girl pulled her sunglasses down. "You don't know?"

"Flo grew up living on a boat," David said. "She's been all over the place. So, where she's from is a relative term, right?"

Flo looked over at him and nodded. "Home is where the anchor drops."

Kia smiled. "That's so cool."

"You guys ready?" Perry asked. "'Cause we got places to go."

"Yeah," JB replied. "We should go over to Bowtie first and set up camp. Then we can paddle over to the beach."

"Good idea," David agreed. "It's the last weekend before school."

"Will it be crowded?" Flo asked.

"Not this early on a Friday," Perry said. "And some people are still leery about going out in public with all the 'Rona stuff. But there are only a handful of cool sites."

JB had only one kayak, but it was for two people; they quickly had it in the water and the group was soon paddling back under the bridge.

"Let's head around to the point," David suggested. "The wind's out of the southwest, so there'll be fewer mosquitos there."

Just past the bridge, David led them into what appeared to be a creek or river branching off to the south. After paddling around a bend, Flo saw a small sign on a thin stretch of sand to her left that read *Bowtie Island*. They weren't paddling up a creek, but a narrow waterway separating the two islands. Two blue kayaks were pulled up into the small cove, near the sign.

They continued east, along the island's southern shoreline. Ahead, a much smaller island lay just off the point. David angled for the gap.

"It doesn't look like anyone's there," JB said. "Come on!"

He and Kia started paddling harder and having two people in one kayak with a longer waterline length, they quickly pulled away from the group. The couple had obviously been kayaking together for some time. They paddled in unison, except when JB, in the back, paused to adjust course.

Flo leaned forward, gaining more purchase against the water, and started paddling faster. She knew she couldn't keep up with the tandem, but she was bound to try. David stayed right with her, but Perry started falling back, then gave up to join Jill, who wasn't trying to race the others.

JB steered their boat toward a small beach, right on the point, a sliver of white sand extending beyond the mangroves. When they landed, he and Kia got out and pulled their sixteen-foot Perception up onto the sand.

David and Flo landed on either side of them and did the same.

JB looked at Flo as she climbed out, then over to David. "I knew you could almost keep up," he said to his friend. "But where'd you ever find this Amazon woman?"

Flo blushed.

"She's on the UF swim team," David said. "But we met down in Belize last winter."

"A swimmer, huh?" JB said, looking toward Flo again. "I'm impressed." He bowed with an exaggerated flourish. "I dub you Zon."

Flo giggled, but liked it. Getting a nickname in a tight-knit group was like being a part of it.

Perry and Jill pulled up onto the beach and the group began to unpack everything from the kayaks. David disappeared into a gap between some mangroves, a pack slung over one shoulder. A moment later, he returned empty-handed.

"We got it," David said. "Nobody else around."

"Hell, yeah," Perry said, slinging a pack over one shoulder and grabbing another.

"Just inside the tree line," David said as Perry passed him, headed toward the same gap. "The best site on the island. That high ground just to the right."

Twenty minutes later, the boys had three small tents set up, all facing a well-used fire pit in the sand. They quickly stowed all their gear inside the tents.

"Our stuff will be okay here?" Flo said, noting that David had put both his pack and hers into the same tent.

"South of the Caloosahatchee is greaser territory," Perry said. "Greasers don't steal from each other."

"Greasers?"

"It's a Fort Misery thing," Kia said, tossing her pack in JB's tent. "Try not to let them get you wrapped up in it."

"Throwback terms that our parents and grandparents used," David said. "Fort Myers was mostly working class back in the fifties, before Cape Coral existed."

"Yeah," Perry chimed in. "Then some Yankee developer thought the cape would make a good place for wealthy retirees. Greasers on the south side of the Caloosahatchee and frats on the north island."

"Cape Coral isn't an island," Kia said. "It's a cape."

David laughed. "If it's surrounded by water, it's an island."

"The swamps on the north side don't count."

"When it was called Redfish Point," Perry said, "everyone knew it was an island."

"Come on," Jill said. "Let's go to the beach."

Back in the kayaks, they retraced their route around Bowtie Island and back under the bridge. Then they paddled toward the northern tip of Big Hickory Island and the open Gulf of Mexico beyond.

Driving from the marina to the Country Club had only taken David and Flo a few minutes; it was only four miles away. Then from there to where they were now, though it had taken half a day to get there, was really only ten or twelve miles from the busy city, Flo estimated.

Yet, it seemed as if they were far, far away, paddling around some cove in the Bahamas, or the Mexican coast. It was wild and wonderful.

"It always scares me coming all the way out into the ocean," Jill said. "There could be sharks."

Flo paddled up next to her. "My dad taught me a fool-proof way to test if there are sharks in the water. Wanna try?"

Jill stopped paddling and turned toward Flo. "What do I have to do?"

Flo dipped a hand into the water and held it up. "Just get a little water in your hand like this."

She waited until Jill had done so. "Okay, now taste it." Flo demonstrated by putting the water to her lips.

As Jill tasted the briny water, Flo announced, "If it tastes warm and salty, there are sharks nearby."

Jill spit the water out and looked over at Flo with a smug expression. "That's not funny."

"Seriously," Flo said. "If you're in saltwater that's warmer than eighty degrees, there's probably a shark within a couple hundred yards. Definitely within a quarter mile. It might only be a foot long, but it's there, all right."

"How do you know?" Jill asked, as they started paddling again.

"I've dived with them hundreds of times," Flo said. "People don't usually see them because they're timid and swim away. When you do see them, it's because they're curious."

"A guy got bit by one over on the east coast last week." Perry said, as they neared the beach.

"Probably in the surf," Flo said. "Or low visibility. Sharks test to see if something is food by biting it. If it's not food, they spit it out. They don't like the taste of humans."

The group reached the sand and scrambled to pull the little boats up as small waves lapped the shoreline. There were other clusters of kayaks, canoes, and people farther down the beach where the sand got wider. Flo and her friends had landed on the very tip, where they could see into the inlet all the way to the bridge, look out over the turquoise waters of the Gulf of Mexico, or across the inlet to the beaches on Lovers Key. Several jet skis were pulled up onto the sand over there.

They spread several large towels on the sand, anchoring them from the wind with whatever they could, including a small cooler. The girls wiggled out of their shorts and the guys pulled off T-shirts. Then all six raced toward the water, splashing until it was deep enough to dive in.

The water was cool and inviting on Flo's skin as she dove headlong beneath the waves. She opened her eyes and dolphin-kicked toward deeper water, staying just a foot above the sandy bottom.

When she surfaced, David was swimming after her, several yards behind, with the others even farther back. She reached with her feet and could just stand on her toes if she tilted her head up. She chose to hover instead, with her knees drawn up, making slow, scalloping movements with her hands.

David stopped swimming and stood close to her. "How do you go so fast underwater?"

At six feet, he didn't have to stand on his toes.

Flo squinted up at him in the bright sunlight, still paddling her hands like a puffer fish. "Ever see dolphins swimming in front of a boat?"

"Sure," he replied. "Lots of times."

"When they're underwater, they barely have to move their tails to keep pace. But when they break the surface to breathe, they have to swim harder."

David closed his eyes and tilted his head toward the sun, as if replaying a favorite scene in his mind.

"You're right," he said, then looked over at her. "How come?"

"It's mostly due to wave creation," she replied. "On top of the water, you leave a surface wake. That takes energy, and it's energy robbed from speed. Plus, under-water, there's no surface tension, so slightly less drag."

"Physics?"

"I've had a good swim coach."

"So, you and your mom stayed in one place a lot?" he asked. "To be coached."

"My coach lives on a boat, too," Flo replied, putting off the question that was on her mind. "She was an Olympic swimmer and we'd see her several times a year."

"The Olympics?" David said. "That's pretty cool."

"Why'd you put both our packs in the same tent?" Flo finally asked.

David cocked his head. "Huh?"

"I thought there would be a boys' tent and a girls' tent."

"We're in college, Flo."

She thought about it a moment, then moved closer to him, so she could stand on his feet, with her hands clasped behind his neck.

"I'll sleep in the same tent with you, David Stone. But—"

David kissed her on the forehead. "I know. And I'm not pushing you into anything. You have to sleep some-where, and we only brought three tents. Besides, your dad would kill me."

"No, he wouldn't," Flo said, smiling. "He likes you."

"No, he'd kill me. And it would be slow. And there wouldn't be any sign that I ever existed afterward."

"He doesn't hurt good people."

David took her hand and pulled her toward shore. "Come on. Let's dry in the sun."

CHAPTER SIX

Twenty minutes after David and Florence left, Savannah had *Sea Biscuit's* engines running, and I'd tossed off the lines and joined her on the flybridge. Since it was her boat, I was the crew.

We idled down the Caloosahatchee, drinking coffee, while the dogs made their way up to the foredeck and sat on either side of the anchor windlass, watching the world go by.

The sights around us were all familiar to me, yet foreign at the same time. I'd grown up in Fort Myers and had explored every inch of the waters for miles around. Billy and I had canoed, camped, fished, and hunted these waters and the inland swamps as kids. Sometimes, we brought other friends, but mostly, it was just the two of us. Maybe we bonded because neither of us had siblings—I still don't know.

"I'm not real crazy about this," Savannah said, after twenty minutes of talking about anything other than what was on her mind. "What if Flo calls?"

I kissed her cheek as we idled past Punta Rasa toward the Sanibel Causeway, then pointed toward the high, arching bridge. "Where they're going is about twelve miles that way." Then I moved my pointing finger just a few degrees westward. "Where we're going is twelve miles that way."

Savannah turned to me and smiled. "What's out there?"

I punched the GPS numbers into her chart plotter from memory and clicked *Go To*. Back in the day, we'd used radio and television antenna towers and other landmarks to estimate where the spot was, sometimes taking hours to find it. Sometimes we didn't find it at all. But while I was in the Corps, technology had spread to the civilian market and Pap was one of the first people in the area to have GPS on his boat. By then, Billy and I had told Pap about our secret spot.

Pap had taught me to navigate by the sun, moon, and stars, and much later, my friend Rusty had helped me sharpen those skills. But Pap wasn't one to ignore tools that made life easier, and he and I used his new toy to find it every time for some years until he passed away.

"Decades ago, they didn't dump as far from shore as they do now," I replied. "About three miles off Big Hickory Island is a spot where the county dumped a bunch of concrete bridge pilings, culverts, steel girders, and big slabs of concrete deck."

"Uh-huh."

"Billy and I saw them dump it," I continued, "not three miles offshore. After the barge left, we found the spot and marked it with a lobster trap float."

"And that's where we're going? Your secret childhood fishing hole?"

"It became a reef," I said with a grin. "Great place to free dive for snapper, grouper, and lobster. Maybe even a hogfish or two."

"Where did David say they were camping?"

"Bowtie Island," I replied. "It's just inland from New Cut, at the north end of Big Hickory."

"So, if she needs us, we'll be closer."

"Twenty minutes away," I said with a grin.

We passed under the causeway and Savannah adjusted our course due south, skirting Little Sanibel Island. Once clear of the shallows, we turned toward the south-southeast, paralleling Fort Myers Beach, less than a mile offshore.

"Head out to the five-fathom line," I told her. "I'll put a couple of lines out and see if we can scare up a mahi or tuna on the way."

Sea Biscuit wasn't the ideal boat to troll for gamefish with, but she did have two sturdy rocket launchers on the outboard sides of the transom.

I went into the salon and took down two heavy trolling rods and reels from where they were secured to the overhead. Then I went out the port hatch and aft to the minimal cockpit, where I glanced back at the sea state behind us.

While *Sea Biscuit* wasn't exactly equipped for tournament fishing, she did flatten the water nicely, leaving a trail of calm water between the two bubble trails from the bow wave.

There were probably as many trolling methods as there were combinations of boats and fishermen. But aboard one of my other boats—*Floridablanca* was a similar-sized trawler—I'd found that giving the fish an easy view of a bright-skirted lure against a calm background was the best way to bring the fish up. The flatness of the water made it easier for gamefish to see the bait trolling behind the white water from the stern.

After dropping two blue-and-white skirted lures into the water, I allowed each to trail back about 120 feet behind the boat, in the middle of its water trail, but well behind the white water nearer the stern.

I put each rod in one of the custom stainless-steel rocket launchers that were mounted to the deck and secured against the top of the transom. They angled back enough to extend outside and above the safety rail. I firmly believe it's better to lose a lure and some line to a big shark or something, than to lose the whole rig due to a cheap rod holder mounted on the rail.

"Bring her up to ten knots!" I shouted up to Savannah on the flybridge.

The sound of the twin diesels rose in pitch and soon the boat was moving at a fairly good clip for a trawler.

Savannah had decided to replace the reliable—but outdated—Cat 3208 engines, which Grand Banks had originally installed, with a pair of new engines. Each of the C8.7 engines delivered seventy percent more horsepower than the original, took up slightly less room, and was actually more economical at low speed. With new, lower-geared transmissions, *Sea Biscuit* was a wolf in sheep's clothes and capable of just over twenty knots. For a thirty-ton boat, that was a lot of speed.

It only took ten minutes before one of the reels started to sing. The rod bent in the direction the fish was going.

"Fish on!" I yelled, grabbing the rod, and yanking it twice to make sure the hook was set.

We'd done this a few times on *Sea Biscuit* since our return from the Southern Caribbean and moving *Salty Dog* up onto the hard for refit.

I quickly reeled in the other line to keep it from getting tangled with what I knew from experience was a mahi-mahi. In much of the Caribbean and Atlantic, it's called a dorado, due to its striking gold and green coloring. When I was growing up, the common name for the gamefish was dolphin or dolphinfish. But people started to use the Hawaiian word so landlubbers wouldn't think we had Flipper on the grill.

Savannah slowed the boat as I fought the mahi. It jumped high in the air—a big bull dolphin, flashing green and gold. Then it did a tail dance before submerging once more. Finn and Woden barked each time the fish jumped out of the water.

Mahi in Hawaiian means strong. There is no word for "very" in that language. Instead, a word is repeated for emphasis. So, mahi-mahi means "very strong," and this one was no exception.

Hopping on one foot as I fought the fish, I kicked the lid open on the big cooler. Unlike my tournament fishing boat, *Gaspar's Revenge*, Savannah's boat lacked in-deck fish boxes.

I braced my thighs against the transom and fought the fish for more than five minutes as he slowly exhausted himself. Finally, I opened the transom door to the swim platform and managed to get the fish up to the back of the boat. I grabbed the gaff off the rail and quickly had it aboard. In seconds, with Finn barking at it furiously, I had the fish in the cooler, then put the lines back out.

Where there was one, there were more.

Over the next hour, I boated two more dolphins and released three. Then I rinsed and stowed the rods and reels and went back up to the flybridge with Savannah. That was enough food for the three of us for several days.

"How many?" she asked, as if she wasn't keeping count.

"Hooked seven, boated six, and kept three."

"That's a start," she said, referring to her large double freezer.

"I promise I'll fill the ice box by the end of the day," I said, standing between the two forward-facing seats. I looked at my watch. "It's still early; just zero-nine-hundred. When did Florence say she'd call you?"

"At noon, six, and before bed," she replied. "Or is that sixteen?"

"Eighteen hundred," I replied. "You add or subtract twelve."

"Wouldn't it be easier if you just used normal time?"

I put my arm around her and pulled her close. "I do use normal time," I said. "There are twenty-four hours in a day."

As we approached the waypoint I'd entered, I turned on the new sonar, setting it to scan forward and down. I was sure of the numbers—I'd dived and fished this spot a hundred times.

"Slow down," I said, "and be ready to turn upwind."

The current was minimal, but *Sea Biscuit* offered a lot of surface area to the wind, which was out of the south-southeast at about fifteen knots. Once anchored, the slow, southerly flowing current would have less effect than the wind.

The bottom recorder started showing a large jumble of debris and before I could say anything, Savannah turned to windward. I left the bridge and went up the port side deck to the windlass.

The depth was nearly thirty feet and she continued into the wind for a couple of minutes, until she was sure we were far enough away that we would have adequate scope on the anchor rode.

When Savannah put the engines in neutral, I unclipped the safety chain from the anchor.

I waited a moment for the wind to bring us to a stop, then toggled the windlass release. The chain clanked and clattered over the pulpit's roller for a moment; then I stopped it and let the wind carry us back more before releasing more rode.

Savannah was watching the sonar, and after several minutes she yelled down that the debris pile had reappeared astern.

I stopped the windlass, reattached the safety chain, and eased off on the windlass a bit, before waving up at her that it was ready. When I did, she reversed both engines, setting the anchor deep in the soft sand.

"It looks like twenty feet to the top," she said, looking over the side. "I can see that it's darker, rather than the usual sandy bottom."

"This used to be one of my favorite spots," I said. "Billy Rainwater and I used to come out here in my little skiff to fish for monster grouper."

"You dive," she ordered. "I'll start cleaning what you've already caught."

"That's a deal," I said. "Hope you can work fast."

"You know I can. Don't you worry about that."

We both went below to change. She put on a lime-green bikini, which brought out her golden-brown skin tone. On the way out, I grabbed my gear from the storage locker—my mask, fins, a weight belt with two pounds of lead, and my mahogany Arbalète speargun.

Savannah was already busy with the mahi, using a large cutting board clamped to the aft rail. We'd added it after our first sea trial with the new engines, to keep from having to bend over to clean our catch on the cabin roof.

"I'll be done with these before you bring up another," she said, challenging me.

I stepped down onto the expansive swim platform and looked up at her. "I wouldn't be too sure about that."

In minutes, I had my mask, fins, and weight belt on, then picked up my speargun and stepped off the platform.

The water enveloped me in its warm embrace. I scissored my legs and surfaced, taking a big gulp of air before submerging and looking down at the bottom.

The center of the debris field was directly below the bow. When movement caught my eye, I folded my body and swam downward toward a good-sized snapper on the fringe of the artificial reef.

The spear tip led the way, but as I approached the fish, I spotted a hogfish just off to my right, rooting around in the sand. I turned and angled toward my favorite eating fish.

Hogfish are a type of wrasse and are a lot more common in the Bahamas and around the northern Caribbean, but they can be found as far north as Nova Scotia and as far south as northern Brazil.

I moved stealthily down on my prey, the sharp tip of the spear tracking the fish's slow movement. Just five feet away, I aimed carefully and squeezed the trigger.

The spear caught the hogfish right in the head. He twitched once, and that was it. As I reeled the line in to head back up with my catch, I looked over the debris field.

It didn't look like a dump site at all now. Where once you could see lobster and fish swimming into and through a maze of busted-up concrete, the pilings and gargantuan slabs of roadbed were no longer visible, having been grown over with hard and soft corals, sponges, and tube worms. The change in the last forty years was phenomenal.

Thousands of small, brightly-colored fish darted in and around the corals, while larger tropical fish—angelfish and parrotfish, and quite a few snappers and groupers, swam slowly around the edges.

Just as I turned to head up, I saw lobster antennas sticking out from a crevice. I angled as I rose—and saw there were at least a dozen antennae sticking out from one spot.

I grinned.

At the surface, I lifted the fish over my head in triumph before swimming to the platform.

"Only you could get a hogfish on the first dive," Savannah said, smiling brightly in the morning sun.

I put the fish and speargun on the platform. "Could you hand me the bull net? I saw a bunch of bugs in one spot."

Savannah opened the small lazarette on the port side and pulled out my big lobster net. Stepping down, she handed it to me and took the hog.

"Any other fish?"

"Tons," I replied, pushing away. "But I want to get these lobster first."

The season had only been open for a couple of weeks and we weren't quite three miles from shore. Could this spot still be a secret after all these years? I focused and breathed in and out deeply, purging carbon dioxide and maybe raising my O_2 level a little. Then I took a deep breath and arched my body, bringing my legs up out of the water to provide weight to drive me down without effort.

Slowly, I kicked to the bottom and approached the part of the artificial reef where the lobsters were hiding. Then I wedged the frame of my net against a squarish, encrusted piling, with the long side resting on the sand. I had the net's handle angled toward me a little, careful not to move suddenly and cause them to dart backward into what was probably a maze of tunnels through the rubble.

One thing I always look for before jamming my arm under a rock to catch a lobster is where the lobsters' antennas are pointed. The long appendages have spines that point away from its body and it uses those spines to fend off predators. All the lobsters' antennas were pointing outward, meaning there wasn't anything dangerous behind them.

With a quick motion of my right hand, I reached deep under the ledge to keep them from scurrying father back, then swept my arm forward.

Instantly, most of the bugs turned and, using their powerful tails to propel them backward out of the hole, shot along the wall and right into my waiting net.

A couple got away, having darted toward me, and then scooted between my legs, but as I pushed off the bottom, I knew I had at least four. I turned the aluminum frame perpendicular, so the net itself was folded against the frame, blocking escape. Then I rose toward the stern of the boat.

"Whoo!" I shouted when my face broke the surface.

Savannah came down to the platform again and I handed her the net. The lobsters flipped their tails as she carried them to the cooler. I grabbed my speargun off the platform once more and finned backward, away from the boat.

One of the bugs flew over the starboard gunwale. Savannah rose and smiled. "Only one short."

I gave her a thumbs up and arched for the bottom again. The freezer was filling up fast.

Over the next hour, I speared two big groupers and four perfect snappers, plus one more hefty hog.

True to her word, Savannah spent as much time waiting as I did diving. Being the tomboy daughter of the owner of a fishing fleet made her no stranger to cleaning and processing my catch.

As I was heading back down for one more try, something out on the sand caught my eye. I slowed my descent and looked in that direction.

It was a dolphin.

Not a mahi, but an Atlantic bottlenose dolphin. It seemed to be playing with something on the bottom and kicking up a lot of silt. Maybe it was rooting for a crab. I swam a few kicks in that direction, always mesmerized by dolphin behavior.

Suddenly, I realized there was a smaller dolphin rolling lifelessly on the bottom in the silted-up water. The mother nudged it, getting its nose under the dead baby, and trying to make it move toward the surface.

I'd seen a lot of dolphins over the years. The baby wasn't a newborn, but it was young—less than a year old, if I had to guess. It was probably born during the spring calving season.

I hung there in the water for a moment, watching the mother desperately trying to save her calf. I couldn't see any wounds on the baby, nothing that would indicate how it had died. Finally, with my oxygen depleted from my lungs, I kicked for the stern of the boat.

"Nothing?" Savannah asked, standing on the swim platform.

"I saw a dead bottlenose dolphin," I said, laying my speargun on the platform, and looking up at her. "It was a baby. And its mother was with it, trying to get it to the surface."

"Oh my!" Savannah said.

I heard the blow right behind me and turned just in time to see the dolphin submerge just a few feet away. She circled me slowly, as if studying me. Then she lifted her head from the water—spy hopping.

The dolphin, every bit of eight feet and four hundred pounds, looked right at me. Then it turned and looked at Savannah. It started flapping its pectoral fins and screeching.

"You have to help her!" Savannah yelled.

The dolphin had appealed to the human mother and somehow Savannah had understood. Not being of the same gender, I didn't understand it, but I knew there was a bond between mother and child in most species, and no stronger bond exists between humans. Often, mothers will help one another for no other reason than they are both trying to raise their young.

I instantly jackknifed my body and started down, looking for the baby. Maybe it wasn't dead. I spotted it as the mother flashed past me. She tried again to push the baby toward the surface, but it wasn't moving. When I reached her, she backed off a little and circled around me, clicking focused sound waves.

It's said that a dolphin's sonar is so acute that it can see inside a person's body. Pregnant women are treated very differently when they're in the water with dolphins. Could she see her baby's still heart?

Very carefully, I put my hands under the calf and pulled it to my chest. It was probably four feet long and would weigh over a hundred pounds out of the water. On the bottom, it was weightless. I felt no life in its inert body. The mother watched me closely.

It was an incredible event. A mother dolphin allowing a human to be so close to her offspring was one thing, but to allow me to touch and carry it was another. I think the mother simply ran out of options and turned to the first being she saw for help.

What could I do? Somehow, she seemed to expect me to bring the baby back to life. And if I could, I would have.

I swam slowly toward the boat, carrying the dolphin calf. I surfaced right at the platform and pushed the body up onto it.

"What's wrong with it?" Savannah asked, kneeling beside the small dolphin.

I moved to the side and scissored myself up onto the platform. "I don't know. I'm fairly sure it's dead."

I left Savannah there and went to my phone in the salon. After contacting Florida Fish and Wildlife, I grabbed two water bottles and went back to where Savannah stood at the transom.

"She's still there," she said. "Swimming back and forth and looking up at me."

The mother dolphin made a slow pass on the surface behind the boat, its body tilted so it could look up at us and see her dead calf.

"Dolphins mourn," I said, watching her slowly glide past. "Maybe not the same way we do, but they know grief and anguish. Fish and Wildlife will be here in twenty minutes. They want to take the body to a private lab in Naples."

Savannah shuddered a little as the dolphin made another pass. I put my arm around her shoulder and pulled her close.

"Are you okay?"

"I just...I don't know. You'll think I'm just being silly."

"You hurt for her," I said, squeezing her shoulder. "I do, too. A parent shouldn't see its child die."

"There's not a mark on its body," she said. "I checked it thoroughly. Still in fishing mode, I guess. The enormity hit me when I saw the mother watching me while I was examining it."

Savannah turned in my arms and sobbed against my shoulder. "She wanted me to... to do something. To save her baby...and I couldn't."

The mother swam past again, her eye fixed on mine as I held Savannah, still sobbing, in my arms. Her up-turned mouth—the ever- present and familiar smile of the bottlenose dolphin—was in sharp contrast to what I saw in the depths of her eyes.

Finn whined and leaned against my and Savannah's legs, nuzzling Savannah's hand with his head. He could see that she was sad and wanted her to pet him. In his mind, I guessed, it felt good to him, so it must feel good to her, as well.

I lifted one hand to the mother dolphin and shook my head, trying to convey empathy.

She stopped and stared for a moment. Then she slipped beneath the surface. I watched as she slowly started swimming toward the west.

CHAPTER SEVEN

There was a knock at the door. A man with a white beard pushed a button that activated a surveillance screen on the corner of his desk. Recognizing the woman on the screen, he pushed another button and the door latch clicked.

The man's private office was in his home. He'd bought the two top-floor, southwest facing units before construction had even started on the twenty-four-story building. The condo was on the tip of Marco Island, one of the most expensive places to buy in all of Florida. Each unit had been designed to be two floors, with the entrance to the living area on the building's twenty-third floor, and a private staircase to the two bedrooms on the top floor. He'd changed the design, joining the two units, making the upper half of one unit his office and the upper floor of the other unit his bedroom suite. The two lower floors were then joined, half making up the well-appointed kitchen and dining room and a luxurious living area. The other half became two large guest bedrooms with private baths.

At a preconstruction price of two million dollars each and an overage of nearly one million, due to many custom changes, he'd invested five million in the project before the condominium even broke ground. It was now valued at twelve million, so Jubal Blanc owned the single most expensive three-bedroom home in the whole state.

The door pushed open and the woman from the closed-circuit monitor came into the office. She was exotically beautiful; tall, and pale-skinned, with jet-black hair that hung well below the crisp white collar of her blouse.

"I have that report you asked for, Senator," the woman announced, as her heels clicked on the imported marble floor.

Jubal took the file she handed him and opened it. "What did you find out about the contractor of record?"

"Woodbury Brothers," she replied. "A state-certified general developer licensed early this year. Daniel and Benjamin Woodbury, along with their wives, are the principles. They came here from upstate New York after selling a similar business in Oswego."

"Is Wells leaning on them, as I asked?"

"Within the constraints of his office. Yes, sir."

Jubal lifted an eyebrow as he looked up from the file.

"He can't actually break the law," Chloe said. "Or even the building code regulations. At least not without raising questions."

"I want them out of there, Chloe."

"Yes, sir," she said, unruffled. "I am aware of that. There just isn't much that can be done...officially."

Chloe Devlin was more than just the senator's private secretary. She was his most loyal and trusted advisor. The woman standing before him wearing a tight black pencil skirt was also his pilot, chauffeur, and bodyguard. He'd hired her ten years earlier, fresh out of MIT. Before he was elected, he'd needed someone smart to predict future trends in the real estate market. Mostly though, he'd hired her on the chance that she'd sleep with him. He'd quickly learned that was out of the question and then he learned of her other skills.

"You have a suggestion?" Jubal asked.

"We're flying up to Tallahassee for Monday's vote," she reminded him. "Perhaps one of your extended family could pay them a visit. But to be honest, sir, the Woodbury Brothers haven't found anything. In fact, they've buried everything deeper with all the fill they brought in at the start of the project."

"But eventually, they'll have to bury water lines and put in a central septic system."

"From what you've told me," Chloe offered, "and the fact that the island is so large, the chances of digging in one specific spot are less than one in ten thousand."

"You have such an analytical mind, Chloe. Let me ask you this. If I had a jar on my desk with ten thousand jellybeans in it, and you knew that just *one* of them was poisoned, would you eat one of those jellybeans?"

"No, sir," she replied. "I don't eat candy. But what's the risk if they do find something? It happened over fifty years ago."

Jubal closed the folder and looked up at her. "I don't want my family name dragged through the mud. If they find that one jellybean, it could ruin my chance at a U.S. Senate seat."

Chloe clasped her hands in front of her. "Sir, with all due respect to you and what you've built and accomplished, your family name *is* the mud."

Had anyone but Chloe Devlin said that, Jubal would have drawn the .38 he kept in his desk drawer and shot them dead on the spot. He'd done it before for lesser offenses. But that had been in his wild, early years, right after his father died.

Besides, Jubal was fully aware that this lovely, demure woman, whom he trusted more than anyone, could kill him before he even got the gun out. And she'd do it with no emotion.

"Get a message to Kurt," Jubal said. "I want a meet. Tonight. At the usual place and time."

CHAPTER EIGHT

The boat from Fish and Wildlife had come hours earlier. They'd taken the body of the dolphin calf to a lab in nearby Naples. The lab was run by a well-known marine biologist who specialized in marine mammals. I'd given the officer my card and asked him if he would have the lab call me when they learned how the little dolphin had died.

We didn't fish anymore. After lunch in the salon, Savannah wanted to talk about what had happened. She was the type of person who had to get all the talk out until she'd resolved whatever emotional turmoil she was feeling. I mostly just listened, offering a nod here or there, until she was finished.

"Let's just stay here tonight," I finally offered. "There's no weather in the area for at least a day."

"Did you talk to Trevor?"

"Yeah. He's got a crew lined up to be there first thing in the morning. They'll finish by evening. He said the *Dog* could be splashed on Monday, once the paint dries."

"That's good," she said, absently.

"What's wrong?"

"It's just that once your boat is back in the water, we'll be at a crossroads, won't we?"

I lifted an eyebrow. "What do you mean?"

"Monday is August 24th," she said. "Since Christmas Eve, we've been having one boat or another refitted. Eight months to the day."

"You're tired of having me around?" I asked, grinning.

"Never," she said. "It's just that...well...where do we go from here? We'll be on separate boats."

I'd brought up the subject of our future last winter and recalled it clearly. "I remember you saying, 'let's just have fun and see where things go,' when I brought this subject up in Belize."

"That was a long time ago."

"It was seven months ago, next Thursday."

She smiled over her coffee. "You remember what day the conversation was?"

"I do," I replied.

"In which direction was your mind going then?"

I took her hand and kissed it. "I've always liked to have a clear vision of what's ahead," I said. "You've always been a free spirit. I simply adapted." I bowed and offered my most courtly voice. "I am fully at your disposal, me lady. Completely open to any suggestion you may have."

Savannah placed her mug on the table and looked down at her hands. "It occurred to me last month, when we flew up to Gainesville to register Flo, that it took just a little over two hours to get there from Marathon."

It was closer to three hours, but I wasn't going to say that. "Yeah?"

She lifted her eyes and met mine. "Wouldn't it take about the same amount of time to drive to Gainesville from Cedar Key?"

"I imagine it'd probably take a bit less," I replied, grinning. "What with traffic and everything. And we'd have to get a car."

"So, let's go there," she said. "To your island."

"And do what?"

I couldn't hide the excitement from my face, and she could see it, letting my question hang for a moment as I twisted on the hook.

"And move in together?" she finally said.

My personal cell phone rang just then. We both saw that it was my daughter, Kim, calling.

"You better get that," Savannah said.

I picked up the phone and touched the *Accept* button, then put it on speaker.

"Hey, Kim," I said. "You're on speaker. I'm with Savannah."

"And I'm on with Marty," Kim said. "Where's Flo?"

"Camping on an island with her boyfriend and some other kids," Savannah answered. "About three miles east of where we're anchored."

"I'll bet Jesse chose the anchorage," I heard my son-in-law, Marty Phillips say.

"Hey, Marty," Savannah and I said at the same time.

"Yes, he did," Savannah continued. "Did he do the same thing with you two?"

The first time Marty took Kim on an overnight trip, I'd actually done just that—never more than a few miles from them the whole time. Just in case anything happened.

"He did," Marty said. "But he doesn't know that we knew."

My mouth fell open a little and Savannah laughed. When she tried to stifle it, she laughed all the more.

"So, what's going on?" I asked.

"You guys reported a dead dolphin earlier and the officer you gave your card to is a friend of ours. He didn't place the name until later and called me."

"Yeah," I said. "It was awful. I was freediving and saw the mother trying to move it toward the surface. I guess it drowned."

"No, Dad, it didn't," Kim said. "I'm at Doctor Angelo's lab now. The calf died from toxins in its lungs. Red tide spores."

"Red tide?" I asked, surprised. "I know it makes some people sneeze a lot and some older folks get sick from breathing it. But a young, healthy dolphin?"

"Doctor Angelo says the pod must have recently been in close proximity to a dense algal bloom," Marty added. "He said it affects the young a lot worse, because of their smaller lung size and lowered immunities."

"But *we* are right here where we found it," I said. "There's no red tide here."

"Dolphins aren't stationary," Savannah said.

"That's right," Kim agreed. "The pod may have come from miles up or down the coast. There haven't been any unusually large blooms reported, though."

"Most of the southwest coast is uninhabited," I said. "A big bloom could go unnoticed."

"We have boats out looking, so we can report which direction it might go and who might be affected."

"Can y'all come out and visit? We're three miles off Big Hickory Island."

"We can't," Kim said. "We have to get back down to Everglades City before dark. When will you be back home? We can come there."

"Next week," Savannah said. "But we might need a couple of days to clean things up."

"She means hang curtains," I said, "and outfit my bunk with frilly skirts and what not."

"Huh?" Kim said.

"We're going to live ashore for a while," I replied.

"Together?"

I grinned at Savannah. "Isn't that the way it's usually done?"

"Aw, Dad. I'm so happy for you both. Just let us know when."

I promised I would, then we ended the call.

"Next week?" I asked.

"Flo starts school on Monday," she replied. "There's nothing holding us here."

The words sounded kind of flippant, but I knew she was very anxious about Florence starting college. The two had only been apart a handful of times. The longest had been two days when Florence had stayed with Charity on her boat. I also knew that Savannah would work it out on her own and needed no input from me.

We took care of a few boat chores, and, as I was covering the helm and instruments on the flybridge, she came up to join me, two drinks in her hands.

I glanced up at the angle of the sun. "It's a bit early for sundowners, isn't it?"

"It's five o'clock somewhere," she said with a smile, placing the drinks on the dinette.

I joined her and we looked out over the port side, our backs toward shore. The Gulf Coast of Florida always provided a beautiful sunset view, rich in color, and there wasn't a cloud in the sky on this particular day.

"Are you okay with what we talked about earlier?" Savannah asked.

I looked over at her. The low sun shone on the side of her face as she returned my stare. "Yes. I've never been more serious."

"Somehow, I doubt that, Jesse. You're the most intensely serious person I've ever known."

Taking her hand in mine, I smiled. "I'd like nothing more than for you to stay with me until we're both old and wrinkled."

She touched the side of my face. "Then that's just what we'll do."

I picked up my Collins glass and looked at the drink. At the top it was pale yellow, fading to orange in the middle, then deep red at the bottom.

"Tequila sunrise?" I asked, a bit perplexed. Savannah rarely poured traditional drinks.

"I call it a 'Hop, Skip, and Go Naked,'" she said. "Rum, OJ, grenadine, Southern Comfort, and 7-Up."

"Hop, skip, and go naked?" I asked, tasting it. "Mmm."

"Was that *mmm* for the drink or the idea?"

"Both."

CHAPTER NINE

Savannah and I had finished a fantastic meal of pan-seared snapper with fresh broccoli and potatoes. Fresh vegetables were something we couldn't get all the time when we were cruising. During the pandemic in the spring, we'd survived on a lot of fish and canned or frozen vegetables we had brought out to us.

Sitting on the foredeck, our backs against the windshield, we could see the Milky Way all the way across the sky. Far to the south, the Southern Cross was just beginning its short arc over the southern horizon. Finn and Woden lay curled on the side decks on either side of where we sat.

Florence had called twice, as she'd promised, once at noon, while at the beach with her friends, and again just before dinner. She said they had a good campsite, well above the water, and on the windward side of Bowtie Island. I had a fairly good idea where they were. Billy and I had camped there many times. With the wind out of the south-southeast, at least they wouldn't have to deal with mosquitoes and biting gnats.

"Do we have to wait a week?" Savannah asked, out of the blue.

"What do you mean?"

She reached over and put a hand on my thigh. I took it in mine.

"*Salty Dog* will be relaunched on Monday," she said. "We're dropping Flo off Sunday afternoon. Can't we leave on Monday?"

"It'll be late Monday before they splash the *Dog*," I replied. "Why the rush?"

"I've only been to your house as a guest," she said. "I guess I just want to become intimately familiar with everything."

She wanted tasks to keep her mind off of Florence. Sitting around in a marina waiting for others to finish their work would be stressful enough. Savannah knew herself well. With little to occupy her time, she'd worry about our daughter.

"Once the *Dog's* in the water, I'll still have to run, test, and check all the systems and everything. But there's no reason we can't leave early on Monday, get settled in on the island, and I can come back up and get her later in the week."

"You'd just leave your boat?"

"*Sea Biscuit* has been your only home for years," I said. "But I have three boats I could live on comfortably, plus a house, and I can only be in one at a time. Right now, only two of those are in the same place—the house on my island, and the *Revenge*, which is docked there. So, I'm at home anywhere, and at the same time, I'm never at home."

Savannah's phone vibrated on the cabin top between us.

"That's probably Flo," Savannah said, reaching for it, "calling to say goodnight."

She turned it over so we could both see the screen and she was at least partly right; it was Florence, though I doubted the kids would be going to sleep any time soon.

"Hey, baby," Savannah said, after accepting the call and putting it on speaker.

"Mom! We need help!"

I was off the cabin top and headed for the windlass before Savannah could respond.

Savannah sat bolt upright. "What's the matter?" she asked, a great deal of urgency in her voice.

"A baby manatee, Mom! I think it's dying!"

I stopped and turned. It was the kind of emergency I *should* have expected Florence would call about, but my mind had immediately jumped to her being in danger, and the fact that she was with David. But she *had* said *we* needed help, not *I*.

"What's wrong with it?" I asked. "Does it seem to be having trouble breathing?"

"Yes!" Florence said. "And I think it's in pain."

"You're near New Pass," I said. "Are y'all comfortable paddling out to deeper water in the dark? We're fifteen minutes away and there's a lab in Naples that specializes in marine mammals."

"Yeah," I heard a man's voice say. It wasn't David. "We can use my tandem."

"We can get it out to you," Florence said, her voice strained from stress.

"Flo and I will go with them to the lab," I heard David say. "JB, you bring our yaks back here."

"We're on our way, Dad," Florence said. "Please hurry."

Savannah went up to the flybridge and quickly uncovered the helm, as I went to the bow and activated the windlass to start hauling in the anchor rode. I heard the engines start just as the hook broke free from the sandy bottom.

A moment later, I had the anchor locked in the pulpit and put the dogs in the cabin before going up to join Savannah.

"Just head due east," I said, powering up the chart plotter.

As *Sea Biscuit* accelerated, I quickly found New Pass and set a waypoint in eight feet of water about two hundred yards off the beach.

"There's your course," I said, as I fished my own phone from my pocket.

I called Kim and explained what was happening as well as my suspicions about it. She said she'd meet us at the lab and then gave me the GPS numbers for the channel that led to it. I scrawled the numbers on a notepad from the chart cabinet.

Though *Sea Biscuit* was faster with her new engines, time seemed to drag as we headed toward shore at twenty knots.

"I should never have—" Savannah started to say.

"This has nothing to do with letting her go," I said. "If we're lucky, she was in the right place at the right time to save a manatee. I'll go down and get some blankets and a bucket to wet them down with."

I wasn't the least bit worried about Savannah at the helm while I was gathering things to make the manatee more comfortable. It was her boat and she knew it very well. Intimately well, as she would say.

From under the settee, I grabbed Savannah's yoga mat, rolled up and secured with a Velcro strap. Then I went down to the aft cabin and took two blankets from the linen closet. On the way out, I retrieved a cleaning bucket from under the sink, along with a short piece of rope to haul it up with. Then I hurried out to the small cockpit.

With the salon and flybridge blocking most of the wind, I managed to spread the blankets on the aft cabin top, next to the dinghy. I overlapped them a little, then rolled out the mat on top of them, and lifted a half-full gas tank from the dinghy to weigh it all down.

Savannah started to slow the boat, so I went to the side deck to look ahead. In the distance, I could discern three light beams, each moving independently back and forth across the water. As we got closer, I could see that the lights were from three head lamps. The one on the right kept shifting to a long, yellow kayak in the center. That would likely be Florence, checking on the manatee in the tandem kayak between her and David.

Sea Biscuit dropped to idle speed as the kayakers got closer. Then Savannah shifted to neutral and shut off the engines. As the kayakers moved toward the stern, she came down to the aft cabin top, then jumped down to the cockpit to turn on the lights under the swim platform and open the transom door. The lights created a glow all around the platform.

I joined her on the swim platform as the three kayaks came around to the stern. The tandem moved into a position with its bow and front seat near the platform. The young man paddling it was a big kid and when he grabbed the platform with both hands, he easily held the boat in place.

Florence and David came alongside and climbed quickly onto the platform. David lashed their two boats together with a short line through each one's lifting handle, then just let them drift away.

The manatee in the front of the two-person SOT—sit-on-top—kayak wasn't moving. It was lying on a large beach towel, which would make it a lot easier to lift. Still, the animal would probably weigh nearly 150 pounds. With David helping me, we lifted by the four corners of the towel and had the animal on the swim deck.

"Up on the cabin top," I said. "I have a spot all laid out."

"It needs to be kept wet," Florence said. "Its skin will dry out fast, even with no sun."

"I'll call you when we get there," David said to the young man in the tandem.

"I hope it's not too late," he replied, gathering up the painter David had tied off to his and Florence's kayaks.

"Go up and get us a half mile out," I told Savannah. "Then turn due south. The GPS numbers for the outer markers are on the note pad."

Florence went with her, both of them talking at once to each other.

I moved up into the cockpit and was able to lean over the rail and grab one end of the towel. David took the other end and we got the manatee through the transom door. I stepped up to the cabin top and put the gas tank back in the dinghy. Then David and I struggled to get the manatee up the three steps onto the roof and then onto the center of the yoga pad.

I heard the double *thunk* as the transmissions were engaged and *Sea Biscuit* started turning.

"Give us a second to get it wrapped up and wetted down," I yelled up to the flybridge.

Working quickly, I tossed the bucket over the side and gently poured it over the injured animal's back. I didn't see any sign of physical trauma. Then David and I pulled one blanket over its back, then the other. I dipped the bucket two more times, thoroughly wetting the blankets, careful to leave the manatee's nose uncovered, but nothing else.

"Okay," I shouted. "Go!"

A moment later, Florence came down and hugged me as the boat started picking up speed. "Mom wants you up there to help her get to the lab. David and I can take care of the baby."

I nodded in the darkness and went up to the flybridge. I checked the chart plotter and saw that we were again making twenty knots and she had the boat centered on the line showing the direction to the waypoint.

Savannah gave a quick glance over her shoulder. "What are the kids doing?"

I looked back to where Florence and David sat on the roof of the aft stateroom.

"They're sitting with it," I said. "Each holding onto the dinghy with one hand and the manatee with the other. They're safe."

"We could go faster," she said. "But you better take the helm. This is already faster than I'm used to."

I held the wheel as Savannah slid out of the helm seat, and then I moved in front of it. After checking the plot line against the compass centered in front of the wheel, I pushed the throttles to the stops and concentrated more on the compass heading, trusting that we were in water too deep for lobster traps.

The thirty-ton boat didn't respond immediately, the way *Gaspar's Revenge* would have, but the digital boat speed readout climbed steadily to nearly thirty knots. For an antique Grand Banks trawler, that was damned fast.

Twenty minutes later, Savannah informed me we were nearing the waypoint. I could see the channel markers and steered toward them as I slowed the heavy boat.

"Everything okay back there?" I yelled over my shoulder.

"It's still alive," David shouted back.

"But it's wheezing and sort of coughing," Florence added.

I steered *Sea Biscuit* into the well-marked channel and slowed to idle speed. I had no idea what the dock arrangement was, and the crescent moon didn't help much, so I was simply following the markers and hoping for the best.

Low-level lights came on ahead, flickering to illuminate a long dock that paralleled the channel. As we got closer, I could see that there was a large turning basin dug into the mainland and the dock was on the north side of it.

There was a center console tied up to the middle of the dock and two people were loosing its lines. I assumed they intended to move it to make room. So, I steered for that spot.

"Take the wheel," I said to Savannah. "I'll get the lines and fenders."

Sea Biscuit's fenders were stored in racks on either side of the bow to make them easy to get to. I glanced at the dock ahead to get an idea how high it was above the water and in minutes, I had the fenders secured at the right height on the port side.

The dock lines were secured to heavy bollards just above deck level and fed through hawseholes. The bitter ends were coiled neatly and made fast on the top rail.

I got the midship spring line first, tossing it to a man on the dock, then started aft.

"I assume you're the one bringing in an injured manatee calf?" the man asked, while quickly looping the line around a dock cleat.

Just as I started to answer, Savannah reversed the engines and then used them to maneuver the big boat sideways. I waited until she finished.

"Yeah," I said, handing the stern line to another dock hand. "It's less than a year old and struggling to breathe. My name's Jesse McDermitt."

"You're the same man who found the dead dolphin calf?"

I moved forward on the teak side deck. "Yes, I am. What are the odds?"

"Infinitely high," the man said, as I threw the bow line toward him.

He had it knotted to a cleat in seconds, then looked up at me. "I'm Doctor Salvatore Angelo," he said. "Most people just call me Sal or Doc."

"Come aboard, Doc," I said, unlatching the opening in the side rail and securing it. "Your patient is back here."

The doctor stepped aboard and followed me back to the side steps up onto the cabin roof, aft the salon.

"He's breathing," Florence said, as we approached. "But it's still a wheezing sound. That can't be normal, is it?"

Savannah joined us and held my arm as the doctor knelt on the deck and produced a stethoscope from his pocket.

"No, it's not," he said, as he placed the end of the device against the side of the manatee.

He moved it around to several places, I guess checking the heartbeat and respiration.

"Can you help us get it inside?" he asked, standing.

By then, several people, most of them about Florence and David's age, were standing alongside the boat.

I pointed to one young man who was a head taller than his companions and looked more like a weight-lifter than a biologist. "You stand ready at the opening—it's about a hundred and fifty pounds."

The young man nodded and stepped forward as I moved around to the animal's tail. David and the doctor each took a corner at its head and we easily lifted the animal with the beach towel.

We carried it across the roof top and down to the side deck, where they handed their corners to the big kid on the dock. He held his end high as I shuffled forward, handing the other two corners of the towel to others on the dock.

The doctor turned to a woman of about thirty with short, brown hair. "Take it straight to Exam One," he said. "Get oxygen going and start an IV with antibiotics. Take a culture swab from inside its nostrils. I'll be right there."

The woman nodded and hurried after the others.

I opened the doors to let the dogs out before jumping down to the dock. Finn was instantly at my side, but Woden remained on the boat with Savannah.

Just then, Kim and Marty came out onto the dock and hurried toward us.

Florence jumped down to the dock next to the doctor. "Is it going to be okay?"

He ignored her and turned to Marty. "What are you two doing back?"

Kim hugged me and then double-hugged Savannah and Florence.

"This is our family," Marty said, shaking my hand.

Introductions were made all around. I don't know if anyone else noticed, but I could see Marty sizing David up.

Kim and Florence had instantly hit it off when I'd told Kim about her half-sister. And Marty had easily fallen into the surrogate big brother role, though he and Kim were more than a decade older than Florence.

Doc turned to Florence. "We won't know if it will survive until we check the slides and run some tests. It very well could have the same problem as the dolphin did earlier today."

Savannah had related what had happened earlier in the day, when Florence had called at dinner time.

"Red tide?" I asked.

"Will your dogs be okay outside? They can't come into the lab."

"They just need to pee on a tree," Savannah said. "Then they'll get back on the boat."

We followed him toward a cluster of low-slung buildings.

"To be more precise," he said, responding to my question and holding a door open for us, "brevetoxicosis is what killed the dolphin calf, caused by the marine dinoflagellate Karenia brevis, commonly called red tide algae."

Once inside, I noted a large waiting area with dozens of chairs along the walls.

Doc saw my expression. "We also do tours here," he explained. "As part of our ongoing fundraising to rescue and treat marine mammals and reptiles."

"So, it's not the algal bloom itself?" I asked.

"The Florida red tide algae produce several toxins," he said. "Including certain brevetoxins, which have potent neurotoxic and hemolytic properties that can be fatal to fish, aquatic mammals, birds, reptiles...even humans."

"There's a bloom near the coast up toward Tampa Bay," Marty said. "But no large blooms have been reported this far south since last year."

"This is a recurring thing?" Savannah asked.

"To one extent or another, yes," I said. "I remember a nasty red tide when I was home on leave in '94. Usually it's not too bad, though."

"That one lasted two years," Doc said, "and wiped out ten percent of the West Indian manatee population. In recent years, the blooms have become larger, but historically there have been worse incidents."

"What causes the larger blooms?" Florence asked.

"Long periods of heavy rain," Marty said. "Like we've been having down in Everglades City."

"Yes," Doc agreed. "Heavy rains create an upwelling from deeper water, miles offshore, bringing the dinoflagellates to the surface. After that, a lot of things must be exactly right for the algae to flourish and displace other non-toxic algae. If all that comes together—salinity, water temperature, competition, and several other events—and if the wind is blowing onshore for a length of time, the bloom can move closer to shore, where it can impact land animals."

"So, the bigger blooms," Florence began, "happen just by chance? It's not a seasonal thing? Does human pollution contribute?"

"I believe, and most will disagree, that stormwater runoff can carry man-made nutrients in the form of nitrogen and phosphorous into the water, which is exactly what Florida red tide algae feed on."

The short-haired woman from the dock came through a door and approached us. "K. brevis," she said. "I'm certain of it."

Doc nodded and put his hand on the woman's back. "This is my wife, Karen." Surprisingly, he introduced her to each of us by name, as if he'd known us all his life.

"You're a marine biologist, too?" Savannah asked.

"No," Karen replied. "I'm a microbiologist. Sal and I met after a lecture at Mote Marine Lab and I came here to study Florida red tide."

"Is the manatee going to be okay?" Florence asked. "I'm the one who found it."

Karen smiled at her. "Yes, she will live. Did you happen to see her mother?"

"*Her* mother?"

"Yes. The baby you saved is a girl."

"I made a point of looking around for the mother before I called the others over. But I didn't see her."

"It's possible we can still reunite them," Doc said. "We know a good many manatees in this area from their scar patterns and have identified more than a dozen who calved this past spring."

"Scar patterns?"

The doctor glanced at me for a moment and I nodded. Then he turned back to Florence. "Nearly all of the slow-moving West Indian manatees in this area, those over the age of three, have propeller scars on their backs."

CHAPTER TEN

After I slipped the lines, Savannah backed away from the dock. She easily turned the big trawler around in the confined space of the man-made lagoon and we were soon idling out of the channel. The reflection of a waxing crescent moon pointed the way as it neared the horizon.

It was late and it had been an arduous day.

Once in deeper water, Savannah stood and said, "I don't know about the rest of you, but I could use a bite to eat."

"Good idea," I said, sliding into her spot behind the wheel. "Why don't you go give your mom a hand," I said to Florence. "David and I need to talk."

She eyed me suspiciously, then followed Savannah down to the galley. David moved up from the aft dinette, where he and Florence had been sitting, and took a seat on the port bench, across from me.

"I know what you're gonna say," David said. "Flo and I aren't—"

I cut him off mid-sentence, before he said something we'd probably both regret. "How well do you know the waters here?"

"The water?"

"I grew up here, but it's been a long time. Currents and eddies change. There used to be an eddy about a mile off Gulfside City Park. We'd sometimes just drift all day, circling around and around, and never had to drop an anchor."

"I know where you're talking about," he said. "But it's more east of the park, closer to the lighthouse. I thought you wanted to talk to me about Flo."

I glanced over at him. "She's my daughter, but she can make her own choices in life, David." I turned to look ahead again. "So that eddy has moved, huh? Do you know other currents farther to the south?"

"You're trying to figure out what the dolphin and manatee might have had in common?"

I shrugged. "Something like that."

David was a good, wholesome kid, though a little bookish, as Pap would have said. He was smart and picked up on things quickly. But he had a streak of out-doorsman in him, too. It was evident in his fascination and love of nature and the sea.

"Besides both being mammals," he said, "they don't have much in common. They live in totally different habitats—inshore and offshore."

"Dolphins still come into the shallows to feed in the Ten Thousand Islands?"

"Not very many people know about that," David said. "Perry and I have seen them a few times. They seem to favor—"

"The lagoon behind Picnic Key?"

He turned and looked at me. "How long ago are you remembering this from?"

"More than forty years," I replied, though it seemed like yesterday.

Billy and I had been canoeing and stopped to camp on the little island. It had about a hundred yards of white sand beach, a few sea grapes, then a big, shallow lagoon on the east side. We'd watched as a pod of dolphin chased a large school of mullet into the lagoon at low tide. Then, in a line, they rushed at the fish, which caused the mullet to do what mullet do. They leapt from the water, stranding themselves on a sandbar. Then the dolphins forced themselves up onto the sand, turning sideways to pick up the flopping fish.

"I told Perry," David said. "He didn't believe me that dolphins could teach things to other dolphins. Do you know that's longer than dolphins live?"

"They pass information down generationally," I said. "What they do there, they learned from previous generations. My grandfather told me about them. He'd watched them herd schools of fish into the shallows behind Picnic Key and feed there when he was a boy during the Great Depression. They went out onto the sandbar and scooped up the mullets to sell at the fish market."

David let out a low whistle. "Ninety years," he said softly. "At least two generations of dolphins."

"My friend, Billy Rainwater, told me that his people have known about them doing this for hundreds of years."

"And manatees are in that area, too," David said, making the connection. "Do you think that's where a bloom is happening?"

"It could be," I said. "The wind's south-southwest now, but it'd been blowing onshore most of last week."

"And they got a ton of rain down there," David said. "Almost non-stop for a week. Runoff from the Everglades would probably have a lot of dissolved fertilizer from Big Sugar."

"Don't blame everything on 'the man,'" I said. "The sugar fields are farther east, and most of the runoff there flows into either Biscayne Bay, via the Miami River, or on down into Florida Bay."

"What else could cause high nutrients?" he asked.

"We don't even know that it was a large bloom," I said, though I figured it likely would be. "But there are lots of ways fresh water can carry nutrients into the Gulf."

"Let's go look," David said.

I laughed. "Go look for what?"

"You have this big boat," he said. "Let's go look for a big red tide bloom."

"Mom and I were just talking about that," Florence said, stepping up to the flybridge behind us and placing a tray on the dinette. "Let's do it, Dad. David and I only have two days left of summer."

"Too bad you left your kayaks," I said. "*Sea Biscuit* can't get very close to shore."

"Call Perry," Florence said, nudging David. "Tell them to pack up and paddle out. We have a mission."

"Whoa," I said. "They might not be quite as excited about this idea and it would take us all night just to get there."

"JB will," David said, digging out his phone. "He's a marine science major. And Jill will want to do it—she grew up here, too. Whatever JB and Jill do, Kia and Perry will follow along."

I looked back at Savannah, who nodded.

"Okay, call them," I said, turning north. "But don't be surprised if they tell you to take a long walk on a short pier."

David paused for a moment. "Perry's just as likely to hang up on me. I'll call JB."

A moment later, David was relaying what had happened at the lab and asked if the "gang" wanted to help in the search for a large algal bloom.

David nodded his head as he ended the call. "JB and Kia will definitely help. He said he'd talk Perry into it."

I bumped the speed up to ten knots and stood. "Take the wheel," I told David. "Keep us on a heading of 345° at this speed. Savannah and I need to check something."

Florence squeezed onto the helm seat beside David, pointing out the compass and crucial engine gauges to him. Savannah followed me down to the salon, where I dug out my laptop.

"What are you doing?" Savannah asked, sitting down next to me.

I opened the lid and waited for it to boot up and for the camera to recognize me. "It's what *you* are going to be doing," I said, clicking the *Soft Jazz* icon on the desktop. "I'm going to call Rusty. When Chyrel comes on the screen, ask her if she can access satellite views of the Ten Thousand Islands area for the last three days."

"She's probably asleep."

"I've never known her to be sleeping before zero-two-hundred."

As the video feed opened, I dug my cell phone out of my pocket and called the Rusty Anchor Bar and Grill, knowing that Rusty's cell would be in the office on a charger.

Rusty was more than just my best friend. He was the keeper of all information worth knowing in the Keys. His family had lived on the same property his bar now occupied for several generations. He knew just about everyone, and anything having to do with the water, diving, or fishing, he was the guy to ask.

"Rusty Anchor," a woman's voice said, as I went forward and sat at the lower helm.

The voice was vaguely familiar. "Who's this?" I asked.

"The Rusty Anchor Bar and Grill."

"No, I meant who are *you*?"

"Sorry," she said. "I just started and this is my first Friday night. Let me try again—Rusty Anchor Bar and Grill, Amy speaking."

Now I recognized the voice. "Amy Huggins?"

"Yes. Who's this?"

"Hey, Amy," I said, remembering more clearly. "This is Jesse McDermitt. Is Rusty around?"

Amy Huggins was the widow of a soldier killed in Ecuador. A few years ago, I'd helped her recover some stolen emeralds. Her late husband had secreted them inside a brick newel post during the construction of their home on No Name Key.

"Jesse!" Amy practically squealed. "It's so good to hear from you. Are you in town?"

"No," I replied. "I'm in Naples at the moment."

"Beautiful area," she said. "Rusty's out back. Hang on. I'll go get him."

I knew the phone at the bar was an old rotary phone with a cord. Though limited, compared to a cell phone or even a landline with a wireless receiver, it had its advantages. If the power went out, the phone still worked, so long as the phone lines stayed up. It got its power from the line.

While I waited, I listened to the bar sounds. Music was playing out on the deck and I could hear several people talking and laughing. Though I couldn't tell what was being said, aside from an occasional word or sentence, it sounded like they were having fun. That was the kind of place the Anchor was.

A moment later, I heard a rustling as someone picked up the receiver. "Hey, you old barracuda! Where the hell are ya?"

"Off Naples," I said. "Got dock space for a couple of boats on Monday? Semi-permanent berthing?"

"*Salty Dog* and *Sea Biscuit*?"

"Yeah, we're planning to stay ashore for a while. Florence starts college on Monday."

"Ah, man, that'll be great! I've missed your ugly mug."

"You looked in a mirror lately?"

"Don't need to, bro. I can look in the eyes of a Playboy bunny to see *my* reflection."

He was talking about his wife, Sidney, who was pictured once in the men's magazine, many years ago, when Rusty and I were stationed together in Okinawa, Japan. Not the centerfold or even a feature, but one of a group of Southeast college girls. Rusty had fallen in lust with her from that picture, and one day, she just showed up at the Anchor, driving a beer delivery truck. Even in bare feet—and she almost always wore heels—she towered over Rusty's five-foot six-inch frame. But they made a great match in so many other ways.

"You're a lucky man, my friend," I told him, and meant it.

"Is that all you called about?" he asked. "'Cause ya know your slip is yours for life. I can put *Sea Biscuit* just opposite you on the end."

"Thanks," I said. "There is something else. Have you heard anyone mention a big red tide in the Ten Thousand Islands area?"

"Hang on a sec," he replied. "Dink took a guy up there scouting for snook just the other day. He's here somewhere. Lemme find him."

With one ear, I listened to the sounds of the bar again. With the other, I listened to Savannah and Chyrel on the video conference. It sounded like they were looking at images together.

There was a loud thunk and a rattle of bottles. "Dammit, Dink!" I heard Rusty yell.

Dink was a local guide who had perpetual sea legs and was very accident prone on land. I imagined there were probably a lot of people who thought his name was Dammit Dink.

"Hey, Jesse," Dink answered. "Rusty said you were asking about the Ten Thousand Islands?"

"Hey, Dink. Yeah. He told me you were up there recently. See any sign of red tide?"

I could tell by his voice when he spoke next that he was cupping the mouthpiece on the receiver. "Yeah, I did. Took a client up there to scout out some spots for when snook season opens on the first. Saw a bunch of dead fish, way in the backcountry east of Dismal Key. I didn't report it."

"What day was that?"

"This past Thursday morning," he replied.

"Why didn't you report it?" I asked.

"Nothing really to report," he said. "A bunch of dead fish, but no sign of what killed them. It wasn't a huge kill, maybe fifty or sixty fish washed up in a cove. My client didn't see it and, like I said, it was all in one little place and way back."

I understood what he wasn't saying. "Way back" was a local term. A lot of people knew about the backcountry of the Keys and Southwest Florida's wild coastline. Way back meant a place where a canoe or kayak was needed.

Or exceptional local knowledge and a flats skiff with a poling platform. Dink had both. He earned a living taking people out to catch fish, and he was one of the best on the water. Taking clients all the way up to that area was expensive, especially so with it still being catch and release season for snook until September first, and Dink charged top dollar. He could do that because he always put his clients on fish.

A red tide problem would close the fisheries in a large area. Not that Dink or the other guides had to be told not to catch distressed fish. By now, he'd spread the word among the guides, and it had gone out to others to avoid that area. Most guides I knew didn't need the government telling them where they could and couldn't fish. The sea told them that and more. They considered the government to be meddling in things it knew nothing about.

"Nobody talking about a big bloom?" I asked. "One that would affect dolphins and manatees?"

"Something like that, I'd a reported it. You know me, Jesse. But no, I haven't heard anyone say anything about a big bloom, except way up toward the middle coast."

I asked him for the GPS numbers, which I was certain he'd recorded.

"Hang on a sec," he said, putting the phone down to dig out his ever-present notepad. He read off the numbers and I jotted them down.

"Thanks, Dink. Put Rusty back on?"

"If I hear anything, I'll tell Rusty," Dink said.

Then Rusty came back on the phone. "I know, I know. If I hear anything about anything in that area, I'll call ya right away. And it's all secret squirrel, hush-hush stuff you can't talk about, right?"

"Nothing secret," I said, maybe too defensively. Savannah looked up at me. "I found a dead baby dolphin this morning and Florence found a nearly dead baby manatee. Both showed signs of red tide toxin."

"Is the sea cow gonna be okay?"

"The guy at the lab said she'll survive and felt confident that they could reunite her with her mother."

"You took it to Doc Angelo?"

"Yeah. You know him?"

"Smart cookie, that guy," he said. "Met him once or twice. I'll let you know if I hear of anything. What time on Monday do you figure on getting here?"

I calculated the distance in my head. "Just after sunset. We'll run straight through from Fort Myers on *Sea Biscuit*, then I'll go back up and get *Salty Dog* later in the week."

"We'll keep a light on for ya."

I laughed. "Tom Bodette has a better radio voice, so don't quit your day job."

We said goodbye and I ended the call as I slid in beside Savannah.

"Hey, Jesse," Chyrel said on the screen.

"Were y'all able to find anything?" I asked.

"Not really," Chyrel replied. "At least nothing resembling a red tide bloom."

"We looked at satellite imagery from two years ago," Savannah said. "The last big bloom up off St. Pete Beach. It was easily identifiable because of the color. But the satellite had been nearly overhead. The only recent images she found are at a more oblique angle."

"'Not really' usually means there *was* something."

"Yeah," Chyrel said. "Two days ago—Thursday afternoon when the clouds went away—satellite views of Southwest Florida revealed a lot of dark water flowing out from several locations."

I remembered what Doc Angelo had said. "Nutrient-rich runoff from all the rain the area got the last few weeks."

"Most scientists think there's no correlation," Chyrel said. "But if a big bloom is going to happen, it'll need food."

"Can you pinpoint the sources?" I asked.

A large, but very localized bloom might not kill a lot. But it could decimate everything in a confined area.

"Five locations," Chyrel said, typing away. "Sending the coordinates to your email."

"Thanks, Chyrel," I said. "If you see any more recent images, let me know."

"You got it," she replied, and then the screen went black.

I went back up to the lower helm and raised the lid on the navigation desk, then returned to the table with Savannah's spiral bound chart book of the Gulf.

Flipping through it, I found the chart showing Naples to Cape Sable and turned the other pages over flat. I opened the email and used an erasable marker on the plastic-coated page to mark each location.

I checked my watch—2300. "From Big Hickory to the first location is forty miles," I said. "Then another forty to the farthest one."

"We should go to the farthest one first," Savannah said. "*Sea Biscuit* can run at twenty knots all day long with the new engines."

"We'll run fifteen," I said. "We won't be able to search until it's light, anyway. And that'll give everyone a chance to rest a little before we start. Some of these spots, we'll have to anchor and kayak to, or leave someone on the boat."

"Why are we doing this again?"

I shrugged. "Do you remember the last weekend of summer before your first year of college?"

Her eyes drifted a moment, and I wondered where they were taking her. A single weekend in her past that she remembered, and I didn't know anything about.

"Do you remember yours?" she asked.

"I didn't go to college until after my first tour in the Marines. And I went to boot camp the weekend after graduating high school. I remember that weekend very well. Going to bed before sunset on a Saturday, knowing Billy was probably tearing up the shrimp."

Savannah rose and picked up the chart book. "That's a bit different than mine," she said with a coquettish smile. "Come on, let's go pick up some college kids."

CHAPTER
ELEVEN

The bright lights of the big Caterpillar 962M front end loader pierced the night as Dan Woodbury turned the key and started the engine. To his right, Ben fired up the other of the two behemoth earth movers.

The sky had cleared Thursday afternoon, several hours after the county inspector had left. By early evening, the dump trucks had started to arrive. Dozens of them, one after another. The pile of sand in front of the construction trailer had grown longer and wider until the trucks stopped coming just after dark.

Ben had arranged the rental of the two very large, fully enclosed wheeled loaders so they would be able to work regardless of the weather, which, so far, had remained dry, even if the ground wasn't.

Dan hoped his luck would hold out. The expense of renting large equipment and bringing in tons and tons of sand would be lost if they didn't finish the project by Sunday night.

The previous morning, Friday, the brothers had started quite early, arriving well before dawn. They'd moved sand from where the trucks had dumped it out to the edge of the island and then along the shoreline, creating and widening a makeshift road in the shallows along the western bank. They'd worked all day and into the night, never stopping. They ate sandwiches in the cabs of the big Cats for lunch and dinner, even as they continued to work. The dump trucks had come all day, arriving before the brothers had moved all the sand from the previous evening.

Just as they'd done on Friday, Dan and Ben had arrived before dawn, fully intent on working straight through again. The sand road now stretched more than halfway along the island's coast and the trucks were due to start arriving again just after first light.

The loaders were equipped with CB radios, just like the trucks, which allowed Dan and Ben to talk to one another and coordinate the dumping as the trucks arrived. There was still a large mound from the previous evening that had to be moved.

With the opportunity to get two of the larger loaders, Ben had changed their earlier plan of having the trucks back up on the sand road they were creating and dumping their loads at the end. The two big Cats could move a whole dump-truck load faster than the trucks could back into the right spot. If one of the trucks got stuck, they'd lose valuable time. But the new plan was working very well and they'd kept pace with the arriving trucks all day long.

Dan checked the loader's gauges and, satisfied it was ready to work again, raised its bucket and put the machine in gear, driving it toward the end of the mound of sand. As he reached it, he lowered and leveled the bucket and mashed the throttle. The engine whined as the big tires bit into the ground.

Just as the machine was about to stop or lose traction, Dan deftly lifted and tilted the bucket a little, getting it as full as possible. Then he lifted the throttle, tilted the bucket upright and raised it. He backed away from the mound and drove around it, following the tracks from the previous day to the beginning of the road they were building.

A few minutes later, after having dumped his load, Dan backed up to where Ben was waiting with another load, then headed back for more.

The brothers alternated like that for a couple of hours, slowly diminishing the size of the mound and lengthening the road.

"Where're the trucks?" Ben called over the radio.

Dan checked his watch. The sun had been up for a while and he saw that it was nearly eight o'clock.

He grabbed the mic and pushed the button on the side. "They should be here already. Give Charly a call. See what's holding them up."

"No need," another voice said over the radio. "Sorry we're late."

"That you, Charly?" Ben asked.

"Yeah, and I have four trucks right behind me," came the staticky reply. "We're about a mile away. Be there in a few minutes."

"Thanks, Charly," Ben said. "Same spot as yesterday, but start dumping at the end nearest where we're working, okay?"

"There wasn't a lot of room there when we finished last night."

"There is now," Ben said. "We've just about moved everything."

The trucks kept coming all day, and the two giant earth movers never shut down. By early evening, they were nearing the west end of the island with the sand road and were well ahead of schedule.

At the end of the day, after the trucks stopped delivering, Dan and Ben shut down the machines. The engines ticked as they cooled in the gathering darkness, and both men climbed down.

Dan stretched his stiff and aching back as his brother approached.

"We got this," Ben said. "And with a day to spare."

"Plenty left," Dan said, pointing toward the mound of sand by the construction trailer. "What do you say we go ahead with pulling the fill back and put this sand in its place?"

Ben turned and surveyed the work they'd accomplished. Dan could see his brother measuring the work to be done and the time they had.

"Yeah," he finally said. "I think we can. So long as it doesn't rain."

"We still have a good ten loads sitting here," Dan suggested.

Again, his brother looked at the edge of the island, then at the mound that was left over.

He pointed along the length of the new sand road. "The fill is shallow along the edge, there," he said. "Down to only a few inches at the nets. And it's mostly dried out now. We can take out native soil there, right alongside the sand road, and go down about two or three feet below the original grade."

Dan nodded his agreement, trusting his brother's mental calculations. "I see what you're saying. The sand road will hold back the seawater and we can use these last ten loads to start backfilling alongside what we've already got."

"Leap frog," Ben said, with a grin. "We just keep the inside lane longer than the outside."

"We have a little light left," Dan suggested.

"Let's do it."

Each returned to the loaders and started them up.

"We'll both start taking it out," Ben said over the radio. "Just dump it off to the side and once we get enough out to run level, you keep removing and I'll start replacing each scoop with sand."

An hour later, the mound in front of the construction trailer was gone and the sand road was as wide as a four-lane highway for twenty yards before the right half ended.

"How long do you think it will take to do the rest?" Dan asked, as the two men met at his loader next to the mound of fill they'd dug out.

Dan had gone deep with his bucket, making sure to take out enough of the original grade to have three feet of nothing but sand when Ben put it in. The expensive fill dirt made up less than half of the content of the mound. The rest was native topsoil, mostly sand. But once it was spread out, it wouldn't matter much.

"Half a day," Ben said, pushing a big rock with his booted foot. "We got a lot done. Hopefully, it won't rain tomorrow."

Dan looked down at the rock. It was the size of a cantaloupe. There weren't many rocks in this part of Florida. In fact, Dan couldn't remember seeing any rocks on the island at all. They'd found broken pieces of concrete, which they attributed to old porches or driveways from back when the island had been a mobile home park in the 60s.

Ben was looking at the rock, too. He pulled his cell phone from his pocket and clicked on the flashlight app, shining it down. "What is that?"

"Too thick to be a part of any driveway," Dan said, squatting to look closer. "An Indian clay pot maybe? There used to be Indians in this area."

Dan rolled the rock over with his hand.

Suddenly, he jumped back, landing on his butt, and scooting away.

"It's a friggin' skull!" Ben said.

CHAPTER TWELVE

I could tell Perry was high as soon as they boarded. I'd smoked more than my fair share during a long bender of a cruise that lasted over a year and a half. I could smell it on him and knew the type. I stepped in front of the transom door as he started up.

"Hand it over," I said.

"Huh? Hand what over?"

"The weed," I replied. "I'll hang onto it and give it back to you when you leave the boat. But if a Coast Guard or Fish and Wildlife vessel comes within a mile, you lose your stash to the sea."

"You can't—"

"Yes, I can," I said flatly. "Possession on board a pleasure craft can result in confiscation and sale at auction. Hand it over or buy the boat and take your own risk. The price is half a mil."

"Just give it to him," Perry's girlfriend said. "I told you not to bring it anyway."

Perry looked around at the others, then shrugged, and pulled a small plastic bag from his pocket. "I want it back," he said, slapping it in my palm.

"Under the conditions I outlined," I said, stepping back, "you'll get it back. Welcome aboard."

"Come on," Florence said, I'll show you where you can put your stuff. Don't mind our dogs—they won't bother anyone."

"You have dogs on your boat?" Kia asked. "What kind?"

"Big," Savannah replied. "But like Flo said, they're gentle giants."

The largest of the three young men, JB, held back as the others shuffled down the side deck and into the salon.

"Thanks, Mister McDermitt," he said. "I told him to just bury it at the camp and he could get it later. He's the only one of us that does that."

The moon had set and though I couldn't see his face clearly, I heard sincerity in his words.

"You're the marine science major, right?"

"Yes, sir."

"Tomorrow, you're gonna get some real world experience on just what you'll be doing for the rest of your life. Rest whenever and wherever you can. It'll be a long day."

After stowing their kayaks on the foredeck, we got underway and I asked everyone to come up to the flybridge.

"You're all adults," I said. "But I want each of you to call or text someone right now and tell them what we're doing. Preferably your parents. The name of the boat is *Sea Biscuit*, and she's a Coast Guard- registered forty-nine-foot Grand Banks, home port Beaufort, South Carolina."

"I'm the registered owner and captain," Savannah added. "I'm Flo's mom, Savannah Richmond. I have a six-pack license and Jesse is a sea captain of unlimited tonnage. That's Jesse McDermitt, with an I and two Ts. You can tell your parents you'll be perfectly safe and back in plenty of time to get up to Gainesville on Sunday."

"Do it now," I said. "If you think they're asleep, text them. We're not moving until everyone does."

"I really don't have anyone to tell," Perry said. "I live with an uncle and he's in Mexico."

"Text him anyway," Florence said. "It's called a float plan. When I was growing up, Mom never left an anchorage without letting someone know where we were going and when we'd arrive."

They all busied themselves with cell phones as Savannah restarted the engines. I set a waypoint on the chart plotter south of us and two miles off Marco Island, then entered the GPS numbers of the site that was farthest to the south as a second waypoint. The two lines made a dogleg with the first half almost due south, then turning south-southeast.

"We'll head southwest until we're five miles offshore," Savannah said, with a quick glance at the chart plotter. "Then turn due south for thirty miles to the first waypoint."

"What should we do about watches?" I asked.

She glanced back at the kids. "What do you think?"

"You and Florence take the girls down and get some sleep," I said. "Once we're far enough offshore and headed south, I'll let David or JB take the helm while I get a little sleep on the bridge. They seem to know their way around a boat. You and the girls can relieve us at zero-four-hundred and you and Florence can do the same thing. That way, either you or I will be on the bridge and can still rest a little."

"That one I know," she said, turning toward deeper water. "Four o'clock."

The watch arrangement was obvious, but nobody grumbled. The girls would sleep while the guys drove and vice versa. And during the time each of us had with them, we'd teach them how to operate *Sea Biscuit*.

They were adults and I was pretty sure the other two couples were sleeping together. From what David had started to tell me, combined with what Savannah had reported from her conversations with Florence, she and David weren't. Maybe this camping trip was to be it, but what did I know?

I did know young men, though. I'd trained thousands and used to be one. Without the girls to impress, they'd do and learn what I told them. The minds of the young were like dry sponges, and every month was but a single water droplet of learning. It soaked in deep. Especially when there were no distractions.

Before going to bed, Savannah brought up two Thermoses of coffee and kissed me goodnight. Finn followed her and settled himself behind the helm seat. I switched on the autopilot and opened the cabinet for a mug. When I filled it halfway, David's head came up from his phone. He was directly downwind of me.

"That smells good," he said.

I handed him a mug and the thermos. "Comes from a little farm in Costa Rica, called Hacienda la Minita. I'd like to visit it someday." I turned to the others. "You college boys grab a mug and come up here. It's time for Navigation 101."

"We know how to use a GPS," Perry said. "And if it breaks, we know where the North Star is."

"Congratulations," I said. "So do most ten-year-old girls. Besides, we're going south, not north."

The moon had set and I'd all but extinguished the back lights on the compass and chart plotter. My eyes had adjusted to the ambient light of the stars, the night sky was clear, and visibility was unlimited. Ahead, I could see our guidepost very low on the horizon.

"Turn off anything that makes a light," I said. "Look off to starboard, toward the horizon. Pick the darkest spot and stare at it for a minute or two."

After a moment, I told them to avoid looking off the port bow. That was where the glow of Marco Island lay, far in the distance.

"Each time your eyes pass over that glow, it'll take a few seconds for your pupils to adjust to the darker sky to the west. If you fire up one of those cell phones, it'll take two minutes. We're in eighty feet of water and it's only going to get deeper, so we're not worried about lobster traps. But you've seen palm trees float up on the beach, right? Hitting one could do a lot of damage. In two minutes, this boat will have traveled the distance of ten football fields. Maintaining night vision is important."

I stood and put a hand up, shielding the glow of the city. "There's Crux, the Southern Cross, dead ahead, where the Milky Way meets the horizon. But look a little off to the right of our course. Your eyes are fully dilated now, so it's difficult to see what you're looking at directly. Peripherally, your night vision is much better. Look for four bright stars in the form of a cross standing upright on the horizon."

"I see it," Perry said, also shielding his eyes from the glow.

"Me too," David added. "I remember seeing it a lot better in Belize—higher in the sky."

"I don't remember that," Perry said.

JB nudged him with a shoulder. "Because you and Jill disappeared every night at sunset."

"The North Star—Polaris—is directly above the north pole," I said. "It guided early mariners until they left the safety of the Mediterranean and voyaged too far south to see it. But there isn't a pole star for the south pole. If there were, we couldn't see it above the Tropic of Cancer. Just as those early mariners couldn't see Polaris when they traveled south of the Tropic of Capricorn. We can only see Crux from spring to fall this far north, and only for a few hours before and after midnight. But it's not the celestial south pole."

"How's that help to navigate, then?" Perry asked. "If there isn't a pole star?"

"Crux points to the celestial pole. If you were to lie on your back at the south pole this time of year, it'd still be almost twenty-four hours of darkness, and you'd see Crux like the hand of a clock, spinning around a black void directly above you."

"So, south is where it's pointing?" Perry asked.

"Exactly," I replied. "The distance to the celestial pole is about four and a half times the length of the cross itself. Then draw a vertical line up to the horizon from there, and that's south."

"I get it," JB said. "So, as the earth spins, it'll appear to move, but all we'll see will be like the needle of a tach, when you rev the engine."

I nodded. "Over the next few hours, it'll start leaning to the right. But it'll disappear over the horizon before it ever gets close to horizontal."

"I bet down in Brazil they can tell time by it," JB said.

"Yeah, but it's like a twenty-four-hour clock. Straight up like it is now is local midnight. Nearer the south pole, where it stays dark during what we call summer, it would be inverted at local noon."

"So, how long have you and Flo's mom been together?" Perry asked.

"Well," I said, grinning, "we've obviously *known* each other for over eighteen years. But we only got back together about a year ago."

"And she's the captain?" Perry asked, somewhat mockingly. "Even though you have a higher license?"

"*Sea Biscuit* has been Savannah and Flo's home since she was born," David offered. "It's her boat."

For the next hour, I instructed my "crew" on ship operations at night. I set the radar alarm for three miles, assigned a short rotation of about forty-five minutes each to watch for anything in the water, and told them if anything happened, to wake everyone on the bridge.

We made the long run uneventfully, as *Sea Biscuit* gobbled up the eighty-five-nautical-mile distance to our first destination. While I'd rested on the bridge, they'd talked a little, but always with one of them keeping a sharp eye on the water ahead of us.

Savannah and the girls came up at 0400 to relieve us with Woden tagging along behind. By then, the three young men were exhausted. Finn followed us down to the salon.

"Your dogs don't even need to be told what to do." Perry said. "They change shifts too."

"That's nothing on our part," I said. "They just started doing that on their own. David, you can take Florence's V-berth. There's a third cabin to starboard with twin singles."

I turned in and managed a solid four hours of deep sleep in the cabin. To some, the drone of the big engines below the salon and the rising and falling swish of the bow wave would prevent sleep. To me, they were a lullaby.

The sound of the engines slowing woke me. Light was shining in through the port side portholes. I dressed quickly and went to the galley to start a pot of coffee.

The pot was full, so I took the Thermos drying in the sink and filled it, then started another pot. Carrying my lifer juice, two bowls, and a bag of dry dog food, I made my way up to the flybridge with Finn following behind me.

The two girls, Jill and Kia, were sleeping at the dinette and David and Florence were sitting on the forward-facing port bench. Savannah was at the helm, her feet up on the dash, as the three of them talked quietly.

The second Thermos and three half-full mugs sat on the dash, so I simply placed my Thermos on the dash with theirs, then put the bowls on the deck and filled them. Finn and Woden started right in on their breakfast.

Florence looked up and whispered, "Morning, Dad."

Taking a sip, I put my hand on Savannah's shoulder and looked at the eastern sky. "Good morning."

The sun had just cleared the mangroves and palms on shore. The view was incredible. The Southwest Florida coast is almost entirely uninhabited until you reach Flamingo, around the other side of Cape Sable. We weren't going that far.

I knew I was admiring a false shoreline—nothing more than a big sandbar, really. Beyond it was sawgrass for miles, with occasional cypress hammocks dotting the landscape—The Everglades.

"We're two miles from the first site," Savannah said, as I glanced at the chart plotter. "Finish your coffee, I need you on the bow."

"Relax a minute, Mister McDermitt," David said, rising from his seat. "I'll get the windlass and watch for any coral heads."

"There won't be any," I said. "Unless they've grown in the last ten years."

David scrambled down to the side deck and went forward to the anchor windlass as Kia came and stood behind Florence, next to me. "Is that where the bloom is happening?"

"It's one of five places we've identified," I replied, still watching the shoreline ahead. "One that *might* be where a bloom could thrive and grow."

The coast of Southwest Florida, once you pass Marco Island, is the last bit of real Florida left. It's an extremely inhospitable environment on shore, with billions of mosquitoes, biting gnats, crocodiles, snakes, and alligators. But the view from just offshore is picturesque and stunningly beautiful.

Patches of white sand beach glistened in the morning sun. Coconut palms swayed in the light breeze. The palms were surrounded by sea grapes and flowering morning glories and sea lavender, all backed by a practically impenetrable wall of mangroves.

As we got closer, we entered the wind shadow created by the mainland as it blocked the south-southeast wind. The waves subsided as the scent of land reached our nostrils. I breathed deep, relishing the smell of the lavender, mixed with the rich, briny scent of the backcountry. There was also the faint smell of decay—centuries-old plant and animal remains, which had settled on the bottom of the primordial ooze. I imagined it was a place similar to this where life first began and where the first sea creature ventured onto the sand.

As Savannah throttled back to an idle, Perry and JB joined us. Perry headed to the dinette where Jill was sitting, and JB had his nose in his cell phone. I knew from experience that it was unlikely he'd have a signal this far from civilization.

He looked ahead, then back down at his phone. "That's Highland Beach," he said, pointing to a long stretch of white sand just north of our course.

"And Broad River just south of it," I said. "That's our first location."

He waggled his phone. "Navionics app."

Savannah shifted the boat to neutral, then into reverse, bringing it to a stop. When she shifted back to neutral again, she called down to the bow, "Which way is the current running, David?"

He stood in the pulpit, looking down at the bottom. After a moment, he turned and yelled back, "Roughly the same as the wind, it looks like."

Savannah turned upwind in eight feet of water. We were within half a mile of Highland Beach, and there was very little in the way of wave activity. On shore, ibises and herons stalked the shallows.

David pointed a little off to port. "There's a big sand patch."

Savannah turned toward where David was pointing. Once over the sand, she shifted to neutral. "Drop it slow," she shouted.

David eased the brake on the windlass and the chain rattled across the roller as Savannah shifted to reverse.

The outflow from the river was visible. Somewhere up there was the source of the runoff. Normally, rivers and creeks in this area carried fresh, clean water from the Glades to the Gulf. The plants filtered it and the snail's-pace movement of the water allowed the sediment it carried to fall to the bottom. It was usually tinged a light tan color from dissolved tannin, but it carried no sediment. What was coming out of Broad River was more than that.

"I doubt we'll find anything here," I said. "But let's get the boats in the water and spread out."

The kids turned to the task with excitement at the prospect of another adventure, and within minutes, had all the kayaks in the water. I went down to the aft cabin and got my go-bag from the bottom of the hanging locker. I checked the Sig Sauer 9mm that was in the bottom of it, and after a moment's indecision, due to being around the kids, I slipped it into its holster and slid the holster under the waistband of my shorts, behind my back.

I also removed a small black box and opened it. Inside were five miniature communication devices that fit in the ear and had bone mics that curled around them and pressed against the bone at the jaw hinge. I pocketed four of them and grabbed the handheld VHF radio from the charger in the salon.

Returning to the flybridge, I handed one of the earwigs to the three young men. "Just push the button on the side and put it in your ear like an ear bud," I told them. "We can keep in touch with each other with them, so long as we stay within a couple of miles of one another."

I demonstrated, and once they all had them in their ears, I said, "Comm check. There's no volume control. Just push it in deeper if you can't hear me okay."

"Like you were right beside me," Perry said.

"Loud and clear," David responded.

"These things are cool," JB said, giving up the race and settling into an easier rhythm. "Are they waterproof?"

"To a depth of one hundred feet," I replied.

"Too bad people can't talk underwater," he quipped. "It'd be cool to dive and talk."

"They work very well with a full-face mask," I said.

Savannah came up from the salon with seven big, two-liter bottles of water in a pair of canvas totes she called "boat bags," then passed them out. "I'll stay on the boat this time," she offered. "What's the plan?"

The others turned to look at me.

"If there *was* a bloom caused by last week's rains," I began, "the onshore winds might have pushed it toward shore and maybe up into the lagoons and estuaries. A friend reported a localized fish kill north of here. Two days ago, the winds backed around to the south-south-east and any algae that was blown inshore might be pooled in lagoons with no northern outlet. So, don't waste time looking toward the south."

"That makes sense," JB said. "Will we be able to see the algae in the water?"

"Maybe," I replied. "Maybe not. If you paddle right into it, you'll likely see it, but you'll probably smell it first. Red tide produces a potent toxin in the water, so we're primarily looking for the aftereffects—dead fish. If any of you start showing any sign of respiratory problems—a cough or scratchy throat—paddle out as fast as possible. Document anything you find with pictures or video."

I turned to Savannah. "I have the handheld and can stay in touch with you. We have earwigs to talk to one another. If we find anything, I'll let you know on channel sixty-eight."

Turning back to the group, I said, "We'll split up here. David and Florence, head south of the river's mouth, but not too far. We're looking for a bloom that will be flourishing due to the runoff. Once you check the area immediately to the south, leapfrog past us and check north of the beach. Perry, you and Jill slip in behind the beach and head north. Check the little bays and lagoons.

JB, Kia, and I will go up into the river a ways and see where this discharge is coming from. Stay together. It's really easy to get separated out here."

"You and Mister Rainwater spent a lot of time here, when you were younger?" David asked.

I looked off to port at the long stretch of sand. Billy and I had camped there many times, as well as at just about every other piece of high ground between Cape Sable and Fort Myers.

"Yeah," I replied. "A lot of time."

We got into the brightly colored kayaks and started paddling away from *Sea Biscuit*. JB and Kia immediately started setting a faster pace than necessary. They weren't going full tilt, but I got the sense that JB was testing me, as he kept looking to see where I was.

He was tall and rangy, maybe an inch or two shorter than me. I matched his pace without appearing to put a lot of effort into it, taking long, deliberate strokes. They had double the power with nearly the same resistance. Nearly the same, because I was a stickler about maintenance, and my kayak's hull was kept polished and free of imperfections that caused drag. It slipped through the water easier. The difference was microscopic, but I had another advantage.

For the average male adult, the span between fingertips, with arms outstretched, is usually within an inch of their height. So, young JB probably had a reach of about seventy-three or seventy-four inches. I'm six foot three, but my reach is more than two inches greater than that—over seventy-seven inches. And I knew how to use that to my advantage.

Soon, JB's furtive glances to see how far he was leaving the old man behind became strained. I maintained a long, steady churn, making it look effortless.

Just a salty old sailor out for a paddle.

Within an hour, we confirmed what I'd earlier believed. The dark water coming out of the mouth of the river could probably help a bloom flourish, but we didn't see any sign of a red tide in the area.

The place Dink had seen the recent fish kill was farther north. Both wind and current would have pushed the algal bloom that direction.

I knew Fish and Wildlife, as well as dozens of volunteer organizations, watched for the eventual red tide to return, but I didn't see any harm in adding a few more eyes.

And this *was* the kids' last weekend before classes started at the university. It'd be nice if they remembered it as the weekend they helped rescue the baby manatee and did something to save others.

CHAPTER THIRTEEN

The Woodbury brothers had agreed to sleep on what they'd discovered. When Dan arrived at the job site Sunday morning, Ben was already there, sitting on the steps of the trailer with a large, brown paper cup from the 7-Eleven store in his hands.

Dan climbed out of his truck and walked toward him. Both men nodded to one another in the morning daylight.

"It's probably a centuries-dead Indian," Ben said, his voice lacking conviction. "Maybe even the survivor of a Spanish shipwreck or an escaped slave. Nobody has lived here since the sixties."

Dan nodded again. He'd been trying to convince himself of the same thing all night. In excavating behind the sand road, he'd kept his bucket at a depth of maybe thirty inches below the original grade. Not really deep enough for a grave, but who knew what this island had looked like two hundred years earlier? It might have been the mainland and the barrier islands were farther out.

"Or it could just as easily be a burial mound," Dan said, slapping his work gloves in this hand. "And we disturbed it."

"It could be just about anything," Ben said, looking up at his older brother. "But if word gets out, no matter *how* it got here, it'll be the nail in our coffin."

That was the crux of what both had been thinking. If the skull were ancient, scientists would move to shut them down until they could recover the rest of the remains and sift through the sand of the whole island. The Tribal Council had far-flung powers in South Florida. If it were more recent, the skull could have come from a murder victim, hastily buried in the soft soil. That would definitely shut things down.

In twenty-four hours, the county inspector would return. The flow of rich topsoil draining away from the island development had been stopped, and there wasn't any rain in the forecast for several days. But the project had practically tapped them out. Wells would ask why the sand they'd brought in was partially in the shallows and not completely backfilled on dry land. The county could just as easily shut their job down and bring in a crew to finish the work, and they might uncover more bones.

"If you hadn't turned it over with your foot," Dan said, then sighed. "I don't know what to do."

"There's a first," Ben said, looking up at him with a half grin.

Though Ben had said it in jest, it was close to the truth. Dan was not an indecisive man. He'd always had a clear view of what he was doing and why.

"What do you think we ought to do?" he asked.

Ben's smile left his face. "I see you brought your work gloves."

Dan looked down at the worn leather gloves he was holding. He'd absently grabbed them out of the passenger seat when he exited his truck. Then he looked to his right, where the big Cats sat in cold silence, mute to any decision the brothers might make.

"Continue the job and wear blinders?" Dan asked. "Just pretend we didn't see what we saw last night? Where is it, anyway?"

"I put it down at the end of the sand last night," Ben replied.

"Can you live with the uncertainty, Ben? It might even be someone recently drowned or murdered. This place has been abandoned for decades."

"Isn't this what you pencil pushers say is a margin call?" Ben said, then took a drink of his coffee. "Everything we own is right here, Danny. Our hopes for the future and for the kids. We're at the end of our damned rope, here. We're overextended and teetering on the cliff, man!"

Just then, the sound of a diesel truck crossing the bridge drew their attention. Dan turned and saw a Dodge Ram approaching the island, its tires humming on the road and clacking on the bridge's expansion joints.

"Get the loader started," Dan said. "Get that next load of sand in place, now!"

Ben sprinted to the loader and climbed inside as Dan walked out toward his truck to see who was coming. He knew what he'd just told his brother to do—hide the evidence. They had no choice. They had to ride it to the end. If the bones were discovered later, he and Ben would deny any knowledge of it.

They only needed to sell one more lot to be liquid again. Two would give them breathing room to continue the project at full speed.

The big Cat's powerful engine started as the black Dodge dually turned toward Dan and came to a stop beside his truck.

Ben drove off toward the end of the inside road, where the skull lay in the trench Dan had dug the previous evening.

"Mornin'," a woman said, getting out of the driver's side.

She was older than Dan, not homely, but very rough-looking. Her hair was disheveled, and she dressed like a man—baggy jeans, a red-and-black flannel shirt, a black windbreaker, and boots. It was only when she walked that Dan was certain she was a woman.

The passenger door opened, and a younger man got out, coming around the front of the truck in a leisurely fashion. Though the sun was barely above the horizon, he was wearing dark sunglasses.

"Something I can help you with?" Dan asked.

"More like what I can help *you* with, asshole," the woman said.

"Excuse me?"

"You hard a hearin'?" the man asked. "Ma said we was here to fuckin' help you, man."

"Who are you and what do you want?" Dan demanded. "This is private property and I have work to do."

"You listen to me, jerk wad," the woman said, pulling back one side of her windbreaker to reveal the butt of a gun sticking out of her pants. "From this day on, I give the orders. Name's Kurt Blanc and this here's my boy, Donnie Fortress.

Dan froze at the sight of the gun. "What do you want here?"

"My uncle asked me to stop by," the woman with a man's name and mannerisms said. "Senator Jubal Blanc. Ever hear of him?"

Dan had heard the name, but aside from that, he knew nothing about the man, or even if he was a state senator or represented Florida up in Washington. Dan didn't follow politics.

"I've heard the name," he said. "But that's about it."

"Are you the contractor here?" the younger man asked.

"I done told you to shut the fuck up and let me handle this!" Kurt roared at her son.

Dan's eyes darted back and forth between the two. The dynamics were simply weird. He could hear Ben's loader backing up now—the deed done.

"Well, are ya?" Kurt asked, taking a step closer.

"Yes, I'm the developer, Dan Woodbury."

"And that'd be your little brother, Ben, out there in that loader?"

Dan nodded, but didn't speak, wondering how the woman knew who they were.

"Tell him to get his ass over here," Kurt said. "The three of us need to talk."

Dan backed up to his truck, and the woman moved forward. Dan noticed she stayed well beyond his reach. And judging by the scar on her left cheek, she was no stranger to fighting.

He reached in and took the microphone from the truck's CB and keyed it. "Ben, I think you better come up here."

"What's going on?" his brother asked.

"I don't know. Just get up here."

He tossed the mic onto the seat and turned to face the strange woman. "Just exactly what do you and your son want? There isn't much of value here."

"There is to us," she replied. "Y'all find anything interestin' while digging around out there by the beach?"

Dan couldn't keep the surprise from his face as his jaw unhinged and fell open.

"Dammit!" Donnie Fortress said. "They found 'em, Ma!"

"Dint I tell you to shut the hell up, boy?"

Them? Dan thought. *He'd said we found* them, *not* it.

The loader turned and started toward where Dan stood by the trucks with the two strangers. Finally, it stopped and Ben lowered the bucket with a thud, shut off the engine, and climbed down.

"What's going on?" he said, approaching his brother.

"She's got a gun, Ben."

Ben stopped short of his brother and looked at the man and woman who'd arrived in the Dodge.

"What do you need a gun for?" Ben asked.

"Depends," Kurt said. "Seems like you dumb fucks done dug somethin' up out there that shoulda never been dug up. So, I can either shoot your sorry asses and have Donnie use that loader to bury you ten feet down in the salty brine what's under this island or we can negotiate."

"Dan," Ben said, stepping up beside him. "What the hell's this woman talking about?"

"I'm talkin' about the dead," Kurt said. "You seemed in a big-ass hurry to run out to the end of that...whatever the fuck it is you're building, with an empty loader. I seen ya push dirt down into that hole. Trying to cover something up?" She grinned, showing stained, yellow teeth. "Only it weren't there no more."

Dan swallowed hard. How this woman found out, he had no way of knowing. But she had, and she now had the skull, so the cat was out of the bag.

Dan shifted uneasily. "Where is it?"

"We took it," the woman said. "And that's all you need to know."

"Who was it?" Dan asked.

An ugly smile slowly spread across the woman's face again. She was missing a couple of teeth and those that were left were stained dark yellow. Dan had seen it before. She was a crackhead.

"Just some old slut that died a long time ago," Kurt said. "Nobody important, and there ain't nobody alive to miss her. The real question is what're you two gonna do about it?"

"What is it you think we ought to do?" Ben asked.

"You're gonna forget ya ever saw them bodies, assbite!" the young man snarled.

Kurt wheeled and punched Donnie hard. It wasn't a hammer-type blow—the way Dan had seen some women fight—but a solid punch from a meaty left fist. The blow dropped the younger man to one knee, stunned, blood flowing from his nose.

"I ain't gonna tell ya again, Donnie! Shut the fuck up!"

Donnie wasn't the only one startled by the sudden violence of the attack. Dan had seen his share of fist fights and had been involved in a few. But he'd never seen a woman strike a man with such ferocity.

Especially not her own son.

She turned on Dan and quickly drew the gun from beneath her windbreaker. Pointing it at Ben's chest, she expertly thumbed the hammer.

"Now, if you don't tell me what I wanna know," she said in a menacing tone, "I'm gonna kill your little brother first."

Dan held up both hands, palms out, stepping in front of Ben. "No, no, I'll tell you anything you want to know. Just don't hurt anyone."

"What'd you dig up?" Kurt demanded.

"A skull. We found a human skull."

"How many besides the one you put out there?"

"How many?" Dan parroted. "Just one. How many are there?"

"And brother Ben thought he was goin' out there to bury it with that loader?"

"Yes!" Dan said, willing to agree to anything the woman said.

She lowered the gun but didn't put it away. "Well then. That makes you 'complicit,' as Uncle Jubal would say. 'Accessory to murder after the fact.' Ain't that what he said, Donnie?"

The younger man staggered to his feet, tilting his head back, while wiping and pinching his nose. "Yeah, Ma."

"Uncle Jubal checked you two out real good," Kurt said. "You fuckers are feelin' the pinch and runnin' outta money, is what he said. One more little delay, and this island will turn back into the dump it's always been. Ain't that right?"

"What's one thing have to do with the other?" Dan said, not admitting to anything.

"You ever hear of the Flat Tire Killer?"

"The what?" Ben asked.

"Started way back...ah hell, I don't know...just after the Korean War. Unsolved murders continuing up to just before I was born in 1970."

"Almost twenty years?" Dan asked, trying to remember if he'd ever heard of it.

"Story I heard," she began, pure evil reflecting in her eyes, "for about fifteen years, more'n fifty women went missing. Prolly more, just nobody cared enough to file a report about 'em. Mostly, they come from over on the east coast. A good half of 'em, at least, were buried right here."

"How do you know all this?" Dan asked.

"The Flat Tire Killer was my grandpa—Uncle Jubal's daddy."

"Look," Ben said, obviously confused and in a rush, "I don't know if this has anything to do with why you're here, but a bunch of kayakers are coming up the creek."

CHAPTER FOURTEEN

We'd spent all day yesterday paddling through the maze of cuts and shallows that made up part of the Ten Thousand Islands. Not all of it; that'd take weeks, but we knew the locations of possible big blooms, if what Doc Angelo had said was right.

The first three locations had yielded nothing unusual, except for the high outflow of darker-than-usual water. We'd covered twenty-four miles of the wild Florida coast and then it was another twenty-five to the fourth site. After arriving late in the afternoon, the crew was exhausted. So, we'd dropped anchor in Gullivan Bay, not far from Dismal Key, where Dink had seen the kill. I wanted to look there before going on up Coon Key Pass to Goodland Bay.

I'd rousted the crew from their slumber at sunrise. JB was like me, instantly awake and ready. The others... not so much.

There was another site, fifteen miles farther north—the last of those Chyrel had identified in her first email. During the night, she'd emailed me the location of a sixth one, just north of Marco Island in Rookery Bay, a large inland waterway accessible only by kayaks and canoes. Getting to it involved paddling north from Hurricane Pass for several miles.

I was unsure if we had the time. To reach these four places and get back to Fort Myers with enough time for the kids to get to Gainesville meant pushing hard.

I checked my phone's GPS. "Should be just ahead," I told David and JB, as we paddled through the flats off a hook-shaped peninsula.

The others had stayed aboard *Sea Biscuit*, while the three of us paddled deep into the backcountry. The distance to the boat was only about three miles, but we'd paddled more than that to get to the coordinates Dink had given me. There were no straight lines in the Ten Thousand Islands.

There was a time when I'd had no electronic aids to fish the backcountry. Billy and I had simply loaded his canoe into his father's old truck and driven down US-41 until an interesting place appeared.

The hook-shaped island had a sandy beach that stretched for nearly half a mile. Then it disappeared around a stand of white mangroves growing on high ground near the base of the peninsula. I remembered camping there a few times.

"Just beyond those mangroves," I said, pointing ahead. "There's a small cove.

David glanced over at me. "Those don't look like mangroves."

"There are three kinds," JB said. "Red mangroves grow right up out of the water near the sea. Those are the island builders, trapping sand and dropping leaves to create soil. Black mangroves grow in mud a little farther inland in brackish water. And white mangroves grow on dry land and look more like regular trees."

As we paddled past the point, the evidence of a recent red tide was plain to see. The white sand along the shoreline was littered with dead fish, flies and crabs swarming all over them.

Fortunately, the wind was at our backs. Otherwise, I'm sure the stench would've driven us away. We paddled closer, spreading out a little.

"There must be hundreds," David said.

JB reached over the side and plucked a dead mullet fingerling from the water. "More like thousands."

The crabs began to scatter as the bows of our kayaks got close to shore. This was more than Dink had reported. A lot more. From what he'd said, I was expecting to find a few dozen dead fish. Looking up and down the beach, the line was unbroken. Dead fish of all kinds were washed a good two feet up onto the sand and piled on top of one another in the shallows.

How could so many be in one place? The islands that made up this part of Florida actually numbered more than ten thousand, as the name would suggest. Some said it was closer to twelve or fourteen thousand, though nobody knew for certain. The waters moved freely through and around them, controlled by the everchanging tides, winds, and currents. The dead fish might have been blown into this area.

"Tens of thousands," I said, pulling my cell phone out of my pocket.

I had two bars, which was surprisingly good. I snapped a couple of pictures, north and south of our location, then put them in a text to Kim, along with the GPS coordinates.

"Let's spread out," I said. "Move downwind and look into any coves like this."

Kim called me as soon as JB and David paddled away to the north.

"You're a long way from the Gulf," she said, when I answered.

"The others are on *Sea Biscuit*, anchored in Gullivan Bay."

"Who's the young man with David in the one picture?"

"A friend of his from college," I said. "His name's JB Bradford, a marine science major. He's part of the group Florence and David were camping with and we decided to look for what killed the little dolphin and almost killed the baby manatee."

"I forwarded your pictures to Doctor Angelo. He just texted me back and said he'd have a couple of research assistants there within an hour. How'd you ever find it so far back?"

"I had a Dink," I said, paraphrasing a line from the movie *Crocodile Dundee*.

"Ah, I should have known. But why didn't he report it himself? That kill looks to be at least three days ago."

"When he saw it, he said it was small and very localized, just a few fish. This island acts sort of like a funnel—it's over half a mile long, with a deep cove at the north end."

"Will you be in the area long?"

"We're heading back to the boat soon if we don't find anything more here," I replied. "There's another place just up Coon Key Pass I want to check out and two more north of Marco."

"More tips from Dink?"

"From Chyrel."

"Oh," she said, sounding surprised. "I didn't know Armstrong Research was into environmental concerns."

Kim had been bugging me to retire completely, worried I was too old for the dangerous situations I sometimes found myself in.

"She's freelancing," I said. "But Jack is concerned about trying to right a lot of things wrong in the world."

Jack Armstrong was a billionaire several times over. He'd been very wealthy before 9/11 and afterward had put together a group of uber-wealthy patriots to do things the federal government couldn't. He'd lost his wife and only child in the World Trade Center.

"Jack and Jesse," Kim said. "Twins separated at birth. I can meet you over in Goodland. Today's my day off. You're not going to paddle all the way up the pass, are you?"

"No, we're taking *Sea Biscuit* up to Goodland and taking the kayaks from there," I said. "We have an extra one."

"I'll bring my board," she said, meaning her stand-up paddle board, or SUP.

"Suit yourself," I said.

We ended the call, and I started paddling again.

Up ahead, a small crocodile, maybe five feet long, was slowly stalking a threesome of sandhill cranes that were wading along the bank, stalking prey of their own. I smacked the water with my paddle, sending an arcing spray toward the little family group.

With their seven-foot wingspan and a weight of only ten or twelve pounds, the mother and father could easily fly away. The young one had only recently fledged and probably hadn't taken flight to test his new feathers yet. Instead, the trio high-stepped up onto shore and crossed over the dune to the other side.

These long-lived native birds were joined every winter by their cousins, the greater sandhills, which could fly three hundred miles a day when they came down from the Great Lakes area.

The croc disappeared beneath the surface. He'd find another meal somewhere. Hopefully not an endangered species.

At 0800, I rounded up my fellow paddlers and we started back to the boat. I radioed Savannah and told her she'd see us at the north end of Turtle Key.

When we paddled out into the bay, the others were preparing to hoist anchor. Finn was first to notice our approach and barked once, standing on the foredeck with his tail wagging. Woden soon joined him.

Savannah started the engines and looked down as we passed the port side. "We're ready as soon as you're aboard."

The dogs followed us to the little cockpit and we climbed aboard, both dogs melting at my feet.

"They act like you've been gone forever," Perry said.

"That's typical Lab behavior," I said, rubbing their flanks. "Woden didn't used to be like this. He's always been very stoic and aloof."

We were soon underway, navigating the narrow channel toward the town of Goodland.

"Kim's going to meet us at the public boat ramp," I told Savannah when I got up to the flybridge.

"How come?" she asked, carefully steering the big boat.

"She and Marty have different days off," I replied. "Maybe she's bored."

She pointed to the fuel gauge. "I can fill up there, too."

"Yeah, but let's go upriver, closer to the site first. I can take most of the kids to check it out, while you come back for fuel."

Kim was waiting at the floating dock when we arrived. In some areas, where tides barely changed a foot, fixed docks were the norm. But in places where the difference between high and low tide could be twenty feet or more, floating docks were required. Otherwise you were constantly re-tying the lines. This area got about four feet during a full moon king tide. Tying up tight to a fixed dock at high tide in a place like this could find your boat hanging from one side six hours later, or worse, snapping the lines and drifting away.

Though she's said it was her day off, Kim wore her uniform cap with the Florida Fish and Wildlife patch. She also had her badge and sidearm clipped to the belt of her cargo shorts.

"I thought you were off duty," I commented, taking her SUP, and passing it forward to David.

She waited until the boat's fenders bumped the dock, then stepped over. "I am," she said. "But in some places around here, guys tend to be a little over-aggressive toward women who are alone."

Finn and Woden greeted her, allowing her to scratch their ears for a moment before heading back up to the bridge and the shade of the Bimini.

"Back out the way we came," I told Savannah. "Then left around Walker's Marina and head upriver."

"You're a cop?" Perry asked, surprise and paranoia registering on his face.

The others gathered and Florence did the introductions. She looked at her sister with obvious pride. "My sister's a sworn officer with Florida Fish and Wildlife."

JB let out a low whistle as we passed the marina, where a pair of go-fast boats were tied off to an outside face dock.

"I wonder what one of those costs?" he asked rhetorically.

"More to operate than to buy," I said. "And if you have to ask either, you can't afford either."

Both boats were Cigarette 42X models, one painted in a garish red and black checkerboard motif and the other with even more outlandish green and orange lightning bolts.

I never could understand that. As if screaming across the water at a hundred miles an hour wasn't flashy enough, almost every go-fast I'd ever seen had been painted to draw attention while sitting still.

Ten minutes later, we were creeping slowly northward along the small town's eastern shoreline toward Goodland Bay.

"See that green marker?" I said checking my watch. "Number 7?"

Savannah nodded.

"There's a deep hole just to the northeast of it, about twenty feet. We'll anchor there long enough to get everyone in the water."

I turned to the others who'd all assembled on the bridge. "It's nearly zero-nine-hundred." I pointed to the bridge visible to the northwest. "The discharge was coming from just beyond that bridge. That's Marco River, which separates Marco Island from a small, uninhabited bunch of mangroves called Turtle Island. We'll splash here while Savannah goes back to the marina to refuel."

"Are you sure it's uninhabited?" JB asked. "I can see a couple of loaders over there."

I got Savannah's binoculars out of the cabinet and trained them on the bridge. Beyond the high span, I could see the once densely covered island stripped bare. JB was right. There were two big Caterpillar front end loaders, plus a large utility trailer of some kind, and a pickup truck. A new bridge connected Turtle Island to Highway 92.

"Looks like the island's being developed," I said. "Could be the source of the runoff."

"We're still a couple of hours from home," Kia said. "Will you have time to get to both?"

"We don't have to take time to anchor," Savannah said, studying the chart plotter. "This holes plenty big and there's no current. It must be slack tide. Why don't y'all paddle up, check it out, then continue on to the next location? It's only a few miles by kayak and in the manatee zone, you can go faster than *Sea Biscuit*. That'll give me plenty of time to gas up then circle around Cape Romano and Marco Island to meet you. If someone will stay back to help guide me, we can probably get to Hurricane Pass about the time you finish checking it out."

"Good idea," I agreed. "Let's get the boats in the water. Who all is going?"

Everyone nodded, ready to go exploring again, except Kia. "I got a little too much sun already," she said.

"Kia can guide me through the shallows, then," Savannah said. "If we get there early, we'll anchor just off the beach."

Within minutes, we had the kayaks and Kim's paddle board in the water and were shoving off. Savannah expertly turned the big trawler around and started back the way we'd come.

As we approached the high bridge crossing over to Marco Island, I noted a beach with several canoes and kayaks on it off to the right, with a parking lot adjacent to it. Little businesses like that had sprung up all over the area since I'd lived there, with the advent of eco-tourism.

Going under the bridge, I heard a big diesel engine start. A moment later, one of the loaders we'd seen moved out onto the beach on Turtle Island. It pushed sand ahead of it for a moment, then started backing up. Finally, it went back inland and the sound of the engine died.

As we approached the island, I could see four people gathered around three pickups near where the loaders were parked.

"You kids wait here," I said, checking my GPS app. "The source of the runoff is right there where they're working. I want to talk to the guy running the loader."

"I'm going with you," Kim said.

"Me too," JB and David both chimed in at the same time.

"Okay," I allowed. "But the rest of you stay out here in the middle of the river."

As soon as the loader had started, I'd felt a cold chill run down my spine. Though JB and David were unarmed, they were both capable young men, and Kim and I were both armed.

We split up. JB had opted for a single instead of paddling his tandem alone. The four of us spread out and approached the sandy shoreline.

I could tell right away that it wasn't native sand. Across the river the sand was powdery, bleached white by the sun. The beach ahead was darker and the sand looked coarse. Beyond it, the island's soil looked dark and rich, muddy with puddles of standing water.

A man with shaggy blond hair wearing a black windbreaker separated from the group and started toward us.

Kim and I moved ahead. Reaching the shallows, she stepped off her board and I climbed out of my kayak. We were still a good fifty feet from the beach, though.

"That's far enough," the man shouted in a high-pitched voice.

As the figure got closer, I realized it was a woman dressed in men's clothing.

David and JB both climbed out of their yaks behind us, as Kim and I sloshed forward in the knee-deep water.

"Are you deaf, motherfucker?" the woman shouted, sweeping the right side of her jacket back.

"Gun!" Kim shouted, pushing David to the side, and drawing her Glock. "FWC! Hands where I can see them!"

I didn't waste time with a warning but had my Sig up and leveled at the woman in half a heartbeat.

She jumped to the side, pulling her own gun out and firing wildly.

Kim and I both returned fire, she with her feet firmly planted, and me advancing with every shot toward the woman. Fifty feet is a long distance for a handgun.

The woman scrambled behind a pile of sand, ducked for a moment, then rose, and ran headlong toward her friends.

My eyes tracked her as Kim and I both moved faster toward shore. One of the woman's friends ran to a black pickup and got in. Before we could reach shore, the pickup fishtailed in the loose soil and headed toward the new causeway, with the woman chasing after it, screaming. At the foot of the bridge, the truck stopped, and the woman got in.

Kim and I made it to shore and with our guns pointed at the two remaining men, we spread out and moved toward them.

"FWC!" Kim shouted again. "On your knees with your hands behind your head!"

The two men complied, dropping to their knees as the black pickup roared away across the causeway.

"Who are you?" Kim asked, pointing her weapon at the taller of the two men.

"Dan and Ben Woodbury," he replied, obviously shaken. "I'm Dan. We own this island."

CHAPTER FIFTEEN

"Y ou good for nothin' prick!" Kurt shouted at her son when she climbed into the truck. "The fuck you doin' runnin' off like that? I've a mind to kick your ass."

"Who were those guys?" Donnie asked, turning north onto Highway 92, and accelerating.

"Cops," Kurt said.

"Cops on kayaks? What the fuck?"

"Keep driving," Kurt said, taking a glass pipe from the glove box to settle her nerves. "Head to Marley and Willy's house. We're gonna need his help."

Donnie glanced over at his mother. "Ma, Willy's crazy."

She glared back at him. "You think I don't know that, dumbass? His kinda crazy is just what those fuckers need. Now shut up. I need to call Uncle Jubal."

As Donnie drove, Kurt dug her phone out of the pocket of her jeans. Jubal's personal assistant answered immediately.

"Lemme speak to Uncle Jubal," Kurt demanded.

She'd only met Jubal's assistant a couple of times and, though the woman was always dressed very conservatively, Kurt sensed there was something dangerous about her.

"He's in a meeting," the assistant replied. "Do you have something to report?"

"Oh, I don't know," Kurt said, trying to control her voice, "just a bunch of cops waitin' to ambush us and then shootin' at us. Put Jubal on, bitch."

"Gunshots?" Chloe asked, unfussed. "Was anyone killed?"

"I think I got one of 'em. There was six against just me."

"Never mind that," Chloe said. "Did you speak to the developers?"

"Yeah, I spoke to 'em. They found one of C. Roy's playthings, but I think they woulda played along if the cops hadn't got there. Are you gonna put Uncle—"

"No," Chloe interrupted. "As I said, he's taking a meeting downstairs."

"I don't give a shit!" Kurt said. "Maybe you ain't hearin' too good. You need me to come down there and—"

"What?" Chloe said, cutting her off once more. "The senator is in a meeting. If you feel the need to come here to his office, Kurt, feel free." The woman's voice dropped low and menacing. "His meeting won't be interrupted, and I'll kick your ass all the way back down to the ground floor."

Kurt was stunned. Nobody had ever talked to her that way. "Who the fuck do you think you are?"

"You have a phone in your hand," Chloe said. "Google it. In the meantime, I'll find out who the responding officers were and get any mention of what happened quashed."

There was a click, and when Kurt looked at her phone's screen, she saw that the woman had hung up on her.

"That bitch!" Kurt shouted, banging a fist on the dash.

"Who, Ma?"

"Uncle Jubal's almighty gatekeeper. That Chloe slut."

"She's hot," Donnie said, slowing as he reached the intersection at US-41.

"What's her last name?" Kurt said, looking at her phone.

"Somethin' like devil," he replied. "Suits her. Man, what I could do to that ass, if I—"

"Devlin," Kurt said, tapping the screen. "Chloe Devlin."

She scrolled through the search results, opening one page after another. "Here she is," Kurt finally said, turning the phone to show Donnie a picture of the woman.

Kurt scrolled down the page, slowly reading Chloe Devlin's biography from a company she'd worked for while in college.

"Says here she's a kick boxer," Kurt mumbled. "MMA, whatever that is."

"Mixed martial arts," Donnie said, almost gleefully. "Cage fightin'. No holds barred."

"I'll cage that bitch next time I see her," Kurt said. "Says she's also a rifle and pistol shooter. Coupla trophies."

Kurt went back to the search results and continued scrolling. "Uh- oh," she said, tapping on a news headline from five years earlier.

"Says here she killed a man," Kurt said. "In a bar up in Orlando."

"Reckon Uncle Jubal knows about that?"

Kurt looked over at Donnie. "I found it on Google, dipshit. Course he knows."

"Who'd she shoot?" Donnie asked, as he turned off the highway onto the poorly maintained crushed shell road that wound through the swamps to the family homestead.

She lowered her phone and stared straight ahead through the windshield. "Din't shoot him," she mumbled. "She beat him up and run him outta a night club. Then he come back in with a blade. Story says she took the pig-sticker from him and nearly cut his head off with it."

.

CHAPTER SIXTEEN

J B had been hit during the gunfire exchange, but it was barely a nick on the outside of his left shoulder. I'd gone into the Woodbury brothers' construction trailer, found a first aid kit, put a couple of butterfly strips on the wound, and bandaged it.

Kim had called in the shooting on her cell phone. Marty was on his way, but deputies would arrive before he got to us.

"Maybe you should go with the others," Kim said, after ordering the two brothers to sit on the steps of the trailer.

"No. Those two will tell deputies that we both fired back and took them into custody, and you won't be able to explain that."

"Yeah, but—"

"No buts," I said. "My gun's legal and I have a permit. You know that. I was shot at in the presence of a law enforcement officer and under Florida's 'stand your ground' law, I was perfectly within my rights to return fire."

My middle daughter looked at me, an expression of concern in her eyes.

"Besides," I said, "JB needs to be checked out by a paramedic."

"He *needs* to go to the hospital," she said, loud enough for him and David to hear.

"Nah," JB said. "I don't need a hospital. I have classes tomorrow."

"Perry!" I called to where the others were waiting down on the beach. "Are you okay taking the girls out to the boat?"

"No problem," he said, stepping closer and looking at Kim. "You don't need us for like a witness or something?"

"Y'all go ahead," Kim replied. "I got this."

David walked down to the beach and hugged Florence, and then he shook Perry's hand and said something I couldn't make out.

In the distance, I could hear the wail of a siren approaching. Perry, Jill, and Florence got into their kayaks and started paddling down the river in the same direction we'd been going when we arrived.

A few minutes later, a cruiser with Collier County markings came across the causeway, lights flashing. It stopped behind the brothers' pickups and two deputies got out.

Kim walked toward them, pulling her ID from her pocket. "Officer Kim Phillips, FWC, Law Enforcement Division."

"Sergeant Robin Watson," the guy on the passenger side said, as he came around the hood. "This is Deputy Drew Blake. What do you have?"

"One civilian injured," Kim said. "Just a flesh wound but I want him to see a paramedic, at least. The shooter escaped in a newer model, black Dodge dually. A woman about fifty years old, blond, heavyset, wearing jeans, a red flannel shirt, and black windbreaker. The driver was younger, but too far away to get a good look at. Nor could I get the tag, except that it was Florida."

The two deputies exchanged a look, almost as if they recognized the description.

"Check Rescue's ETA, Drew," Sergeant Watson said to the other deputy.

"On it."

"What about those two?" the sergeant asked, nodding toward the brothers.

"Property owners and developers," Kim replied. "I haven't had time to ask them much of anything, but the shooter and her accomplice had just arrived when we came under the bridge."

"And those guys?" he asked, nodding toward us.

"My father, my sister's boyfriend, and a friend of his," Kim replied. "We were on a private excursion."

He glanced down at Kim's bare feet, civilian attire, and the gun clipped to her belt. "Do you always open-carry when off duty?"

Kim smiled at him. "If you were a woman in this area, wouldn't you?"

He grinned back at her as a gray-green F150 turned onto the causeway. It had FWC markings on the side.

"Point taken," Watson said. "Your call, Officer. You're first on scene and have authority far beyond Collier County. Whatever the county can do to assist, just let us know."

Kim grinned at me and bobbed her head toward the brothers. I fell in beside her and we walked toward the trailer. Marty got out of the pickup and headed toward us.

"That deputy knows who the shooter is," I said, keeping my voice low.

"I know, Dad."

"He didn't ask many questions."

"Like he said," Kim began, "FWC is a state agency with federal powers in some cases." She looked at me and grinned the way she had when she was a teenager. "That means I outrank him."

"I got the call there was a shooting," Marty said. "Is everyone okay?"

"Yeah, but the shooter got away," Kim replied, then turned her attention to the older of the two men. "Mister Woodbury, can you tell me anything about the woman?"

"Nothing other than what she looked like," Dan Woodbury replied. "And you saw her yourself. They pulled into the yard here and she immediately went down to where you were. She didn't say a word to either of us."

Kim glanced from one man to the other. "So, neither of you have any idea what she was doing here or why she fired on us?"

"No clue," Ben Woodbury replied. "We were just getting started on our day's work. Which, by the way, we're behind schedule on and have an inspection in the morning."

Kim looked back to where David and JB were standing. I followed her gaze. Her board and our kayaks were behind some brush near the tip of the island. The work area where we'd seen the loader operating was completely visible from the trailer. But not our approach. There was no way the woman had seen us coming. The only one who could have seen us approaching would've been whichever one of them was running the loader on the beach and had driven it back to the trailer.

No, there had been some sort of interaction between the woman and the brothers, and Sergeant Watson knew who she was. Of these things, I was certain.

And there were too many people in the immediate vicinity who were withholding the truth or outright lying. Woodbury was, for sure.

To warn the others? I wondered.

Another siren could be heard in the distance. "That'll be the paramedics," Marty said.

"Did either of you get a tag number?" Kim asked.

"No tag on the front, like back home," Dan said. "And when the shooting started, we both hit the dirt."

"And you never saw the man or woman before? This is a really small town."

"We're new here," Ben said. "And we work seven days a week."

185

I turned and walked away from the group toward the island's interior, scanning the area. The ground was flat and muddy, not a tree, bush, or even a blade of grass in sight, except the clump where we'd landed our boats. I knew this place had once been densely covered—mangroves along the creek that bordered one side of the island, sea grapes, palms, and dense saw palmetto in the interior, and beachgrass along the dune on this side. Billy and I had discovered abandoned trailers here in the early 70s, but there was no bridge connecting it then. I'd often wondered how the trailers had gotten there, or, if there had once been a bridge, where it went. The land had nearly reclaimed everything by then, pulling the trailers down into the primordial muck of the Everglades.

The sight of the barren wasteland nearly made me sick. In a matter of months, another part of old Florida would disappear forever. I didn't blame the Woodbury brothers. If they didn't develop it, someone else would. The stream of people arriving in the state every day eclipsed the number of people dying or leaving by almost two to one.

A hundred years ago, there were less than half a million people in the whole state, Miami was nothing more than a small trading outpost of about three hundred individuals, and the seven-square-mile island of Key West was the state's most populous city, accessible only by ship or ferry.

There were now well over twenty million in the state and Miami had more residents than the whole state had when the city was first incorporated. Once Henry Flagler had extended the East Coast Railway there from Palm Beach, the city grew fast.

Where the construction trailer stood was the highest point on the island and seemed to be on native soil, unlike the sand on the beach. As I moved away from the trailer, the ground got mushy and dark. The smell of it hit me—that sickly sweet smell of plant decomposition. And something else.

Reaching down, I picked up a dried clump of soil and broke it apart with my hand. There was a piece of vegetation in it—part of a blade of sawgrass. I sniffed at the clump of dirt, confirming my suspicion.

Clouds were beginning to gather out over the 'Glades to the east. I turned and strode back toward where Kim and Marty were questioning the Woodbury brothers. Sergeant Watson was headed that way, too.

"Where do you want us to cordon off?" Watson asked. "We can have a forensics team here with metal detectors to find any spent shell casings."

"The only ones you'll find will be in the water, where we were," Kim said. "The shooter had a revolver. But she left some clear tracks in the drying mud over where our boats are. We'll want casts of those."

"Tell them to step on it," I said. "Weather's approaching. It'll be raining in less than an hour."

A low, rolling thunder from way out over the 'Glades reached our ears, as if punctuating the need for urgency.

Dan and Ben looked toward the east, then looked at each other. I could sense far more worry in their expressions than a rainstorm should cause. It rains just about every day in South Florida.

I knew that a good forensics team could find a lot more than the woman's tracks. She'd dived behind a beachgrass sand berm.

There could be hairs, clothing fibers, a button from her shirt, any number of things that could put her behind that dune.

That physical evidence, along with eye-witness testimony of her actions, would put her away for a good five years. The crazy blond woman had fired on a law enforcement officer who'd identified herself.

Somehow, I didn't think it would be the first stretch behind bars for her.

"Where'd you get your fill dirt?" I asked the younger brother.

He looked up at me, confused. "Why?"

"It's not from around here," I said. "Just wondering where you had it trucked in from."

"I got a deal from a guy in Okeechobee."

"Dredging from the lake bottom?" I asked.

"How'd you know?"

I handed a hunk of the dried clay I'd broken apart to Kim. "Smell that."

She did, then passed it to Marty, who in turn handed it to the sergeant.

"Smells like...garlic," Sergeant Watson said.

"It reeked of it when the trucks brought it in," Dan said.

"It's phosphorus," Marty said.

"The muck at the bottom of Lake Okeechobee is loaded with it," I said. "When the water in the lake is high, the increased pressure leaches the phosphorus into the water. This was dredged several months ago, during the dry season, when the muck held more un-dissolved phosphorus."

Dan shrugged. "Phosphorus and nitrogen are good for lawns."

"Yeah," I said. "It's good for all kinds of plants."

Then I looked off to the northwest, where I was sure Savannah was now anchored and worrying.

CHAPTER SEVENTEEN

The midday sun beat down on the old house, just as it had for the last 113 years. Built just after the turn of the last century, the house had been added onto and remodeled twice, as it was passed down from generation to generation.

The first major renovation had been in 1954, using funds from a VA loan. In 1969, it had been rebuilt with an addition, the interior walls stripped to the bare studs to add electric wiring and plumbing. The funds for that project had come from a life insurance policy. Fifty years later, the old house was in dire need of further repair and modernization.

But the current owner liked the old ways. She liked her privacy. And most importantly, she didn't want to appear to be worth as much as she was. Being part of the poor, downtrodden masses had its advantages.

The screen door slammed shut at the front of the house as the owner stepped out. She was in her sixties, with gray hair in a knotted bun not quite centered on her head. She was a big woman, tall and wide in the hips, as her mother had been. She wore a tan, unflattering, sleeveless dress that hung loose down to her thick knees.

The screen door's hinges creaked as two men came out. They were giants, having to turn their broad shoulders through the door. One was clean-shaven, wearing jeans and a T-shirt. The bigger man looked more like a lowland gorilla in clothes than a man, with facial hair covering most of his face and long, unkempt graying hair hanging over the rest.

"Who ya think it is?" the smaller man asked.

"The system don't say who it is," Marley Blanc replied. "Only that someone's comin' down the road."

The sound of a diesel engine could be heard and soon a black pickup rounded the last bend before the house.

"It's just Kurt and Donnie," Marley said. "Willy, go open the barn door."

The big, bearded man went around the side of the house to a barn that looked in worse condition than the house. Looks were deceiving, though. Both structures were solidly built and would last another hundred years with nothing more than new tin on the roof now and then.

Willy Quick opened the big doors to the barn. Inside were his and Marley's pickups as well as the car belonging to Willy's friend, who had come out to the old place to pick up a batch of coke. Willy had just brought a load in from Mexico.

Smuggling drugs into the Everglades was a lot easier than taking them into a big city, which was the final destination. Deliveries were made offshore, using a number of flat-bottomed bateaux with outboard engines, as well as a couple of speed boats. They brought the product into the maze of the Ten Thousand Islands, each to a different location, where the drugs were transferred to airboats. These could traverse very shallow water and skim across the sawgrass, bringing the load to Marley's house.

The barn was cavernous, with room for at least half a dozen cars. More, if Willy pulled his boats out. It was built right at the edge of the swamp and had back doors that Willy could use to get his own airboat in and out without a trailer. It was there that the drugs were finally offloaded, and transported by land to Miami, Orlando, and Tampa.

His bass boat was on a trailer and needed the tow dolly if he wanted to launch it from the barn. But he usually towed it with his truck to a public boat ramp.

Keeping the boats and vehicles out of sight had been Willy's idea, as was the pressure switch in the shell road where it met the highway. It set off a doorbell in both the house and the barn, warning them of visitors.

DEA and the sheriff's department's helicopters flew over sometimes. Without the flashy vehicles and boats visible, the place looked like it was intended to—a ramshackle cracker homestead, barely this side of abandoned.

The black Dodge pulled into the barn and Willy closed the outer doors, then went over to the main door and stepped inside. "You're not supposed to be here till tomorrow," he said to his common-law wife's only child, ignoring Kurt's ignorant spawn.

She slammed the truck's door and looked at the giant. "Uncle Jubal needs some help with somethin'."

Once inside the house, the five of them sat down. Kurt and Donnie's visit had interrupted Willy's careful weighing of the cocaine.

"You said ten ounces even, right?" he asked his friend.

"Yeah. I can probably do a little more next week."

Willy looked at Kurt. "You gonna re-up since you're here?"

"That ain't why we came," Kurt said. "This shit can wait."

The big man looked up from his triple beam scale and glared at Kurt. "I do things in my own order."

"Let's get this outta the way," Marley said, her voice gravelly from fifty years of smoking two packs of cigarettes a day, plus all the marijuana, crack, and meth. "Anything concerning my brother can wait."

"Uncle Jubal 'bout got me killed!"

Willy looked up from the scale. "How so?"

"I got people waiting, Willy," the other man complained, eyeing the coke on the scale. "Your family squabbles can wait."

"Shut the fuck up, Quint," Marley snapped. "You ain't in no damn hurry on a Sunday, and we both know it. You'll spend the rest of the day holed up somewhere with a couple of coke whores."

The man knew when to shut up, Willy thought. Gotta give him props for that.

The two of them had been around the Blanc family nearly all their lives. Marley was older than them by a few years, but Willy didn't care. Since her mother, Bertha, had died five years ago, Marley had been the clan's matriarch.

Her brother, Jubal, had left at an early age, thinking the family's activities too reckless. He'd made a fortune in real estate but wanted power—the kind of power that went with a title. But the fortune he'd made paled in comparison to what his mother had amassed after murdering her husband.

Willy and Quint were both aware of the depths of the family's depravity and they knew all the secrets. Few other outsiders did.

"Uncle Jubal sent us 'round to talk to them developers," Kurt said. "Sure enough, they uncovered one of the graves."

"And you convinced them to cover it back up?" Willy asked.

That was one thing they all agreed on, even Jubal. His concern was the sullying of his name, as he had higher political ambitions. He and Marley, as well as Bertha before her, didn't want the attention an investigation into C. Roy Blanc's fantasies would bring. There were even more bodies buried in the abandoned subdivision north of the highway in the Picayune Strand.

But not all of those were from C. Roy's activities fifty years ago, and many weren't women. Willy had his own secrets.

Kurt nodded. "I had 'em convinced, but then the cops showed up."

"Cops on kayaks," Donnie added.

Willy looked at him as if he were one of the dogs. "Kayaks?"

"One was ridin' atop one of those big surf boards what you paddle standin' up."

"And you're sure they were cops?" Willy asked Kurt.

Kurt stood and paced the room. "Two of 'em was for sure. A man and a woman. She yelled that she was FWC and I could see her badge. She tole me to put my hands up. Well, I pulled my pistol and got off a couple shots, then dove behind some bushes. At least two of 'em shot back at me before I skedaddled back to the truck and we hauled ass outta there."

Willy's eyes, partially covered by his hair, cut to the door. "Did anyone follow you?"

"No," Kurt said. "Weren't a soul on the Tamiami the whole way here. One way, nor the other."

"A woman with Fish and Wildlife?" Willy asked. "Can't be many of them. What'd she look like?"

"Tall," Kurt said. "Maybe five-nine. Blond hair, skinny. She weren't in no uniform, but she did have a badge on her hip."

"Sounds like that husband and wife team over in Everglades City," Willy said. "The guy with her have dark hair, maybe an inch or two taller? Both about thirty?"

"She was 'bout that age," Kurt said. "But the guy with her was older. Near as tall as you. Not as big, but no slouch. Sandy hair over his ears and a tattoo on his forearm. He looked too old to be a cop."

Willy's friend's eyes lifted from the product on the scale. "A skull tattoo on his left arm?"

"You know him?" Kurt asked.

"If it's the guy I'm thinking," he said to Willy, "and she just described him to a T, we both know him."

"What the fuck you talkin' about, Quint?" the big man growled.

"Our senior year, Willy. Last game of the season. The guy who busted my shoulder and killed any chance I had at college and the pros."

"Yeah," Willy said, "I remember that. What was that guy's name?"

"Jesse McDermitt," Quint Robbins replied.

CHAPTER EIGHTEEN

After leaving Kim and Marty to finish their investigation, David, JB, and I paddled the two miles to the north end of Marco River. *Sea Biscuit* rode at anchor just offshore.

Needless to say, the rest of the expedition was over. At least for the kids. I hadn't mentioned anything to the others about the possibility of the Woodbury brothers' runoff being the catalyst of a red tide event, but I wasn't finished digging.

And what did the crazy woman have to do with it? Probably nothing, directly. But I'm not a big believer in coincidence.

I knew Savannah had her heart set on getting back to my island to busy herself with turning it into a home for us. And part of that plan involved helping to keep her mind off Florence being away, so I didn't want to disappoint her.

As we'd paddled out, I considered just the two of us continuing our own investigation. That might accomplish the same thing. If not, and she really wanted to get to the island, I could come back in the *Revenge* and maybe bring Rusty or Jimmy. We hadn't had an adventure in a few years.

But first we had to get the kids back to Fort Myers, and then up to Gainesville. Florence had said she was just going to ride up with David, since we'd already moved all of her stuff up there. She only had a backpack full of clothes to take with her and was leaving some of her belongings on board. That way she wouldn't have to carry things back and forth when she came home for holidays or long weekends.

Home? I thought.

My house only had one bedroom. There were three other houses on the island, all the same size, shape, and configuration. Jimmy's place used to have two bedrooms, but after Hurricane Irma nearly wiped my island clean, we'd rebuilt his the same as mine. Kim and Marty had a place there, as well. But they only stayed over once in a blue moon. The fourth house had to remain a bunkhouse. At least for another year.

I'd bought my little island right after I'd retired from the Corps. The sale came with the stipulation that a fish camp be built on it within ten years, and then it had to remain a fish camp for twenty. I'd built my house and two bunkhouses the first year. At the time, the bunkhouses were meant to house door kickers, not fishermen. But it satisfied the county. Jimmy's house had been built later and one of the bunkhouses was converted for Kim a couple of years after that.

I was coming up on the end of the time period that stipulated the need for the one remaining bunkhouse. Florence could stay in Kim and Marty's place until that period ended in the spring. Then I could remodel the remaining bunkhouse into a place for her.

We arrived back at New Cut and dropped JB and Kia off there, where they'd parked near the campsite. They promised to pack up everything for the others and get it to them after class on Monday.

Then we dropped Perry, Jill, and David at Port Sanibel Marina, where a friend was waiting to take them back to where they'd parked their vehicles on upper Hendry Creek.

By the time we got back to our marina in Fort Myers, it was midafternoon. David was already there, waiting.

"Are you sure you have everything?" Savannah asked.

It was the third time she'd asked Florence the same question.

"Yeah, Mom," Florence replied. "Don't worry. I'll be fine. If I forgot anything, I can just replace it."

"You have the credit card we got for you?"

Florence did her eye roll thing. "Yes. *And* the debit card for the account you opened for me in Gainesville. Nothing's going to happen."

"The credit card's for emergencies," I reminded her. "We'll see that there's money in your account."

They hugged, then Florence stepped over to me. "Remember rule six," I said, more to David than Florence. I hugged her and whispered, "If you need anything, just tell me. I'll move mountains for you."

David loaded her pack in the back with his and then suddenly, Savannah and I were alone.

"This is gonna be weird," she said. "Which one is six, again?"

There were ten rules for dating a Marine's daughter. I was kind of partial to the last part of rule number six.

"If you make her cry," I replied, "I'll make you cry."

We turned and the dogs led the way down the pier to *Sea Biscuit*. Woden kept looking in the direction David's truck had disappeared.

"How old was Florence when you got Woden?"

"My mom bought him for Flo's seventh birthday," she reminded me as we stepped aboard and went down to the salon. "For the whole first year, the only time they were apart was during his daily training sessions."

"No wonder he and Finn get along so well," I said, trying to get Savannah's mind onto anything else. "They're about the same age."

"I think it's just that they're both well-adjusted boat dogs."

She had a point. Dogs belonging to cruisers did seem calmer. I guess it probably had to do with the many slips and anchorages they visited where they were always coming into contact with new people and their pets.

"What do you want to do for dinner?" I asked. "We could go out."

"You mean, like on a date? Just the two of us?"

"Unless you don't want to," I said. "We have plenty, and I can grill."

"Let's do that," she said. "But I'll cook. I know you want to get up to the yard and see how *Salty Dog* turned out.

"You sure?" I asked.

"Go," she replied. "Just be back in an hour for sundowners before dinner."

I kissed her and left, with Finn tagging along beside me. We walked down the dock to the parking lot, then took the shortcut through the mangroves to the boatyard next door.

Two guys were working beside my boat. One was packing up tools and the other was removing masking tape from the boot stripe.

"You the owner?" the guy stowing the tools asked as I approached.

"Yeah," I replied. "Jesse McDermitt. Looks like you're all finished."

He was a younger guy, maybe in his mid-thirties. Like his partner, he was dressed in white pants and a white, long-sleeved shirt—typical painter attire.

"I still wanna come back in the morning before she goes in the water," he said, wiping his hands on a rag from his pocket. "Name's Lee Cushing."

I shook his hand and looked at the *Dog*. The white hull above the red water line stripe gleamed with fresh polish. The blue antifouling paint below it looked slick and unblemished.

"No way just the two of you did this."

He laughed. "No. Trevor said you were in a hurry. The rest of my crew just left. There were six of us working all day."

"And Trevor already settled up with you?"

"Yes, sir, he did. Said he wasn't sure if you'd be back by the end of the day."

"We want to splash her early," I said.

"No problem," Lee said. "We'll be here before the sun comes up to do any last-minute touchups. His lift driver doesn't come in until eight and as soon as he lifts her, we'll paint the bottom of the keel. The paint dries superfast, even in the water. It just needs twenty or thirty minutes of air drying. She'll be in the water by nine at the latest."

I walked around the hull, checking out the job they'd done as they finished packing up their tools. Cushing and his crew did good work.

Once they left, I climbed the ladder to the cockpit. Finn barked from below. I think he preferred *Salty Dog* to Savannah's boat. I knew he liked the *Dog* better than my other boats.

Except maybe the little Grady-White. Its forward casting deck was just the right height below the bow for Finn to stand with his front paws up on the anchor locker hatch, his face in the wind like a Mack truck's hood ornament.

"I'll be right down," I told him. "And your boat'll be in the water tomorrow."

I unlocked the companionway hatch and went below. At the nav station, I turned on my laptop. It was like the other laptop computers I had on my other boats, and on *Sea Biscuit*. I found that lugging one from boat to boat was a pain.

I sat down to run some online searches using generic phrases like "Goodland woman arrested" and dozens of variations. But I didn't come up with anyone who looked like the woman on Turtle Island.

Finally, I called my friend, Billy.

When he answered, we exchanged pleasantries for a moment. Billy wasn't much of an idle talker. When I described the truck and the woman, he asked. "Was she with a half-wit Butthead look-alike?"

Now that he mentioned it, what little I saw of the woman's accomplice, he did resemble the cartoon character a little.

"Who is she?" I asked.

"Kurt Blanc," Billy replied. "She's the daughter of the leader of the Blanc clan who live all over the Faka-hatchee and Picayune Strands. Surprised you never heard of them."

"I left town at seventeen," I reminded him.

"The family's been running weed and coke in through the backcountry since the sixties."

"Still doesn't ring a bell."

I didn't follow local news much when I was a kid. Still don't. Neither had Billy. We were just a couple boys who lived in rural Southwest Florida and liked to fish and hunt.

"One of them went and got himself elected to the state senate," Billy said. "They've got the sheriff, a couple of assistant DAs, and at least one county judge in their collective pockets. These aren't people to trifle with, Jesse. Step on one of their toes and heads will pop up all over the 'Glades saying 'ouch.'"

As he talked, I searched the internet for her name. Lots of references came up for men. I added the words "Florida woman" to the search and found an arrest report with a picture of the woman we'd encountered.

"How many of them are there?"

"Not all of them have stuck around," Billy replied. "The smart ones left and the really dumb ones are in prison or dead. But it'd be a safe bet that there's at least forty adult siblings and cousins."

"Major players?"

"Marley Blanc is the matriarch. Big woman, Early sixties. Nothing happens out there that she doesn't know about. Her mother, Bertha Blanc, is the one who set up the smuggling operation. She died a few years back."

"The mother?" I asked. "A drug kingpin?"

"Her husband, C. Roy, died about fifty years ago. Some say he had a weak heart, some say cancer, and some folks think she poisoned him."

"No investigation?"

"It was 1968, Kemosabe. War protests, acid, sit-ins, and free love were enough to keep the law and the press busy. Besides, he was just a poor cracker living in the swamp."

While some might take offense at the cracker remark, Billy and I knew the true meaning.

Cattle was big in Florida. The industry was ranked twelfth in the nation and number one of all the states east of the Mississippi River. What they called cowboys out west were cow hunters in Florida. There were no vast, open plains here. And the cattle weren't so easy to find.

Finding them was one thing but getting them out of the tangle of saw palmetto and brush was sometimes a whole different story. So, Florida's cow hunters used long bullwhips that they would crack in the air above where they knew a cow was hiding to drive it out. That's how they became known as crackers. And not all Florida crackers were white.

Billy went on to tell me what he knew about the rest of the family. C. Roy and Bertha Blanc were born in the thirties and he was eight or nine years older. She was just sixteen when she gave birth to the oldest of their seven children in 1955, and twenty-eight when she had the last one in 1967. Seven kids in twelve years.

The oldest of their children, Jubal Blanc, left home at a very young age, Billy told me. Apparently, the senator had a few run-ins with local law enforcement before he was sixteen. He'd eventually gotten into real estate and was now quite wealthy. As far as Billy knew, he'd never married.

His sister, Marley, had only one child, Kurt.

"Odd name for a woman," I said.

"There's a lot of stories going around about how Kurt got stuck with that," Billy said. "Personally, I think Marley was either drunk or high."

He also told me that of the seven siblings, two were dead. A brother named Darby Blanc had gotten into an altercation with a neighbor who shot off one of his ears. He'd later died of an accidental, self-inflicted gunshot to the head.

"A lot of folks think it was no accident," Billy said. "That the neighbor just finished what he'd started. The same year he died, Dreama Blanc had been murdered by her ex-husband, Eugene Quick."

"Funny thing is," Billy continued. "Eugene's cousin now lives with Marley and is helping her run the operation. His name's Willy Quick."

"Willy Quick," I repeated. "That name's familiar."

"Should be," Billy said. "Same age as us and played offensive line for Everglades City."

Quint Robbins had also gone to that school. I couldn't help but wonder if the two were still in contact. Was it possible that Robbins had sent his friend's clan after me for embarrassing him on the dock? Could his grudge really run that deep?

"Two of Marley's sisters," Billy went on, "Jo Blanc and Sue Roy Blanc, along with Kurt, run drugs throughout the smaller towns down there. But most of what they bring in goes right into the Miami pipeline."

"None of these women married?" I asked.

"You mean the Blanc name?" he asked. "Yeah, but they keep their last name. They're a weird bunch. All the women are big and rawboned. They run everything. Most of their kids are born out of wedlock when the moms are still in their teens. It's been rumored that Kurt's father was one of her uncles."

"Sounds like a rough bunch of rednecks."

"One of the brothers, Pistol Blanc, left the state and never came back. Scuttlebutt says he's hiding out in West Virginia from a possible rape charge in Monroe County ten years ago."

"Anything else you can tell me about them?" I asked. "Known hangouts or where any of them live?"

"You might catch one or two of them out at Gator Den on Faka Union Bay."

"That place hasn't burned in hell yet?"

"At least three times," Billy replied with a chuckle. "It's like herpes—it keeps coming back. Marley's place is on the old river, not far from there. You need some backup?"

"Thanks, Billy. But we're leaving in the morning to take Savannah's boat down to Marathon. I'm going to come back later in the week to get *Salty Dog*. Might bring Rusty with me."

"Call me when you get in. We'll burn some steaks. In the meantime, I'll see if I can find out anything more about what Kurt's up to these days."

"Thanks, again, Billy."

"You be careful around these particular whites," he said. I could visualize the grin on his face at the play on words. Blanc was French for white. "Some of 'em would need a lot of killin'."

CHAPTER NINETEEN

The next morning, we woke early and met Lee at the boatyard. There wasn't much to do until the lift operator arrived, but true to his word, Lee went over every inch of the hull, mostly by touch. He and his helper hit a couple of spots with a fine grit block sander and repainted a few areas. Once the big Travelift was on scene and the thick slings put in place, *Salty Dog* was lifted a couple of feet from the spot she'd rested for several weeks. The lift held the *Dog* in place for a few minutes as Lee painted the parts of the keel bottom that had been resting on blocks of wood.

By 1000 we had *Salty Dog* in a slip and I'd checked all the bilges and thru-hulls for leaks. Satisfied, I locked her up and an hour later we were underway aboard *Sea Biscuit*.

The *Dog's* sea trial would be the move down to Marathon.

It was 140 nautical miles to the Rusty Anchor, give or take. We encountered a squall about halfway, but it was more rain than wind. We just set the autopilot, maintaining eighteen knots, and went down to the lower helm station until we'd plowed through it.

The sun was setting as we finally passed under the big arch of the Seven Mile Bridge, spanning Moser Channel. I was at the helm with Savannah, and the dogs were at their usual station on either side of the bow.

Puffy clouds to the southwest, high above the horizon, took on a pale pink glow, which began to fade to a burnt orange color as we passed Boot Key and rounded East Sister Rock into Vaca Key Bight.

Savannah stood beside me, also watching the display of light and color. "You love it here. I can tell."

I looked over at her and smiled. "I love most of it," I said. "The islands, the water, the reefs, the people. The way everything seems to be balanced and calm."

"Except when it's not," she said, as if reading my thoughts.

I'd been thinking about Kurt Blanc. There were several facts that just couldn't be ignored.

She'd seen us as clearly as we'd seen her.

The shooting happened just three days after Quint Robbins had failed to get his revenge at the marina. That was too close together to be a coincidence.

Quint Robbins and Willy Quick had been teammates in high school and probably friends. They both still lived in the same very rural area. Both men were big and the area they lived in very small. There was almost zero chance they didn't still associate with each other.

All these facts had me concerned not just for Kim, but also for Florence.

"I'm worried about her, too," I said. "It's a big, scary world."

Savannah took my arm as I made the familiar turn to line up with Rusty's channel. "She's not as timid as you think she is. After all, she's your daughter."

I pulled the throttles back to idle, and then shifted to neutral, letting the boat drift about a mile offshore. Then I gathered the woman I loved into my arms and I kissed her.

"I only wish I'd been there when she was growing up," I said. "It seems I have a history of not doing that."

She frowned. "You had your work and we would have been a distraction. Even though you weren't there in a physical sense, in a way you were always with her. As she grew, I began to see a lot of you in her. She's strong and smart, and very capable."

We watched the sun go down in silence, each lost in our own thoughts. After the last of the sun disappeared, I heard a cheer far in the distance. I could see the lights at the Anchor, bright against the dark backdrop of dense foliage that shielded it from the rest of the world.

I put the engines in gear and brought *Sea Biscuit* up to a high idle, turning the bow toward the channel again. As we approached the point where the channel became a canal, I slowed the boat down to a crawl.

There were a lot of people at the Anchor. Several of them, Rusty in the lead, started toward the far end of the canal where the boardwalk looped around the turning basin to the side where we were going to dock *Sea Biscuit*.

At the mouth of the canal, I reversed the engines and brought the big boat to a full stop. Then, using the engines alone, I turned the boat around and backed her toward the last spot on the western dock.

The canal was long, and going all the way to the turning basin at the end where Rusty kept his salvage barge was the only other option in the narrow confines. At least if we wanted to be facing the sea, ready for a quick departure.

Not that we were planning, or even considering, going anywhere else. During the last eight months, we'd always known where our next port-of-call was going to be. But now, we had no plans. Still, I always preferred to back in.

I just liked being prepared in case I had to move fast.

Savannah went down to put the fenders out and ready the dock lines, as Rusty and perhaps a dozen others approached. My friend and business partner, Deuce Livingston, was among them, along with his wife, Julie. She was Rusty's daughter and my goddaughter.

Jimmy and Dink caught the lines Savannah tossed and within minutes we were tied fast.

"Welcome home!" Rusty shouted up to me. "Damn, it's good to see you again, bro."

I shut down the engines. "Good to be seen, Rusty."

Savannah opened the rail and we both stepped down onto the dock. It really was good to be home again.

Rusty hugged Savannah, then me. Sidney and her niece, Naomi, were there, and they and Julie swarmed Savannah, all talking at once. Fortunately for Savannah, that's how her mind often worked. She could discuss two or more topics at the same time, with two or more people.

Her quick mind kept me on my toes.

The four women started walking toward the end of the canal.

"How long ya stayin', *Capitán*?" Jimmy asked.

Jimmy had worked for me in one way or another almost since I'd arrived in the Keys. He'd helped me bring the first *Gaspar's Revenge* down from a Miami auction a week after I retired from the Corps. In fact, he'd been instrumental in finding her. I'd hired him on the trip back and he'd helped build my fishing and diving charter business.

"Semi-permanent," I replied, clapping my old first mate on the shoulder. "We have a couple of new residents on the island, too."

"We do?"

"Savannah is moving in with me," I replied, smacking my hand to my thigh twice. Finn and Woden jumped down to the dock and stood on either side of me. "You remember Woden?"

"For real?" Deuce asked, tying off a spring line.

"For real and certain," I replied. "How've you been, Deuce?"

"Great," he replied. "Investigating corporate swindlers, cheating spouses, the occasional abduction. Nothin I'm not used to."

"It's amazing what you can get used to," I said, paraphrasing a line from the movie *Roadhouse.*

We followed the women around the end of the canal and up to the bar. The parking lot was practically full, as was the dinghy dock.

Music came from out on the back deck and several diners sat on the side deck, enjoying a meal, and watching the sunset show.

You couldn't see the sun set over water from anywhere on Rusty's property. But except for a few weeks around the summer solstice, you could see the sun *rise* over water, just off the tip of Key Colony Beach.

Still, the setting sun was pretty dramatic to watch from the deck, as it slipped down among the masts and rigging of the boats in the canal and disappeared beyond the trees on the other side. It was a Keys thing.

"Here," Savannah said, handing me her phone as I stepped up beside her at the bar. "It's Flo."

I put the phone to my ear. "How was the first day?"

"Oh, Dad! It was incredible! I only had *four* classes today. Then David showed me around the campus in the afternoon, until I met with the swim team before dinner. I have three different classes tomorrow, then alternate through the week, four, three, four, three, four and practice every evening. I'm in an accounting class with Jill, and David's an aide in my computer science class. Everyone I've met has been real nice."

"Sounds like you're off to a good start. How's your roommate?"

Over the last few weeks, Florence had talked and video-chatted several times with the girl she'd be sharing a room with for her freshman year. Her name was Lauri Wilson and she was from Destin, a small town up in the Panhandle.

"She's nice," Florence said. "We're both on the swim team, but she's a diver. We had lunch together and I found out she's a psych major. How are Woden and Finn?"

I looked over to where the two dogs lay in the corner, a water bowl between them. "They're fine. I think Woden misses you already. On the trip down, he kept going into your cabin looking for you."

"Aww, I miss him too. And you and Mom. I won't keep you. It sounds like a lot of people there. She just called to tell me you made it to port okay."

"You're gonna check in regularly?"

"I'll call you every night after practice. And Labor Day weekend is in just a couple of weeks."

"Okay," I said. "If you need anything, just call. We'll fly up and get you for Labor Day if you want."

"Can David come down?"

That was something I hadn't figured on.

"Sure," I said, though I was anything but sure. "There's plenty of room on the island."

We ended the call and I handed the phone back to Savannah. "I think Florence needs a car."

"*I don't even have a car,*" she said. "But you're probably right."

Amy Huggins looked up from the other side of the bar, where she was getting a beer out of the cooler. "I have one for sale. I didn't mean to eavesdrop, but it's hard not to from this side. It's not new, but it's very reliable."

"What is it?" I asked.

"A Jeep Wrangler Unlimited," she replied. "I just bought a Keys car and don't really need it."

A "Keys car" was basically any vehicle that could be bought cheap, started and ran most of the time, and you didn't have to worry about it rusting.

"What year is it?" Savannah asked.

"It's two years old," Amy replied. "But it only has a little over eight thousand miles on it."

"Hey, Jesse," Dink said, interrupting. "Did you find that spot I told you about?"

Amy went down to the other end of the bar to deliver the beer and take another order. Conversations with bartenders tend to take longer than with other people.

I pulled my phone out and pulled up the pictures I'd taken of the fish kill. "Yeah, I did. There were a few more than you had me believe."

Dink looked at the images on my phone and let out a low whistle. "I didn't see anything like that," he said. "I'd have called in Fish and Wildlife. That's a major fish kill. You were in the right spot, though. I recognize the white mangroves on the bluff there."

"So, all this happened since Thursday?"

"Had to," he replied, pinching the image, and spreading his thick fingers, enlarging it. "Most of these fish ain't two days dead yet."

"What're y'all looking at?" Rusty asked, stepping between us.

Dink turned my phone so he could see and zoomed the image back out. "This was where I saw the small fish kill the other day."

"That ain't small, Dink," Rusty said.

"It wasn't that big when I saw it." He handed the phone back to me and asked, "When was that taken?"

"Yesterday morning," I replied.

Deuce joined us and looked down at the screen. "Where was that?"

"Up in the Ten Thousand Islands," I replied. "Southeast of Marco."

"What were you doing back in there?"

"Long story," I replied.

The door opened and Tony Jacobs walked in. Tony worked for Deuce and had been a member of his SEAL team years ago. He was a wiry guy, with a shaved head, and skin the color of strong coffee. Originally from North Carolina, he was the son of a farmer and a Sunday school teacher.

Tony spotted us and came straight over. "I heard you were back," he said. "Had to come down and see for myself."

I shook his hand and grinned. "Good to see you again, Tony."

"Jesse was about to tell us a long story," Deuce said, bouncing his eyebrows.

Savannah rose from her stool beside me. "I'm going to leave y'all to your sea stories. I'll be outside with the girls."

She kissed me on the cheek and left.

I turned to Deuce and the others. "Kim and I were shot at."

CHAPTER TWENTY

"What'd you do with the shooter's body?" Tony asked.

I looked around at the four men. There are people who become friends and among them, you might find one or two who would not only ask such a question but grab a shovel. I was very fortunate in that I had quite a few such friends.

"She got away," I said.

"Uh-oh," Rusty murmured. "Another amorous admirer who wouldn't take no for an answer?"

I went on to tell them of the hunt with the kids, trying to find a source of nutrient-rich runoff in the Ten Thousand Islands and how we'd encountered Kurt Blanc.

"Blanc?" Rusty asked.

"You know who she is?"

"No, but there's a whole family of Blancs up in the Goodland area. They're into all kinds of stuff, most of it illegal. Scuttlebutt says they're big players in the Miami coke scene. Callin' those people swamp trash is insultin' to a lot of nasty, two-legged swamp rats. That family ain't nothin' but inbred scum."

"Billy said almost the same thing," I offered. "Anyway, the shooting happened just a couple days after I had a run-in with a guy named Quint Robbins. I'd busted his shoulder in high school football and a guy on his team was Willy Quick, who's mixed in with the Blanc family. I'm worried about Kim and the kids who were with us."

"That's a bit of a reach," Deuce said, stroking an imaginary beard, thinking. His dad had done the same thing when pondering something. "I just can't believe the guy whose shoulder you hurt would hire someone to kill you."

"That's the rub," I agreed, nodding. "It doesn't make any sense to hold that kind of grudge for that long, but somehow they're connected."

"I'm goin' with ya," Rusty said flatly.

"Going where?" Deuce asked. "Don't tell me you're going up there again? Look, Flo's at school a hundred miles from there. And Kim's a cop. No way they'd go after them."

"You gotta go up there to get the sailboat, anyway," Rusty continued, ignoring Deuce's recommendation. "And I done told you I'd help bring her back here."

"Count me in, if you're looking for crew," Tony said. "I like to sail."

"Then I'd better go, too," Deuce offered. "Just to keep you out of trouble."

Jimmy had been sitting quietly on a bar stool, listening to everything. "Um, don't take this the wrong way," he said, twisting a strand of hair hanging in front of his shoulder. "But among smug drugglers like that, all four of you dudes stick out like a drunk at a church revival."

"We're just going for a sail," Rusty said.

"Yah, dude, and I'm the pope."

"It might get dangerous, Jimmy," I said, knowing that he'd want to go. "Probably better if—"

"Screw that, Jesse," he said a bit too loudly, drawing stares. He leaned in and lowered his voice. "You know full well I wasn't always a pot-smoking computer geek. I can handle myself as well as..." He paused and looked around at us. "Well, I can handle myself okay."

I looked in my friend's eyes. Usually, they were red-rimmed, glassy, and he was squinting to hide the fact that he was stoned. I never had a problem with his habit; Jimmy always arrived to work sober and never brought anything on board. He was as reliable as a summer day was long. Now I could see fierce conviction in his eyes.

"Okay, Jimmy," I said. "Do you have any charters scheduled?"

"Three full days," he replied. "But all of them are flats clients I can hand off to Dink or one of the other guys."

"Is the *Revenge* ready?"

"The *Revenge*?" Deuce asked. "Why not take one of the smaller boats up there?"

"Mobility and firepower," Jimmy reminded the former Navy SEAL team leader.

Tony chuckled and I tried to suppress a grin.

Jimmy added, "Yeah, she's ready."

"That, and she needs a little work done," I added. "It'll take us most of a day to get there and two days to sail back."

Jimmy turned toward me. "You're leaving the *Revenge* there?"

"It's a great boatyard and the workers are fast and good."

"Fast and good means expensive," Jimmy said. "I told you on the phone last month the problem was minor and the engines wouldn't need a rebuild till after the season."

"We're not having them rebuilt," I told him. "We're getting a pair of Rolls Royce engines installed."

"You're kidding!"

Jimmy was as laid-back as anyone I'd ever known. There wasn't much that excited him or got under his skin.

Except one thing. Like me, he was a speed junky.

"She's sixteen years old," I said. "I know you take great care of her and she's already one of the fastest tournament boats in the area, but you know as well as I do, technology has come a long way since 2004. New engines and a complete refit, pulpit to platform, keel to antenna mast."

Jimmy started twisting his hair again. "That's gonna cost a ton, man."

"Priced a new tournament boat lately?"

I had. Just after Jimmy told me about one of the engines having a compression problem, I'd started looking. A new boat, comparable to my 45-foot Rampage convertible, would cost well into seven figures. I'd paid nearly half a million dollars for the *Revenge* nearly thirteen years ago. And she was three years old at the time.

Then I started researching engines, emailing and talking on the phone with engineers at Rampage. New engines, electronics, and a full refit would be less than half that. The *Revenge's* hull was sturdy and heavily built. It made good financial sense to keep her.

"Good point," Jimmy agreed. "I have a good lead on a big offshore charter next week."

"Use *El Cazador*," I told him, meaning my thirty-two-foot offshore center console. "Or just let it go."

Jimmy grinned. For the whole time I'd been gone, he'd skippered the *Revenge*. His knowledge and intuition when it came to game fish was uncanny and the clients loved him.

"Rolls Royce, huh?" he asked, practically drooling. "Which one?"

"It's going to be a bit cramped above the engines," I said, delaying his satisfaction. "The new ones will be six inches taller. But they're nearly a foot less in length, which will free up some room. They're also a bit narrower, but not enough that you'd notice."

"What about weight?"

"They'll add a hair over a ton more weight, but the engineers I talked to said it's negligible.

"Which engine?" he asked impatiently.

"The MTU V-10 M96," I replied with a grin. "Over fifteen hundred horses at the shaft."

"What will that mean for speed?" Tony asked.

I shrugged. "I went back and forth in emails with engineers at Rampage and Rolls, and they agreed that fifty-seven knots would be a realistic expectation on a calm day."

They all looked out the windows toward Vaca Key Bight and the Gulf Stream beyond. It was, as usual in summer, flat calm.

"You mean miles per hour, right?" Deuce said softly.

"No," I replied. "Fifty-seven knots. Sixty-five miles per hour."

"That's gonna be a gas hog," Rusty said.

I shook my head. "The new Tier 3 engines are a lot more economical. They'll burn less at wide-open throttle than the old C18s. At cruising speed, we'll add almost fifty percent to her range."

Jimmy turned away from the window and looked at me. "Dude, that can get us to Cancun, non-stop, with no fuel bladders in the fish boxes."

"And get there before sunset," I added. "The engineer said the sweet spot will likely be cruising at around forty knots."

"When are you leaving?" Tony asked.

I turned to Rusty. "My little Grady still here?"

"Where else would it be? After you took off last year, I took the liberty of putting it on the trailer and haulin' it out, so the bottom didn't get all skunky. It's out back on the slab. Tank's full and batteries are charged."

"I want to spend the day showing Savannah around the island," I said, looking around at my friends. "But I'd like to head back up there early on Wednesday."

As Rusty had pointed out to me so many years ago, jobs were for mainlanders. In the Keys, you hustled. Not having time clocks to punch made it easier. All five of us were business partners in one way or another. I owned part of Deuce's security company as well as a share in the Rusty Anchor. Jimmy and Tony worked for us. But both of them had other gigs on the side, as did Deuce and I. Rusty had so many sources of income and now that he was married, he had backup besides Julie.

They all nodded.

Amy made her way back to our end of the bar and I quickly pulled my phone out and ran a search.

"Anyone need anything?" she asked.

I looked over at Jimmy. "How's the island's provisions?"

"Your house and the *Revenge* are fully stocked with canned and dry goods, but there's nothing in your fridge except a case of Red Stripe."

"Just a couple bottles of water for me," I told Amy, flipping through the search results. "What color's your Jeep and how much do you want?"

She opened the cooler and produced two water bottles, placing them on the bar. "It's white, with a three-piece, removable, black hardtop," she replied. "It's a Willys edition with off-road tires, tinted windows, and a bull bar. I'll take thirty."

I flipped through a few more results. There were only ten listed on the site I was searching. All priced close to $30,000.

"Sold," I told her. "Call Pam over at the bank in the morning. I'll leave word for her to make the transfer."

"Just like that?" she said, puzzled. "You don't want to test drive it, kick the tires, or haggle over the price?"

"Just like that," I replied with a grin, as Savannah came back in and joined me. "The price is fair. Drop it off here tomorrow? It's going to be a gift for our daughter when she comes home for Labor Day."

Savannah took my arm and smiled approvingly. "I'm tired. It's been a long day."

"That it has," I agreed, returning her smile. I turned to Rusty. "Key's in the tractor?"

"Yeah. Need any help?"

"We can handle it," I said, then turned to my friends. "Sorry to cut the reunion short, but we're gonna head up to the island now."

We said our goodbyes, then went out the back door. Rufus motioned me toward the kitchen counter.

"Hey, Rufus," I said. "Sorry we can't stay. The last few days have been pretty strenuous."

The old man smiled broadly, displaying large, white teeth, a gap in the middle. Nobody knew how old Rufus was. He worked in the little outdoor kitchen during lunch and dinner and his niece, Kyndall, worked the breakfast bunch, and helped during dinner.

"I and I know all 'bout dat, mon," he said, passing over a small cooler. "Der be some fish sandwiches for yuh."

I glanced at Savannah, who smiled and accepted the cooler.

"Thank you, Rufus," she said. "That will make a perfect dinner."

We stepped off the back deck, headed toward the concrete pad Rusty had built a couple of years ago to store boats.

"How old *is* Rufus?" Savannah asked. "And what did he mean that he knew all about our last few days?"

"I don't question what Rufus says, but he does seem to have an uncanny grasp of what goes on in these islands." I shrugged "I'm guessing late seventies. Nobody knows."

"I think he's older than that," she said. "And I think Kyndall is his grandniece, not his niece."

I didn't know about that, having never pried into the man's past. It was true that Kyndall had much darker skin than Rufus, whose complexion was more like nutmeg. And she was much younger, maybe in her early thirties. She worked efficiently, kept to herself, and didn't speak much. A lot like her uncle. Or great-uncle.

Ten minutes later, the little Grady-White was idling at the short pier by the new boat ramp. I put the trailer back, parked the tractor, then walked down to where Savannah was waiting by the boat.

Finn was up on the forward casting deck, as usual, and Woden just looked confused. He'd never been on this boat before, and I doubted he'd spent more than a few hours away from Florence his whole life.

I untied the bow line and stepped aboard, pushing the boat out as I did so. Savannah quickly released the stern line and did the same.

Shifting to reverse, I let the 140-horsepower Suzuki pull us away from the dock toward deeper water.

"Who all's going back to Fort Myers with you?" Savannah asked.

I shifted to forward and nudged the throttle slightly, turning the little boat toward a spot well off the shoals, which I knew extended out from East Sister Rock.

"Deuce and Tony," I replied, "and Rusty and Jimmy."

"I'm tempted to go with you."

"I know," I said, bringing the boat up on plane. "And you're welcome to if you want. We're leaving Wednesday morning."

Finn stood with his front legs on the bow, head up, and ears back. He looked back to where Woden stood, just beside the console, and barked. Woden then joined him and the two stood at the bow, enjoying the wind.

The truth was, the more I thought about it, the better the idea of Savannah going with us sounded. With Jimmy coming, she'd be alone on the island. Not that there was anything dangerous to worry about. But she'd miss Florence all the more, if left alone.

"No, I can't," she said, her voice raised above the sound of the outboard. "I have people coming out."

"People?"

"Did you really think that Julie, Sidney, and Naomi would sit around while you guys go off?"

"They don't even know," I said.

"Sure, they do," she replied, squeezing my arm. "Julie has some great ideas for your house. They're going to hit a few stores, while I coordinate from out there on FaceTime."

I looked down at her and smiled. "Unbelievable."

CHAPTER TWENTY-ONE

T he headlights from Dan's truck swept the guard-rail of the new causeway as he turned off the highway. It was after midnight and he drove slowly across the short span to Turtle Island.

In early spring, when the weather was cooler, they'd seen crocodiles on the newly built bridge, lying on the warm concrete. A big one could rip a tire right off the rim. Caution was advisable.

Dan's headlights shone on the big, garish sign at the opposite end of the causeway, which proclaimed lots were for sale at predevelopment prices. Dan thought the young couple in swimsuits on the sign didn't quite convey the idea of what he was sure the island would become—a retirement community.

When he turned off what would one day be Turtle Island Boulevard, his headlights illuminated his brother's pickup and the construction trailer. The lights were on inside, but Ben was sitting on the steps. Dan parked next to his truck, shut off the engine, and got out.

"What're you doing out here?" Dan asked, as he strode toward his younger brother.

"I could ask you the same thing," Ben replied.

There was a six-pack of Bud at Ben's feet, two missing. Dan pulled one of the beers from the ring and cracked the aluminum tab.

"I couldn't sleep," he said, taking a pull from the warm beer.

"Ghosts bothering you?" Ben asked sarcastically. He finished his beer and tossed it at an open barrel, missing it completely.

Dan sat down hard on the steps next to his brother. "At least we got the go-ahead from the county."

"Yeah. But at what cost?"

Dan sighed. Fortunately, most of the work by the forensics people had been right behind the trailer, where the sand enclosure started, and where the people in the kayaks had landed. He and Ben had kept silent about who the woman with the gun was. They didn't mention her grandfather, either. Or what he'd buried on their island.

After all the cops left, the brothers had simply continued their work, scraping out the new fill and moving the sand inland from where it had originally been dumped in the shallows. They'd worked without thinking, remembering the woman's words when she'd run off after the shooting.

"What else could we do?" Dan asked. "You heard her say they'd be back when we least expected."

"It doesn't bother you?" Ben asked, sweeping a hand toward the rest of the island. "The fact that there might be a dozen or more bodies buried out there?"

"What good would it do, Ben? It happened more than half a century ago and the guy who killed them has been dead longer than either of us has been alive."

"So, there's nobody around who misses them?" Ben asked. "Is that what you're saying? You think we should just ignore the fact that we *own* the burial site of a serial killer? Move people in and not tell them? What if someone's dog digs a hole in the backyard and uncovers a skull like we did? Or maybe a little kid?"

Dan took a long pull on his beer as Ben opened another one.

"I'll be honest with you," Dan said. "I'm more afraid of *her* than the cops."

"Rightly so," a booming voice spoke out from the darkness.

Ben stood quickly. "Who's there?"

Dan also stood, his eyes trying to pierce the near total blackness outside the cone of light from the trailer's windows. The moon hadn't risen yet, and he saw nothing.

Suddenly, a figure emerged from the darkness, coming toward them from the island's interior. There hadn't been a car drive past the bridge since Dan arrived, and he knew there was no other way onto the island except the causeway.

The man coming toward them was huge. Dan was six feet tall, but this man was far bigger. When he got close enough, Dan could see that he was wearing jeans that were wet to mid-thigh.

The creek at the back of the property was only three feet deep for the most part. Beyond it, there was nothing but swamp for miles.

As he stepped farther into the light, Dan could see he was carrying a backpack by the straps. His face was mostly hidden by a thick, graying beard and long strands of greasy, unkempt hair.

"Name's Quick," he said, his voice barely more than a grunt. "You met my stepdaughter earlier this morning."

"What do you want?" Ben asked.

The giant looked over his right shoulder, toward where the beach had been returned to its original, though now higher, location.

"I see you went ahead with it," Quick said. "That was smart. Find any more bones?"

Dan's mouth fell open. They hadn't been expecting a visit from the Blanc family. But that's exactly when the woman had said to expect them. It was only by chance that he and Ben were here this late.

The jobsite was being watched.

"We didn't exactly have any choice," Dan said, sounding surer of himself than he felt. "And no, we didn't even look."

"Kurt's a relatively harmless girl," Quick said, his head coming back around. "Relative to me, that is. She's my woman's only kid. Oh, she can shoot you or cut your balls off and feed them to you, and she'll still sleep like a baby, but there are lot worse things that can happen to a person. And *I* am that whole lot worse thing."

"What's that supposed to mean?" Ben asked.

The big man glared at both of them, taking a measured step forward. "What it means is the Blancs run everything south of Marco. It means you're gonna do everything we say from here on out. And I mean everything."

"What if we don't?" Ben asked.

The big man took three steps and was suddenly within arm's reach. He towered over Dan by a full head and probably weighed more than the two brothers combined. But it was the look in his eyes, behind the mane of hair, that was most fearsome. He snorted like a bull.

"If you don't, I'll tear the arms and legs off your kids," he replied with a snarl. "Then I'll have my way with both your wives before I do the same to them. Lastly, I'll squash your heads together until they pop."

"What do you want us to do?" Dan asked. "We already kept everything from the police."

"Tomorrow, you rent the biggest, most bad-ass industrial tiller you can find. Then you bring it out here and run it over this whole island to a depth of two feet."

Ben noticeably retched before turning away.

"We'll make it worth your trouble," Willy Quick continued. "What's your most expensive lot?"

Dan looked confused. "Huh?"

"Your most expensive lot?" Quick repeated. "We want to buy it and turn it into a playground for the little kiddies."

"What?" Ben said, recovering.

Quick tossed the backpack on the ground in front of Dan. "This is business to me. A bunch of cops digging up bones of the past will only complicate my business. Use that to build a playground and keep whatever's left over."

With that, the brute turned and lumbered back toward the dark side of the island. In seconds he'd vanished, as if the swamp had just opened its maw and swallowed him up.

"What's in the pack?" Ben asked.

Dan bent over and picked it up. When he opened it, he looked at his brother, dumbfounded. "It's money."

Ben came closer and peered into the backpack. "I don't like this, man," he said, stepping back.

"Like it or not," they both heard Quick say, his voice sounding far off and yet, very near, at the same time. "You're in bed with the devil now. Just remember, the swamp has eyes. You're always being watched."

"What the hell *was* that guy?" Ben whispered.

"Let's get inside," Dan said, tossing his nearly empty beer can into the barrel and heading up the steps.

Once inside, they closed and locked the door, then went to Dan's office in the back of the trailer. There, he opened the pack and dumped the contents on his desk—bundles of $100 bills.

Ben stacked them in five piles, five bundles in each. "This is a quarter million friggin' dollars, Dan. Is it real?"

Dan picked one up one of the bundles and thumbed it. The bills weren't new; the serial numbers were all over the place.

He tossed it on the desk. "Yeah, they're real."

"I bet these people are drug smugglers."

"Or worse," Dan added. "Why would they give it to us?"

"It's hush money. Like he said, we're in bed with the devil, himself. We have to tell the cops."

"We do that and it'll all come out," Dan said. "That we found the skull and didn't report it. That's called being an accessory."

Ben pushed his hair back with both hands. "How the hell could we have known?"

"We could get prison time, Ben. Never mind that the investigation itself would drag on forever. If we don't make that first of the month payment next week, we're done. We only need one deposit on one lot. Then we live to fight another day."

Ben looked down at the piles of Benjamins. "Or we take this and use it to satisfy the bank."

"Look," Dan said, turning toward his brother, "We can get the utilities and the roads in. Then we can decide what to do going forward—either start building homes or sell the remaining lots to another builder and get out still intact."

Ben looked up at Dan. "In for a dime?"

"In for a quarter million dollars."

CHAPTER TWENTY-TWO

The sun was still below the horizon when I woke. There were no lights on in my bedroom but the gathering light outside allowed me to see every detail, what there was.

I'd lived a fairly spartan existence on my island. Always had. Even after Hurricane Irma had practically destroyed everything and we rebuilt, I kept my own quarters simple. It's what I was used to.

Savannah lay beside me, the sheets tangled around her legs and her blond hair hanging across her face. I don't think she'd stirred the whole night after we'd made love. This wasn't simple.

I'd been married twice while I was in the Corps. Deuce's dad, Russ Livingston, had been my platoon sergeant early in my career. He hadn't been able to keep his marriage intact either and often said that if a Marine needed a wife, the Corps would have issued him one. My first marriage lasted six years and three deployments. The second lasted six months before I realized Russ had been right.

As I looked at Savannah, she stirred, stretching her arms and legs as she opened her eyes.

She smiled. "Good morning."

"Ready to get started?" I asked.

She sniffed at the air. "Coffee first."

I'd set the machine up before we'd gone to bed. When we'd arrived back at my island, I'd left the Grady tied to the pier and we'd spent an hour just relaxing and watching the stars from out on the deck. I hadn't been home in eight months and it felt good.

"I'll get it," I said.

Rising from the bed, I pulled on my boxers, then went into the living room. Finn and Woden lay on the big oval rug in the middle of the floor. As one, they rose and followed me to the door.

"Go show Woden around," I told Finn as I opened the door.

I poured two mugs of coffee and returned to my bedroom.

Our bedroom.

Savannah was pulling a T-shirt down over her belly, already dressed for the day.

"Do you usually make the bed first thing?" she asked.

I gave her a lecherous grin as I handed her a mug. "Just as soon as I'm finished using it."

She started pulling the sheets up. "You're finished. You have a lot to show me. Are Rusty and the boys coming here, or will you be going down there to pick them up in the morning?"

"We hadn't decided that," I said. "I'll call Rusty and he can bring them up in his boat."

We quickly made the bed and finished our coffee, then went outside. The sun was just peeking over the horizon.

"There are several fruit trees around the island," I said. "Banana, mango, papaya, orange, and grapefruit. You can have your pick for breakfast."

"Ever thought of raising chickens?" she asked, as we started down the back steps. "You know, for the eggs? They're all over Key West."

Savannah liked omelets for breakfast. Usually, I opted for fruit, but never turned down a bacon and egg sandwich.

"That could work," I agreed, pointing off to the northwest, beyond Kim's house. "There's a tiny island just a few yards off. I own it too. See that big solar array?"

"That's interesting," she said, as we continued down the steps. "I've never seen one like that."

"It folds out in the morning, opening like a flower. Then it tracks the sun across the sky before folding up again. A chicken coop could work out there."

"This is what I really wanted to see," Savannah said, continuing across the sand, past the corner of the house and toward the new aquaponics system.

"We don't have a problem with animals eating our vegetables," I said. "There usually aren't any out here. A Key deer wound up here once, a few years before Irma—a young doe. She got into the lettuce, but we caught her and took her back to Big Pine. And there are very few bugs this far out in the backcountry. Chickens on the little island might not get into the veggies."

I showed her how the setup worked. We now had six tanks, where we'd once had only four. The three higher tanks held catfish, crawfish, and tilapia. The Keys extended 115 miles out into the ocean from the mainland and there are very few natural freshwater ponds or lakes, so freshwater fish were hard to find. There were a number of restaurants up and down the island chain that bought from Jimmy.

"The water from the fish tanks gravity-feeds down to the vegetable tanks," I explained. "It carries a lot of dissolved ammonia and nitrates from the fish waste, which the plants thrive on. The roots of the plants are suspended in the water stream in baskets of limestone gravel. The plants remove the waste from the water and add oxygen. Then the water's pumped back up to the fish tanks. The plants grow three or four times faster than in soil."

"Are they all on one pump?"

"No, each is completely independent. The water from the fish tanks never crosses over."

"Why's that?"

"Jimmy's idea," I replied. "He says fish leave a scent in the water and sensing different species, they might become aggressive."

We went up three steps to the catwalk that surrounded the fish tanks. Each tank was twenty feet long and eight feet wide, with a depth of four feet.

"Each of these tanks holds about five thousand gallons and is segmented by screens of varying sizes to give the fry some protection as they grow. We feed them up at the large end, where the bigger fish are trapped. The smaller ones go that way and when they get too big, they can't get back."

"Wouldn't they grow too big at this end to be able to get through the mesh to where the food is?"

"Not often," I said. "They come out to feed and there are lots of places to hide on the bottom. The fry don't have to go far, as the food is broken up by the bigger fish upstream. If threatened, they only need to swim back through the screen or hide in the coquina rocks scattered across the bottom."

I pulled a dip net from a bracket and pointed to two more nearly identical ones. "Each net has progressively bigger mesh. A couple swipes through each section once a week is all that's needed to move any bigger ones that might get trapped."

Savannah took the net and moved it through the small end of the catfish tank. "How long do the fish take to reach maturity?"

Hundreds of small fry swam through the net's mesh. One was too big and she deposited it in the next section.

"It takes about eight months for the catfish to reach two to three pounds," I replied. "And they reproduce fast. There are about five hundred channel cats in there."

"And the tilapia?" she asked.

"A bit less time," I replied. "Maybe seven months to reach three pounds. I'd guess there are maybe five hundred in that tank, too. In just four months, the craw-fish will be about twenty count per pound. Jimmy harvests all three every other Friday."

"What's over there?" Savannah asked, pointing toward the northeast.

"Just a fire ring," I said. "Somebody left it here before I ever bought the island."

"No, beyond that," she said, walking in that direction. "Out past the trees."

I fell in beside her. "That's the power and water plant," I said. "The battery house has fifty lithium ion batteries, charged by the solar panel, with a diesel generator for backup."

"How often does that come on?"

"The old one ran for at least two hours a day," I replied. "We had older, lead-acid batteries then. The new generator only comes on once a week for a maintenance run. So far, it's never kicked on the generator, though."

She looked around the interior of the island. "You're completely off the grid?"

"Yep. The cistern above my house collects rainwater. In a pinch, and it's only happened once, we can pump water from the *Revenge's* water maker up to the cistern. Waste goes into a macerator, then is injected into a deep well."

We circled the island to the left, stopping at the bunk-house. "This will be Florence's after we remodel it in the spring."

She turned toward the north pier, taking my hand. "Are you sure you're okay with women living here?" she asked, hesitantly. "I mean fish camps, fire rings, a bunkhouse...it's like a giant man cave."

"The fire ring stays," I said. "We can do anything you want to the rest of the island. I wouldn't have it any other way."

We sat down at the end of the T-head, dangling our feet in the water. The clicking of untrimmed claws announced the arrival of the dogs. Finn sat next to me and Woden next to Savannah.

"What do you like most about living out here?" she asked.

I had to ponder that one for a moment. "It's changed over time," I finally replied. "When I built my house, I liked the solitude. Sometimes, I'd go a whole week and not even see a boat go by out in the Gulf."

"And later?"

"I built the bunkhouses to quarter Deuce's team when he was with Homeland Security. I missed the camaraderie of my fellow Neanderthals and helped him train his team. This island became a place for us to stand down and relax."

"And now?"

I looked over at her and put my hand on her bare thigh. "I've been with you for the last eight months. I think I like that better than the solitude. I hope you'll be happy here."

Savannah sighed and laid her head on my shoulder. "I don't see how anyone wouldn't. It's such a quiet and serene place."

I thought back to the times when trouble had come to my shore. It'd happened quite a few times. Once, a psycho gypsy witch doctor had gassed everyone on the island and kidnapped me. Another time, a hired killer had come in the night to kill me and Deuce. And during Hurricane Irma, a crazy Icelandic woman had tried to ambush me.

"Show me the rest," she said, rising from her spot.

We continued the tour and worked for a while—feeding the fish and cleaning up the eastern shore. The prevailing winds always pushed things up onto the beach.

Savannah pointed to the northeast. "What's that island?"

"That's Upper Harbor Key," I said. "It used to be owned by a grumpy old Navy man turned bridge-builder named Woodson until he died. Now Wood's daughter, Mel, owns it."

She looked over at me, surprised. "A woman?"

"She lives there part-time with her boyfriend, Mac Travis. He used to work for Wood and lives there full time, taking care of the place."

"You mean you actually have neighbors?"

I picked up a chunk of fiberglass. It might have been from a boat, there was no way to tell. "Well, they're a mile-and-a-half away, so I wouldn't go so far as to call them next-door neighbors."

She gazed toward Wood's island. It looked like mine and every other key in the backcountry, low and flat. The house Wood had built out there had burned down several years back and Mac had rebuilt it. Then Irma came and he'd been slowly rebuilding ever since. Unlike mine, his house was built in the interior of the island and not visible from the water. So, there was nothing for Savannah to see.

"What are they like?" she asked. "I assume you've met them."

"Just regular people, I guess. He's a commercial diver and catches lobster during the season and treasure during the off-season. He'd be out with his hand, Trufant, pulling traps right now."

"And her?" she asked, turning toward me.

"A lawyer," I replied. "She's worked some pretty high-profile environmental cases. She mostly comes out on the weekends."

"We should have them over some time."

I liked Mac okay. He was a quiet guy for the most part. I guessed him to be a few years younger than me and he appeared capable enough. Like Wood before him, he kept mostly to himself.

Still, if that was what Savannah wanted to do...

"I don't know," I said. "I barely know Mel Woodson, and Mac and I know each other well enough to greet each other by name. He doesn't strike me as a social animal."

"He's a hermit like you."

I grinned. "I'm not a hermit. A hermit doesn't have a beautiful woman on his arm."

We ate lunch and as the afternoon grew hotter, took a dip in the Gulf to cool off. Finn joined us, but Woden stayed on the pier.

"He doesn't really like the water," Savannah said. "I know. Weird for a boat dog, huh? But he just never learned to swim."

"You mean he's forgotten," I said.

"What do you mean?"

"Mammals have a lot of things in common," I replied. "One is the ability to swim. In the womb, all mammals are suspended in amniotic fluid. Humans swim for the first nine months of development. After we're born, some don't return to the sea for a long time and they forget. Finn's mother was a Lab and his father was half Lab and half retriever. She probably had him back in the water within a few weeks of birth."

"Mom got Woden when he was six weeks old, but he stayed with his trainer for two months. When he finally came to live with us, he went back to the trainer every day for several hours."

"Finn and I can remind him," I said. "The ability never really goes away completely."

Finn swam toward us, his ears up. I looked toward Woden on the pier. He was standing, facing the island.

"Someone's coming," I said.

"Who? Your friend Mac?"

I started toward the ladder, Savannah following me. "No, we'd see and hear him. Someone's coming up the back way, between Howe Key and the Water Keys."

We dried off quickly, and I pulled my boxers and shorts on. With nobody around, we'd been skinny-dipping.

"Come on," I said. Both dogs looked to me for guidance.

"*Bewachen*," I said to Woden, ordering him to guard. Before I could say anything to Finn, both dogs took off at a dead run, side by side.

"He's picking up Woden's commands," Savannah said, pulling on her shirt and hurrying after me. "Who do you suppose it is?"

"I don't know," I said, reaching the steps to the bunkhouse. "Wait here."

I went up the steps two at a time and entered the small building. There were three sets of bunkbeds down both walls—room for twelve fishermen. Between each set of bunks was a window and below each window, a small dresser. I went to the first dresser and yanked open the top drawer.

When I went back down the steps, I was clipping a holstered Colt 1911 to my belt.

"You think it's trouble?"

I took her hand and hurried toward my house on the other side of the island. "Won't know till it gets here. But I doubt it."

"Then why the gun?"

I shrugged. "Better to have it and not need it, than to need it and not have it."

In the distance, I could hear the buzz of an outboard motor. It wasn't a big engine, probably less than fifty horses, and it wasn't running fast. Someone was picking their way up through the cuts and sandbars to the south.

Finn and Woden stood at the foot of the south pier, ears up and on full alert. Finn was guarding his home and Woden was standing by his friend.

It was that simple.

Few intruders would attempt to tie up at my dock with either dog there, obviously waiting for them to try.

We walked out onto the south pier about halfway, and the dogs stayed in front of us.

Finally, a small boat appeared, clearing the last of many banks and sandbars at the southern end of Harbor Channel. The boat came up on plane and headed straight for us.

"That's Rusty's boat," I said, noting that he wasn't alone.

I didn't have to check my pockets to know that my phone was on the charger in the living room.

Rusty slowed the boat and came alongside the dock. Deuce tossed me a line from the bow. Jimmy and Tony were with them.

"I've been callin' all morning," Deuce said. "There's been a development."

"What kind of development?" I asked.

Rusty tied off the stern line and stepped up to the dock. "The kind what comes into my bar asking questions about you."

"Who was it?"

"He was sly," Rusty said. "Didn't talk to me at all, just mingled with some of the locals, asking questions. Dink said the man told him his name was Bill Monroe. But when Dink asked if he was related to the bluegrass player, he said the guy didn't know what he was talking about."

"He's in his fifties," Tony added. "How does someone live that long with that name and not know who the king of bluegrass is? Even I know that."

"Real big dude," Jimmy said. "Taller than you and at least three hundred pounds."

"Did he have a scar over his left eye?"

"Yeah," Rusty replied. "You know him?"

"Quint Robbins," I half mumbled. "I put that scar there."

"The guy you got into a scrape with, up in Fort Myers?" Deuce asked.

"Has to be," I replied.

"Course, anyone who knows didn't say anything," Rusty said.

"Dink told me that the guy thinks you're a cop," Jimmy said. "He wanted to know where you lived."

"And it took all four of you to come up here and tell me?"

"They worry about you," Savannah said. "So do I."

Then she turned to my friends. "You're all staying, right? We'll need more food."

"*No problemo,*" Jimmy said. "Tony and I can catch what we need and I'll do the cooking."

I grinned at Deuce. "Grab your gear. You know where the bunkhouse is."

Jimmy stepped down into the little Grady and held his hand up to me. "Keys?"

Tony joined him, with both their wet bags. "We shouldn't be but an hour or so."

I handed Jimmy the key to the Grady, then helped Rusty unload the rest of their gear from his boat. Savannah led Deuce toward the bunkhouse with his gear.

"How's she like it?" Rusty whispered.

"It'll take her some getting used to," I said. "But living on a small island isn't a lot different than boat living."

"You'd be smart to put a ring on her finger, bro. You keep letting them slip away and you're gonna be a lonely old man."

"Says the guy who stayed a bachelor for three decades."

He looked over at me, his face serious. "I ain't kiddin', Jesse. Savannah's a *good* woman. And that don't have nothin' to do with her bein' a knockout. She's strong-willed and independent. You'll look far and wide to find a better match."

I looked ahead, where Savannah was walking and talking with Deuce, as if having four guests show up unannounced was nothing out of the ordinary. I knew better. Living on a boat, moving from port to anchorage, one rarely had a visitor, much less four of them.

My mind drifted to Quint Robbins. It was obvious there was more to this than a high school grudge. Had he sent the woman, Kurt Blanc? What was so important they would shoot at someone who they thought was a cop?

CHAPTER TWENTY-THREE

The white Cadillac Escalade turned off the highway onto a crushed shell driveway. Within a few yards it passed over the sensor buried across the trail and was then swallowed by the overhanging trees.

Jubal Blanc didn't worry that his visit was being announced. He was expected. Besides, they were going to his sister's house.

Riding in the backseat, Jubal ended a phone call he'd made when they left the office on Marco Island.

"ADA Brighton's a fuckin' prick," he said.

Chloe Devlin didn't react to the language, but merely shrugged, a corner of her mouth turning up slightly.

"That was my impression the first time I met him," she said. "He's a Chikkan-obsessed pervert."

"Chikkan?" Jubal asked. "I'm not familiar with that one."

"When we were going down in the elevator with him, that first time? His hand *accidentally* rubbed my ass twice. The third time was with his dick."

"And that's called chikkan?"

"It's Japanese," Chloe remarked. "Men in Japan do it all the time on buses and trains. Like I said, the guy's a pervert."

"I wasn't aware of that, Chloe. If I had been, I'd have—"

"I took care of it," she said. "When more people got on the elevator, I was pressed back against him and *might* have crushed his nuts in my fist like a stress ball."

Jubal chuckled as they entered the clearing where his sister's house stood. "That explains a lot."

"How's that, Senator?"

The barn door opened and she steered the big SUV into it. Willy Quick pulled the doors closed behind them.

"He's wanting to charge those developers," Jubal said. "For withholding evidence. He thinks they know who Kurt is."

Chloe got out and opened the back door. "I can have a word with him," she offered. "I did a little follow up on him and know he spends every other Saturday night at a strip club and hotel in Miami. He goes to the club alone but goes to the hotel with a small crowd."

"Is that right?"

"Yes, sir. He'll be there this weekend."

"Make it happen," Jubal said. "But catch him with his pants down."

He turned to face his brother-in-law. "How are you, Willy? Great work last night with those Yankee developers. We drove past there on the way out. They're playing ball."

"We gotta do something about Kurt," Willy grunted, skipping pleasantries. "But first we gotta do something about the cops she took pot shots at."

"Let's go inside," Jubal said, unruffled. "How's Marley?"

"Bitchy as ever," Willy replied, not attempting to hide the fact that his eyes were crawling up and down Chloe's body.

Chloe wore her usual black skirt and white blouse. Her hair was up in a high ponytail, making it dance whenever she moved. She wore dark sunglasses, now propped up on her high forehead.

"Maybe if you weren't such a douche bag to her," Chloe said, the corner of her mouth turning up again, accentuating the seductive red lipstick she wore.

Willy's dark eyes smoldered. "You know I could rip you limb from—"

Chloe didn't let him finish his threat. "No, fat ass. You can't."

"Now, now," Jubal said. "Let's not go there, again."

The first time his personal assistant and brother-in-law met, she'd come away with a torn blouse and he had a black eye and split lip.

Jubal motioned toward the smaller door and after a moment's hesitation, Willy stomped over and opened it. He didn't bother to hold it open, but just stalked off toward the house.

"He's a prick, too," Chloe said, pushing the door open and stepping out into the sunlight.

"Yes," Jubal agreed, following her. "But he's family. Please try to keep it civil."

"It's hard for me to believe you come from this same stock, Senator."

They entered the house through the front door. Marley was sitting in a worn recliner, Kurt and Donnie on a couch beside her. Willy's friend, Quint Robbins, sat in a straight-back chair he'd pulled from the kitchen. Two rough-looking strangers stood behind him.

"Did you find out anything?" Jubal asked Robbins.

"His name's Jesse McDermitt," Robbins said. "Willy and I know him from up in Fort Myers. The locals down in Marathon weren't much help, but I have a friend at the Monroe Clerk's office. McDermitt owns an island in the Content Keys, north of Big Pine. He has two daughters. Eve Maggio, who lives over in Miami, and Kim Phillips, who's a Fish and Wildlife cop."

"She was the one who shot at me," Kurt said.

"The same boat he was on in Fort Myers," Robbins continued, "was at the place in Marathon, that he owns part of—the Rusty Anchor Bar and Grill."

"What's the name of the boat?" Chloe asked, pulling a cell phone from her small clutch purse.

"It's called *Sea Biscuit*."

"And the two women you saw on the boat with him?" Jubal asked. "Were they his two daughters?"

"I don't think so," Robbins said, shaking his head. "One was too old and the other too young."

"The older one?" Chloe said. "Was she like late forties? And the girl about eighteen?"

"Maybe," Robbins replied. "A damned hot late forties."

"What kind of boat?"

Robbins stared at Chloe, unsure.

"She's my assistant, Robbins," Jubal said. "Anything you can say in front of me, you can say in front of her."

"An older-looking trawler," he replied. "The home port on the stern said it was from Beaufort, South Carolina."

"There's a motor vessel by that name and home port documented with the Coast Guard. It belongs to a Savannah Richmond."

"It's hers, not his?" Robbins asked.

"You said this man was a police officer?" Jubal said to Kurt. It was more of an accusation than a question, left hanging for her response.

"He sure started shootin' like he was a cop," Kurt said. "The woman definitely was. I seen her badge."

"I can take care of that end of things," Jubal said. "I know people with Fish and Wildlife."

"He ain't a cop," Robbins said. "He's retired. A washed-up has- been."

"There's also a Jesse McDermitt listed in the Coast Guard registry," Chloe said, scrolling busily on her phone. "He owns a number of registered vessels. A fifty-foot Seaton pilothouse trawler that's over fifty years old, a Formosa ketch not much newer, and a Rampage sportfishing boat only fifteen years old. He's the primary in one business, Gaspar's Revenge Charter Service, and a partner in McDermitt and Livingston Security, as well as the Rusty Anchor Bar and Grill."

"You found all that on your phone?" Robbins asked.

Chloe waggled it at the man. "It's called Google. You should try it some time."

"Knock it off!" Marley yelled. "Ain't gonna be no belittlin' here."

The corner of Chloe's lips curled slightly. Her trademark smirk.

"This McDermitt sounds like a loose cannon," Jubal said. "And he saw Kurt's face. I'm more worried about him than the girl cop. Her boss is bought and paid for."

"You said he lives on an island north of Big Pine," Chloe said, looking back down at her phone. "Yet his girlfriend's boat was in Marathon?"

"The water north of Big Pine Key is shallow," Marley pointed out. "He probably keeps a small boat at that marina to shuttle back and forth to his island. What's the name of it, Quint?"

"The island he lives on?" Robbins asked. "So far as the Clerk's office knows, it doesn't have one."

Marley leaned forward. "Then how are your boys gonna find it?"

"Can't be too many of them," Robbins replied with a shrug.

"Quite a few, actually," Chloe said, looking at her screen again. "The Content Keys looks like a collection of a good forty or fifty small islands. But only two that show any sign of habitation." She turned her phone to Jubal and pointed to two small specks. "Both are on Harbor Channel. This is an aerial view. You can clearly see one house on this island and several more on this other one. The image is four years old."

"Didn't Hurricane Irma pass through that area?" Jubal asked.

"It did," Willy said. "Almost three years ago. I doubt any of those houses were still standing after that."

"May I?" Marley said, reaching for Chloe's phone.

The younger woman released it without a fuss. Jubal knew that she could take on anyone in the room and win, probably all at once. But she knew better than to step on his sister's toes.

"Only one way to find out," Marley said. "This waterway here," she indicated a line on the screen to Willy, "it's called Harbor Channel. I know it well. It's deep water. You and Quint go with them boys. Take the two go-fast boats first thing in the morning. Find him and kill him."

Kurt grinned in satisfaction, revealing her missing and stained teeth.

CHAPTER TWENTY-FOUR

I woke before sunrise to find Savannah wasn't next to me. I'm usually an exceptionally light sleeper but didn't notice when she got up.

Getting slow in your old age, McDermitt, I thought.

We'd eaten before sunset, Tony helping Jimmy with the food preparation, then we'd sat around the fire ring until well into the night. Mostly catching up, but we also talked a little about the events that'd happened up on the mainland.

I put on a clean pair of boxers and went into the front room. That's where I found Savannah. She was bagging sandwiches and cutting up fruit and vegetables into sealable bowls.

"What's this?" I asked, hugging her from behind.

"You'll need some food for the trip," she said.

"You didn't have to do this."

"I just wanted to contribute in some way," she said, turning into my embrace. "Coffee's ready."

I hugged her, then poured a mug and took a tentative sip.

Strong and black.

"It's only a couple of hours to get up there in the *Revenge*," I said. "She's stocked, except for meat, and we'll remedy that on the way or when we get there."

I heard footsteps on the back stairs and the tick of dogs' claws. Savannah must have let Finn and Woden out.

"What time are Julie and Sidney going to hit the shops for you?"

"We changed our plans," she said. "Julie's picking me up in an hour. Sidney and Naomi are coming too, so we can all brainstorm here a little before we go shopping."

I looked around my little two-room house. "It's almost a blank canvas," I remarked. "I'm not much of a decorator."

"It's very...*functional*," she said, smiling. "But it could use a little color."

"Have at it," I said, opening the door as I saw Rusty walk past the kitchen window.

"Have at what?" he asked.

The dogs came through the door behind him and went straight to the rug in the middle of the room.

"Your wife and daughter are coming up here to go over some redecorating ideas with Savannah."

Rusty looked around at the sparse accommodations. "Yeah, you could spruce this up with a little color."

Savannah couldn't suppress a laugh.

"Are the others up?" I asked.

"Yeah. Jimmy's making breakfast on the grill."

"Go," Savannah said, swishing us toward the door with her hands. "I'll be down in a few minutes."

Rusty and I left and headed down the steps.

"Did ya ask her?"

"Ask her what?" I said.

"To marry ya, ya dumb grunt."

I grinned at Rusty in the darkness. "I don't even have a ring."

"It takes a mouth to ask the question," he said. "You can always get a ring later."

The others were sitting at one of the old wooden tables. They'd been built from heavy cypress planks and were anchored deep into the island's coral and limestone bedrock. They, and the stone grill, were some of the few things that had survived Irma completely intact.

Jimmy looked up from a cast iron skillet where he was moving bacon around. "What time you want to get underway?"

He slid another pan onto a tray on the table. It was loaded with scrambled eggs and slices of pepper from the garden.

"As soon as it's light enough," I replied.

Rusty and I sat down across from Deuce and Tony as Jimmy placed a skillet of sizzling bacon on the table. We each helped ourselves and ate quickly and silently.

The dogs preceded Savannah, who joined us and helped herself to a plate before sitting beside me. "I left a cooler full of sandwiches, fruit, and sliced vegetables by the stairs."

When we finished eating, Savannah told us to go and get the boat ready, that she'd take care of cleaning up.

I held her with one arm and brushed a strand of hair from her forehead. "I'll call you when we get there."

We kissed, then she shooed me away. "Go on, now. I have work to do here."

I picked up two strips of bacon and looked at the dogs. They sat patiently, heads and ears up, waiting. I tossed the two strips, and they each caught one.

"You two stay here and keep Savannah company."

"What do I do with them when I leave?" she asked.

"Nothing," I replied. "Finn knows his way around and there are a couple of islands they can walk to without getting their bellies wet. They'll have fun till you get back."

The five of us returned to my house and headed to the narrow, inside steps that led down to the dock area below the house. Most of the time, I missed having the exterior access. It had been a lot more convenient than going up to the deck, into the house, and down to the docks. But it was also a possible point of entry for someone who wasn't supposed to be there. Giving up a little diminished accessibility for security was a better idea. There were only two ways into the dock area. Through the boat doors, which extended several feet below the surface, or through my house.

I picked up the cooler at the head of the stairs and switched on the lights mounted to the floor beams. The underside of the house was instantly illuminated by four bright, LED lights.

"Wow!" Tony exclaimed, his smile like a kid's on Christmas morning. "Seeing that big beast again just never gets old."

He was referring to my primary charter vessel, *Gaspar's Revenge*, situated on the far side of the dock area. She filled most of her berth, being only a foot shorter in length and height.

My house was fifty feet by twenty feet, with a fifteen-foot deck around three sides. This footprint allowed for dockage below the house that was sixty-five feet wide and fifty feet deep. The *Revenge*, with her pulpit and swim platform, took up nearly all of the fifty-foot berth.

Next to her was *El Cazador*, a thirty-foot Winter Yachts center console with an inboard diesel. It was tight on that side, only twenty-eight feet of lateral room for the two boats, which had a combined beam of twenty-five. But the water was always calm and there was never any current. *Cazador* had the easier spot to back into because she was a single-engine and less maneuverable.

My smaller boats—the ones used for fishing the backcountry—were all on the other side of the center stairwell and dock.

"Go ahead and get everything aboard," I said, as I opened the small cabinet at the bottom of the steps.

I selected the right key and clicked the *Unlock* button on the fob, then tossed it up to Jimmy, already on the flybridge.

The familiar click of the release mechanism on the massive doors in front of the *Revenge* was comforting in some way. I'd been away for a long time.

After Irma, I could have replaced the door system with something more modern, but the spring-loaded hinges were simple and about some things, I like simplicity. Once the latch was released, the doors, which extended below the water's surface, opened without power. The springs in each hinge slowly unwound, pushing the heavy doors against the water. There were hydraulic rams on each hinge that pulled the doors closed, so power was only needed for that operation.

First one engine growled to life, followed quickly by the other. The easy rumble of the twin 1100-horsepower engines thrilled some inner sense and I felt the hairs on my arms stand up.

"I'll get the lines," Tony said, scrambling back over to the narrow walkway.

Like Jimmy and I, Tony was a speed junky.

Rusty and Deuce, on the other hand, were content to move at a slower pace. Rusty's old forty-horse Evinrude was just enough to get the boat to plane, but insured he'd never reach any breakneck speed—maybe twenty-five knots if he were lucky and had a tail wind. Deuce had always been sedated by the wind power his ketch generated.

I could go both ways. I loved the feel of the *Dog* when she heeled over in a stout wind, and I also got a charge out of skimming across the flats in my Maverick at fifty knots. Sidney said I was a transvesselite.

After boarding the *Revenge*, I stowed the cooler and climbed up to the flybridge. Jimmy rose from the helm and moved over to the second seat while I studied the gauges. The fuel tanks were nearly full and both engines' oil pressure gauges were reading nominal.

"Watch the temperature gauges, man," Jimmy said. "The port engine will start moving before the starboard."

That made sense and was probably what first alerted Jimmy to check each cylinder. With one of them losing compression, it wouldn't burn all the fuel as efficiently in that cylinder.

While it might not be noticeable at operating temps, the difference in when the gauges started to move would alert a careful observer that one engine was warming up faster from a cold start. The gauges didn't move until the coolant temperature reached 100°, the lowest readout on the analog dial.

That was going to be part of the refit. An all-new, modern instrument package came with the new engines I'd ordered, complete with computer diagnostics.

The coolant temperature gauge for the port engine began to rise. I started counting in my head. At twelve seconds, Jimmy snapped his finger and pointed at the other gauge. He must have been counting too, because at that moment, the starboard engine's temperature gauge began to move.

"Twelve seconds," he said. "Every time."

Tony stood ready on the port side, dock lines to the bow and stern, currently looped around two cleats, were clutched in his hands. Deuce and Rusty stood ready to haul the lines in when he released them.

"Cast off!" I ordered, putting the starboard engine into forward.

With deft movements, Tony flipped both lines, loosing them from the cleats, then released the bow line for Deuce to haul in.

The *Revenge* slowly moved forward, turning slightly to port with the wheel amidships and only the starboard screw turning. Tony kept the stern line out of the water as Rusty coiled it, then he stepped up onto the gunwale and down into the cockpit. With the lines clear, I engaged the port engine.

Water swirled behind us. With nowhere to go, the prop wash rocked the other boats in the confined space. The new concrete sea wall around the whole dock area rose well above the water, encapsulating each support leg of the house.

As we moved out of the shadows, the stainless-steel pulpit and side rails, as well as the gleaming white foredeck, caught the early morning sun.

I put on my shades. "Saturday night, rock and roll."

"Um, it's Wednesday," Tony said.

Rusty chuckled. "We got us a boatload of squids, bro."

A moment later, I clicked the *Lock* button on the fob as we idled through my narrow channel. I glanced back and saw the doors closing. When I started the turn into

Harbor Channel, the fob vibrated, telling me that the catch had engaged.

I pushed the throttles forward slightly; the powerful engines responded instantly. Though they were sixteen years old and had nearly ten thousand hours on them, Jimmy had maintained them well. The *Revenge* responded like a finely-tuned sportscar—one that weighed nearly twenty tons.

I put my hand on the throttles and could feel the restlessness. The *Revenge* wanted to go pound her way through the sea. I glanced over at Tony and Rusty, sitting on the port bench. Rusty sat sideways, gazing out toward the Gulf, not a care in the world. Tony's dark features were easy to read. His gaze was on my right hand, anticipating the thrill of 2200 horses screaming below us.

Usually, I ran sedately through the channel until I passed Mac's island. There, the channel was nearly a quarter mile wide and there was another quarter mile of flats to his shore.

The current in the channel was maxing out at two knots against us. It would dissipate our wake quite a bit before it even reached the shallows. There was little chance of waking Mac's shoreline.

I pushed the throttles past the halfway mark. Instantly, the stern settled as the massive props displaced tons of water below us. The bow rose and the *Revenge* surged forward. In seconds she'd climbed up her own bow wave like a hungry cat after a squirrel. The bow came down and she continued to gather speed as the big boat started to plane.

Tony stood and braced himself against the railing. His big, toothy smile white against his dark ebony skin. Tony was in his late forties, but you couldn't tell it to look at him. He was fit and wiry, and without a wrinkle. From the North Carolina Piedmont—mostly widely scattered small farms—his parents had taken the family to the coast on vacation once, and, as Tony described it, the worm had turned. He enlisted in the Navy before graduating high school and shipped out four days after commencement.

When the *Revenge* reached thirty knots, I pulled back on the throttles a little. As we approached Mac's island, I didn't expect to see any sign that anyone was there. It was early, but the season was open, and I knew Mac and Tru would already be out pulling lobster traps after an overnight soak.

Turning the wheel slightly, I kept the *Revenge* in the deeper water between Turtlecrawl Bank and the grassy flats to the north of Mac's island.

It was still early, but there'd been a steady southeast wind all night and the sea state beyond the channel was a little choppy. Nothing the *Revenge* couldn't handle. I adjusted the trim and pushed the throttles a little farther.

A quick look at the knot meter told me we had forty knots of boat speed. A glance at the GPS speed on the chart plotter indicated a slightly lower speed over ground, due to the current. Our SOG was just over thirty-eight knots.

I pointed the bow toward the north-northwest and set the autopilot. Then I adjusted it to the precise heading.

I knew from experience there was nothing between my island and San Carlos Bay but water, and it rarely got shallower than thirty feet.

"You're not gonna open her up?" Tony asked, a hint of disappointment in his voice.

"One engine's been having problems," I said. "You in a hurry?"

"Nah," he said. "I just like to go fast."

I checked the chart plotter's GPS speed again and glanced at my watch. It was 0730. I nudged the throttles again, not enough to engage the superchargers, but just about. Our SOG was an even forty knots.

"We're two-and-a-half hours from San Carlos Bay," I announced. "Then another half hour up the Caloosahatchee River to the marina. We should get there about eleven hundred."

"You're not gonna stop at Marco?" Rusty asked.

"Can't get anywhere near where the shooting happened," I replied. "And I have a feeling the root of the problem is a lot farther inland."

Deuce sat on the forward-facing bench in front of the console. He turned his head slightly to be heard over the buffeting wind. "Billy's going to meet us at the marina with two trucks."

"So, that's who you were on the phone with last night?" Tony asked. Deuce nodded.

Billy Rainwater, aside from being a good friend and the best 4x4 builder in south Florida, was also the leader of the Calusa tribe and an attorney. Deuce had retained his services some years ago, and he'd helped the firm with legal questions from time to time. The retainer was one dollar and he'd never billed Deuce for his time, though Deuce and I had both asked him to.

"We'll split up in Fort Myers," I said. "I'm known to these people. Rusty might be since they were snooping around the Anchor."

"They're going to find Quint Robbins," Deuce said to Tony. "You, Jimmy, and I are going to use Billy's other truck and drive down to Goodland."

CHAPTER TWENTY-FIVE

"**I**'m going," Kurt said flatly.

Willy glared at her under the yellow light of the sodium lamps around the parking lot. "You think we need *your* help?" he snarled. "It's on account of your hot-headedness that we're having to go down there in the first place."

"He shot at me, Willy. Nobody does that and gets away with it."

Willy nodded toward the two men walking out onto the dock with Quint. "Them boys are as good as they come."

"I wanna kill that fucker myself," Kurt said.

Willy knew that Kurt was as stubborn as her mother. Maybe even more so. *Definitely crazier*, he thought.

"Okay, but you ride with me. I don't want your momma coming down on me 'cause you drowned."

They walked down and followed the others out onto the floating dock toward a pair of flashy Cigarette boats. The group stopped by the first boat, which was painted in giant green and orange lightning bolts.

Willy pointed to the lead boat, with a more sedate red and black checkerboard paint job. "Quint, you ride with him. We'll go in this one."

They quickly loaded their duffle bags into the boats. In the heavy canvas bags were a pair of scoped rifles and an assortment of handguns.

Willy didn't know what to expect and wasn't taking any chances.

As soon as the engines were running, they cast off the dock lines and pushed off. The unmuffled racing engines in each boat growled at idle as the two Cigarettes made their way down Coon Key Pass toward the Gulf.

"What're ya waitin' for?" Kurt said to the driver. "Get this thing moving."

"It's idle speed all the way to Coon Key," the driver replied, obviously annoyed. "Manatee zone."

"Fuck a bunch of sea cows," Kurt said. "I got things to see and people to do."

"We don't break the law when it's light enough to be seen," Willy explained. "The paint jobs on these boats your ma bought is bad enough; no reason to attract more attention. We'll be there in a little over an hour, don't you worry."

Kurt sat back and muttered expletives under her breath.

At least I won't have to listen to her once the engines get going, Willy thought.

For the next ten minutes, he and Bo, the boat's driver, had to endure the woman's constant, curse-riddled diatribe. Willy assumed she'd hit the meth pipe when she went into the public bathroom outside the marina office. The woman was a hot mess. But considering where she'd come from, it was to be expected.

While nobody outside the family knew for sure, Kurt had been the product of a violent rape at the hands of her uncle when Marley was fourteen. Killing the bastard had been the last thing Jubal did before leaving Southwest Florida.

Finally, they reached the marker showing the end of the manatee protection zone. There, the lead boat, with Quint and Zeke aboard, sped up and they were soon on plane.

Bo advanced the throttles and their boat shot forward. The big engines and buffeting wind were already loud, though the boat was only at half throttle. They quickly caught up to the lead boat and Bo veered away, crossing its wake, and accelerating even more. Once alongside, he throttled back to match the other boat's speed.

The two boats headed due south, toward deeper water. A few minutes out, the other boat turned toward the south-southeast and accelerated.

Willy looked back and was shocked to see that they were already out of sight of land.

Bo also made the turn south, but in a wider arc. When he increased power, the engines screamed as the boat shot forward. He quickly caught up to the other Cigarette, but a hundred yards farther out. Zeke increased his speed to match Bo's.

Willy looked over at the speedometer. They were going over ninety miles per hour, though the ride felt like he was cruising in an old Cadillac Eldorado, rolling down the Tamiami.

Willy reached over and turned the zoom knob on the chart plotter until it showed the whole southwest coastline and the Keys beyond the mainland.

Big Pine Key and the Content Keys were dead ahead as the two boats roared across the light chop. Willy looked over at the other boat. Only the rear third of it was in contact with the water. He looked at his watch. It was six o'clock. At this speed, they'd get there before the clown even got out of bed.

Willy's mind returned to what Quint had said about the two women with the McDermitt guy. "Damned hot" was how he'd described the older one.

I'll have to be careful, Willy thought, glancing back at the psycho meth monster who was his stepdaughter. Meth-heads were, at best, unpredictable.

But when they got there, if the girlfriend and her daughter were on the island with this McDermitt guy, he'd have to get them separate, away from Kurt. Maybe it wasn't such a bad idea to let Kurt kill the guy. She wouldn't be quick and merciful. No, she'd take her time with him.

And while she was doing that, he and the other three men could take the two women out of sight and do whatever they wanted. They were going to die anyway, and it had been a couple of years since he'd last had a good-looking woman.

Bo was concentrating on the water ahead. Willy watched the chart plotter as the boat ate up the miles, using the zoom knob to keep the Content Keys and his quarry at the top of the screen. He was getting more excited every time he turned the knob to zoom in.

Willy knew all the stories about C. Roy, and secretly, he understood why he'd killed all those women. If Bertha had found out he was screwing them, she'd have cut his nuts off. Corpses under the ground couldn't talk.

But Bertha had found out. Marley had told him how her mother had poisoned her father, and how she'd made Marley and Jubal watch him die. It was for that reason that Jubal never took a wife.

Marley was a lot like Bertha. If Marley caught him so much as looking at another woman, she'd kill him.

But look he had—and a lot more.

Never anywhere close to home, though; Willy was a patient man and the family business had him driving all over south Florida.

He'd once gone more than a year without succumbing to his animalistic urge to dominate. But he had no problem taking advantage of an opportunity when one presented itself.

He'd always made sure that the women he'd abducted had a family. Killing them for their silence, like C. Roy had, would just bring too much heat these days. Corpses do talk to scientists. They could find out a lot from a dead body.

Instead, he took their driver's licenses and read their address to them, then threatened their kids. That had always been enough to make them compliant and silent when it was over.

Willy had never had to actually hit a woman, either. That was taboo in the swamp. At three or four times the size of the women he liked, all he needed to do was just grab the one he wanted and drag her off. The big mall parking lots on the east coast were a favorite target.

He simply waited in his truck until a small woman, who'd by chance parked near him, came out when there wasn't anyone else around. He looked for those with bags from toy stores. Sometimes, his wait could be more than an hour. But eventually, he found what he wanted.

He'd always waited until they'd loaded their packages into the back of their car. He didn't want their stuff, and the idea of someone walking by and taking it didn't sit right either. But before they could get in their cars, he simply grabbed them, and carried them to his truck.

Willy didn't have much in the way of preference. Blond, brunette, redhead, white, black, Hispanic. All that mattered was that they were young and small. They were easier to control and usually more docile from the start.

Picking one with a family wasn't hard. His truck sat high enough that he could see down into nearby cars, and the kid seats were a dead giveaway if the women weren't carrying bags from a kid's store.

Women had always held the power in the Blanc family and therefore in Southwest Florida. It'd been that way long before Bertha, and would continue long after Marley. Kurt would be next in line.

That was a scary thought. Inbreeding was common, but usually it was between cousins. Her uncle being her daddy was different. The bitch was touched and the meth didn't make that no better.

Marley was several years older than Willy. He thought she was ugly and fat, but so was he. It definitely wasn't her looks that had attracted him all those years ago.

It was the money and power. The Blanc family had amassed a fortune. Marley had always been fat and ugly, but now she was old, fat, and ugly.

And sitting on a gold mine.

When the old bitch finally died, there would be a power vacuum. Marley's sister Jo was nearly as big and mean as Kurt and both of them wanted to be the leader of the clan. There would definitely be a scuffle. One of them might even end up killing the other.

Willy had only to bide his time. When Marley died and the inevitable power struggle commenced, Willy would snatch the gold and head for Mexico or South America.

The Blancs didn't trust banks. Their business was a cash business and they piled up cash until it took up too much space. Then they converted it to gold and put it in an underground vault in the backyard.

Willy and Marley had the only keys. There was over two hundred pounds of bullion buried back there, and Willy aimed to have it. And he had all the patience in the world.

There was another sister, Sue Roy, the youngest. But she was small and kept to herself most of the time. No threat to anyone.

In 1978, a fourth sister, Dreama, had been murdered by her ex, Eugene Quick. Eugene was Willy's cousin but that hadn't mattered. Willy marked him as dead, even though the cops had nothing and didn't care much about some swamp rat woman, anyway. Willy had tried to kill Eugene a week later and spent ten years upstate for the crime.

Ten years for trying to bring justice? And he walked? That just wasn't right. Ole Eugene up and disappeared the day after Willy's release.

Everyone, including the sheriff, knew Willy had killed him. And everyone knew that Eugene had killed Dreama. But neither of the bodies had ever turned up and Willy knew that Eugene's never would. A woodchipper and manure cannon saw to that.

The Blanc family had rallied around Willy, saying that Eugene must have run off when Willy was released from prison. That was when Marley had claimed the big man as her second husband.

Every now and then, Willy could hear Kurt shouting something from the back of the boat. He pretended he hadn't, as the clicks to zoom the chart plotter came faster. They were already nearly there. He turned the knob again. Just fifteen miles to go.

"What's that?" Bo shouted.

Willy looked up. Far ahead, barely visible on the horizon, he saw something white.

"Binos in the console," Bo shouted, pointing at the dry box mounted in the dashboard in front of Willy's seat.

He opened the door and pulled out the binoculars. It was difficult to hold them steady. The boat wasn't leaping over waves or anything, but the chop created a constant vibration.

"It's a boat," Willy shouted, lowering the glasses. "A big sport fisher."

Bo picked up a small, handheld radio and spoke into it. Willy heard a crackling sound as Bo held the device to his ear, but he couldn't make out what was being said.

Bo put the radio between his legs and turned the wheel slightly to the right. "We'll pass them at a distance," he shouted. "No sense in letting anyone get a close look at us."

Quint's boat angled away with them as the gap to the oncoming boat diminished. With a closure speed of probably 135 miles per hour, it only took a couple of minutes before the fishing boat passed by, half a mile away.

Willy looked back with the binoculars. It took a moment to train the powerful instrument on the passing boat. The name on the stern was *Gaspar's Revenge*.

Where've I heard that? Willy wondered, lowering the binos.

"What the hell are you doing?" Bo shouted into the radio.

Gaspar's Revenge Charter Service, Willy thought, remembering Jubal's hot little assistant telling them that the guy they were after owned that boat.

Looking off to the left, Willy saw Quint's boat slowing and turning. This time, he did hear the excited voice over the radio. "It's him," Quint shouted. "It's Jesse Mc-Dermitt."

CHAPTER TWENTY-SIX

"Got something on radar," Jimmy said. "About eight miles ahead and coming fast, man."

"How fast?" I asked, glancing at the radar screen.

Jimmy studied it for a moment. "This can't be right," he said, adjusting the knobs again.

"What?" Tony asked, moving around behind us to see the screen.

"Closure rate is a little over 120 knots," Jimmy said. "Must be a go-fast boat headed this way."

On the horizon, I could see an occasional spray of white water and flash of bright color. I reached into the upper console and handed Tony a pair of binos.

"Not one," he said a moment later, "but two bogeys. They're turning away slightly, to the west."

"Take the wheel," I said to Tony, who was only too willing to comply.

He handed me the binos as he slid into my seat and I trained them on the oncoming boats. It was a pair of Cigarettes all right. One was green and orange and the other black and red.

"No way," I murmured.

"What is it?" Deuce asked, now standing, and looking toward the boats about to pass abeam.

"I saw those same two boats in Goodland on Sunday."

For a second, I could see a man looking at us through a pair of binoculars. I lowered mine and looked at the two boats speeding past a couple hundred yards away. When I raised them again, the guy had put down his binos and held something else close to his face.

I recognized him.

"It's Quint Robbins!" I shouted.

"They're slowing!" Rusty yelled back.

"I'll take it," I said, tapping Tony on the shoulder.

He stood and I took the wheel and slid back into my seat, just as a loud popping sound could be heard high above us.

"Incoming fire!" Deuce shouted, instinctively pulling his handgun from behind his back.

I jammed the throttles to the stops and instantly heard the superchargers scream as they spooled up. The boat lurched forward and reached its top speed of fifty knots almost instantly.

There was another loud pop, this time off to starboard.

I looked back over my shoulder. Both boats had slowed and were turning around, nearly half a mile back. A handgun was useless at that range and a rifle, shooting from an unstable platform, might as well be.

But someone on the red and black boat was shooting at us with a rifle. And at the speed those boats were capable of, they wouldn't be at a distance for long.

"Tony, break out the Ma Deuce!" I shouted.

If there was anything Tony liked more than speed, it was things that went boom. He'd been a bomb tech in the SEALs. He scrambled down the ladder and disappeared into the engine room.

"That ain't gonna help none, once them go-fast boats get ahead of us," Rusty said.

"He's right," Deuce agreed, heading for the ladder. "I'll man the minigun."

"Wait," Jimmy said, grabbing Deuce's broad shoulder. "No offense, man. But you're a little top-heavy to go dancing around the foredeck at fifty knots. I'll do it."

"Are you sure?" I asked.

"Piece of cake," Jimmy said, and went sliding down the ladder's rails to the cockpit.

"I'll help Tony," Deuce said, and went down after Jimmy.

I glanced back again. Quint's boats were almost a mile behind us, but it looked like they were now at full speed. They'd overtake us in two minutes. Glancing at the chart plotter, I could see that we were less than fifteen nautical miles from my island.

Nudging the throttles again, though I knew they were wide open, I looked down at the cockpit. Tony and Deuce already had the titanium tripod mounted.

We'd once practiced deploying the big .50 caliber machine gun and the two of them together had accomplished it in just over a minute.

But that was some time ago and we hadn't practiced it in a long time.

I concentrated on the water ahead as Jimmy moved out onto the side deck. It wasn't rough, but he had to get out to the bow, where the mounting receiver was installed beside the windlass.

Mounted at shoulder level on both sides of the cabin were grab rails that extended forward to where the side rails started. Jimmy used them to walk sideways on the narrow side deck. He had the heavy pack over his shoulder and nothing behind him for support. Just water whizzing past at fifty knots.

He finally made the foredeck and moved quickly along the rail.

Behind me, I heard the familiar sound of the top cover on the receiver being slammed closed and the side handle chambering a round.

Just then, a bullet cracked into the back of the overhead, sending shards of fiberglass splinters into my right shoulder and back.

Ma Deuce's bark answered back.

Few sounds on the battlefield instilled more fear than the rat-a-tat of the big Browning M2 machine gun as it launched four hundred half-inch diameter projectiles per minute more than a mile downrange. First introduced in 1933 as a crew-served infantry piece, it quickly found a home on ships and patrol boats. In Vietnam, the added mobility of the helicopter made it a fearsome weapon.

On the bow, Jimmy quickly assembled and mounted the small Gatling-style minigun and signaled that he was ready, clipped to the rails at four points.

I looked back and saw that the pursuing boats had split up after Tony's opening barrage. It was obvious that Tony couldn't engage forward, since the cabin blocked his fire, so they were going to flank and get ahead of us, where Tony couldn't reach them.

Their speed was a huge advantage if we were racing. But we *weren't* racing.

"Hang on!" I shouted, as I turned with Quint's red and black boat.

While a cowboy might say, "Never bring a Thoroughbred to a cow-cutting contest," it would also be good advice on the water. The Cigarettes were fast in a straight line, like Thoroughbreds. But as we said in the Corps, slow is smooth and smooth is fast.

I turned the Cigarettes' advantage against them as Tony opened up once more. His rounds were getting closer, but Quint was also firing back.

The boat's driver turned even more to port, away from us, and away from Tony's tail stinger.

I stayed with him, leaning into the turn as much as I dared. Too much and the boat could stumble at this speed. So could the Cigarette. He was forced to slow down to turn sharper.

The orange and green boat overshot us, going wide the other way. They didn't expect me to go on the attack to cut one from the herd.

Suddenly, a loud ripping sound came from the foredeck and what can only be described as an undulating whip of fire reached out from Jimmy's place on the bow. The whip—the visible trail of 7.62mm rounds being fired at five thousand rounds per minute from the electrically operated gun—moved across the water, chasing the go-fast boat. When it found its mark, the M134 minigun chewed through everything, pouring almost eighty rounds per second into the fleeing boat.

A massive fireball rose as the boat stumbled on its chine. Parts of the boat scattered forward and out to the sides from the force of the high-octane blast.

I looked to the northeast. The other boat was two miles away and bugging out, headed north at full speed.

After slowing the *Revenge*, I turned toward the wreckage of Quint Robbins's boat. Large pieces of fiberglass were floating on the surface, some burning. There was no sign of anyone.

Rusty stood at the rail of the flybridge, a handgun pointed down as I circled the wreckage twice.

Robbins and his driver were dead and gone.

"They fired on us," Rusty said. "Ain't but one outcome there."

"Secure the weapons," I called down.

"You gonna call this in?" Rusty asked.

I turned back to the north-northwest, letting the engines idle. Adrenaline was still coursing through me. And I was pissed.

"Think the guys on that other boat are gonna do that?"

He sat hard on the bench seat and leaned forward, elbows on his knees. "I don't know, bro. I kinda doubt it. This vendetta thing is way overboard to be just an old football score to settle."

"Ya *think?*"

"This is how it's been for you all these years?"

"Not always," I said, taking a deep breath. I'd forgotten that for the last several decades, my best friend had done nothing but work hard and raise a daughter alone. "Usually, I arrange for the bad guys to spend time with Bubba in Raiford."

Rusty chuckled then looked up. "You should concentrate on them developers you mentioned. The cop *pretending* not to know, well, you can't lean on him. But them two Yankees, ya sure can."

With the weapons secured, I brought the *Revenge* up on plane and headed north.

"You got a bullet hole in your overhead," Rusty said, noticing the splintered fiberglass above and behind my head for the first time.

I grinned at him. "A couple of inches lower and he might have done some real damage."

"Not much," Rusty said with a chuckle, as the others came back up.

"Everyone okay?" I asked, looking specifically at Jimmy.

The others I wasn't worried about. Deuce and Tony had taken lives in firefights before. Rusty had too, in Lebanon. Jimmy had fired a gun at someone only once, defending Finn.

He just shrugged. "They shot at us first, man."

"That's the right attitude to have," Rusty said.

"What about the three guys on the other boat?" Tony asked.

"They're not going to report anything," Deuce said, adding his assessment to Rusty's. "Those boats are used for one thing—drug smuggling. But I sense there's something far deeper."

"It's a waste of time to go up to Fort Myers now," I said. "I'm certain Quint Robbins was on that red and black boat. By now, the other boat's called ahead and the cat's out of the bag."

"There's an awful lot of them Blancs, Jesse," Rusty reminded me. "But if these people *are* smug drugglers, count me in on whatever you want to do."

I looked around at the others, ending with Jimmy. He just shrugged again, twisting at the end of his hair. "We're all here 'cause we're not all there, man."

Rusty laughed. "You been hanging around Eric Stone too much."

"So, we're headed to Goodland," I said. "Jimmy, take the wheel. I need to make a call."

I went down to the cockpit and into the salon. The sea state required me to use my hands on the overhead grab rails through the salon. I continued down to the master stateroom, where my satellite phone was on the charger.

When I got back out to the cockpit, where I'd have unobstructed access to the satellite, I made my call.

Billy answered on the first ring. "Trucks are at the marina," he said by way of a greeting. "All gassed up."

"Change in plans, Billy. Robbins and his cohorts intercepted us at sea and fired on the *Revenge*."

"So, they're all dead and you don't need my trucks? Still coming up here for those steaks?"

Nothing ever ruffled Billy Rainwater. If you told him the ground behind him was being vaporized and sucked into space, he'd just calmly reply that it might be a good idea to go somewhere else.

"They were in two Cigarette boats," I said. "One got away and probably headed back to Goodland. I saw both of them there a few days ago. That's where we're headed."

"What time?" he asked, unconcerned about the boat that *didn't* get away. "I need to find someone to drive the other truck down there."

"We'll be at Walker's Coon Key Marina in two hours," I replied.

"I know a better place," Billy said. "Away from so many eyes."

He said he'd text me the GPS coordinates and ended the call.

My sat phone chirped an incoming message before I was halfway up the ladder to the flybridge.

There, I handed my phone to Jimmy and told him to plug the GPS numbers from Billy's text into the chart plotter.

"Were you hit?" Deuce asked. "There was blood on your seat when you went below."

"Just some glass shards," I replied pointing at the bullet hole in the gel coat above Jimmy's head.

"Take your shirt off," Rusty ordered. "Let's have a look."

I moved around behind Jimmy, sat in the second seat, and pulled my shirt off.

Jimmy looked up from the chart plotter. "Looks like a private residence. I set a waypoint at the outside marker for Big Marco Pass."

"You still don't figure on contacting the law?" Rusty asked.

I winced as he pulled a sliver of fiberglass out of my shoulder. I'd thought about it. I'd considered calling Kim and Marty. But we didn't have anything substantive to go on. Well, aside from Quint shooting at us with a rifle.

"Not yet," I replied. "I want to get over to that development and talk to the Woodbury brothers."

"What do you figure you'll find out from them?" Deuce asked.

"I don't know. But someone's trying way too hard to keep something hidden. And that just makes me more determined to find out what it is."

CHAPTER TWENTY-SEVEN

Billy stood on a dock behind a house in Isle of Capri, just across the Pass from Marco Island. I was surprised to see David Stone with him.

"What's he doing here?" I asked Billy, as I stepped down onto the dock.

Billy looked from me to David, mock surprise on his face. "Do you know this young man?" he asked. "I just hired him to deliver the other truck."

Though it was likely none of the others saw the mirth in Billy's dark eyes, I did.

We'd known each other since before we started school. We'd made up a game where one of us would make a statement and the other would have to guess if it were true or not. We'd never had to show proof that a statement was true or false; our word was enough. The challenge was to see if one could tell a lie without the other picking up on it. We were blood brothers, and I probably knew Billy better than anyone.

And he me.

"Yeah, Billy," I said, a bit irritated. "He's dating my daughter." I finally turned to David. "And he's supposed to be in class today."

"My afternoon class was canceled," David said. "So, I went home to get some things I forgot, and stopped by Mister Rainwater's place to see if he had any work for me."

I looked back at Billy. "You into computers these days?"

"Computer science is very big in automotive," David said. "Mister Rainwater gives me a batch of chips to re-program for some diesel engine controls sometimes. He didn't say we were bringing these trucks to meet you. What are you doing here?"

I glared at David. Then, ignoring his question, I turned back to Billy. "Who owns this house?"

"A friend," Billy replied. "She's gone up to Martha's Vineyard to ship some things down and won't be back for a week."

"Do you have a key?"

"And clothes hanging in her closet," Billy replied. "I stay here sometimes."

"I'd like to meet this woman one day," I said. "But right now, a map of southwest Florida on a table would be great."

"I have one in the truck," he said. "The back door's open."

David fell in beside me as I started for the house. He glanced nervously back at the others. "What *are* you doing here?"

"Trying to figure out what the secret is behind Turtle Island," I replied. "You didn't happen to bring your computer, did you?"

"No, just my phone."

"See what you can find out about the island," I said, entering the house.

It was an older home, probably built in the 50s or 60s, with a low, almost-flat roof with open beam ceilings inside. The floor was polished terrazzo and the furnishings modern; the cool interior hinted at central air conditioning and the whole house had a beachy vibe. The room we entered was open all the way to the front of the house, and through the front window, I could see Billy at his truck in the driveway.

Glancing around, I spotted a picture on a wooden bookcase and went over for a closer look. Billy was in the photo with an attractive blond woman. They were smiling brightly, on the verge of laughter. It took a good deal to elicit that kind of emotion from my usually stoic friend.

Billy came in and noticed me looking at the picture. He raised a book in his hand. "Got the map."

After we'd gathered around the table near the back door, Billy opened the large book to a map that showed the coast of Southwest Florida from Naples to Chokoloskee—a distance of thirty or so miles, and inland to the Fakahatchee Strand, a good forty miles.

I pointed to Goodland and looked at Billy "The two boats that attacked us were here, Sunday afternoon. If they didn't return here, where would they go?"

"You said they were Cigarettes?"

"Yeah," I replied. "One with green and orange lightning bolts and the other with a black and red checkerboard pattern."

"I know the man who owns them," Billy said. "Zeke Mitchell and his cousin Bo Collier run the boats for him."

"One of the Blancs?" Deuce asked.

Billy shook his head. "Terrance McKay is his name and he's in tight with the Blancs but not related. They use those boats to bring drugs in from way offshore."

"Well, their drug shuttling ability is cut in half now," I said. "The other boat headed back this way. He might have gone back to his slip at Walker's. Is there anywhere else he might go?"

"They *could* go just about anywhere," Billy said. "That's why they don't get caught. Them boys and the Blancs know the Ten Thousand Islands and the rivers upstream better than just about anyone. They race out to a passing freighter to pick up coke, meth, or whatever else they bring in. Then they meet airboats back in there, where nobody can follow."

"The police are understaffed down here," David said. "I heard my dad mention that."

"A flashy boat like that," Billy continued, "it will draw attention anywhere outside of Marco and Goodland— home territory. They're a dime a dozen in Miami, but those two are the only Cigarettes in a hundred miles. They don't draw as much attention here because they're known around these parts. On the days and nights they're not smuggling, those boats are out and being seen. They get stopped and boarded a lot when they're seen, but never when they're not. Radar and speed keep them invisible when they're bringing something in."

"Let's assume they thought we turned back," Deuce said. "Most people would. That'd be the prudent thing to do after such an encounter. But, then again, most people don't have machine guns on their boats."

David glanced up at me from his phone but said nothing.

What Deuce was saying made sense to me. The boat was too easy to spot and if Goodland were its home base, people there would be less likely to notice its comings and goings. And like Quint Robbins, these people were cocky, because they were used to getting their own way. Odds were good that they went back to their home slip.

"Deuce, you and Tony will go with Billy," I said. "Are you okay with that," I asked Billy.

"The Blancs know who I am and where I stand," he replied. "My being with you will come as no surprise to anyone."

"Good," I said. "We'll start at the marina and have a look around Goodland if we find the boat there. Then I want to stop on Turtle Island and talk to the Woodbury brothers. I pointed to Deuce. "I want you three to go inland. Billy knows every dirt track and swamp road around here. You're looking for a black Dodge dually."

"Yeah," Rusty scoffed, "like there won't be many of those around."

"It's a newer model, with dark-tinted windows."

David looked up from his phone. "If you know the name of the owner, I can get the tag number."

I measured him a little differently. "You don't even know what we're doing. For all you know, we could be planning a bank robbery."

David laughed nervously and looked around at the others. "Not if you and Mister Rainwater are involved."

"The likely owner of the truck will be Kurt Blanc," Billy said.

"Do you know what town he lives in?"

"*She* lives in Carnestown," he replied. "Never assume."

David got to work on his phone. "The only thing weird I found about Turtle Island is that a mobile home park was built there in 1965 and abandoned in 1968."

"Abandoned?" I asked. "After just three years?"

"That'd be the year of the unnamed hurricane," Rusty said.

I gave him a doubtful look. "They've been naming hurricanes since the early fifties."

"It's true," Billy added. "You and your mom went to Hawaii that summer when your dad took leave. I remember it rained buckets here for close to two weeks, never letting up."

More than fifty years ago, I thought. It was the last time I'd seen my dad.

He'd been a Marine in Vietnam when he was killed. Just days after returning from that leave Billy had mentioned, Mom and I had flown out to join him in Hawaii for two weeks. My mom took her own life after learning he'd been killed in action.

"I remember reading about that," Rusty said. "The eggheads said it never even reached tropical storm strength. Just a big tropical system parked on the beach up north a ways, then it drifted slowly south for more than a week. My dad was a bit worried about it, but then it headed across the state northward."

"There had been a two-year drought up until then," Billy said. "The dry ground and heavy runoff caused a lot of damage—light poles toppled, bridge aprons washed out, and even some buildings shifted or just plain sank."

I dug the key to the *Revenge* out of my pocket and handed it to David. "My laptop is below the TV," I said. "In the cabinet under it is a small black box. Would you go get the laptop and the box for me?"

"Sure," he replied, rising from his seat.

"And bring the power cord, David. This could take a while."

As soon as he left, I looked at the others. "I don't know much about these people, except that they're violent. Be careful, but if someone engages you, be ready, too. David will stay here and coordinate."

"Good idea," Jimmy said.

"I'd like you to stay with him, Jimmy."

"Dude! That's not gonna happen. I might not be the Rambo type like you guys, but—"

"What about your live-and-let-live attitude?" Rusty asked.

Jimmy looked at him, a serious expression on his face. "When someone tries to hurt people I care about, it's live and let *die*, man."

David returned and handed me the box and laptop, along with the key. I opened the computer's lid and, after waiting for the facial recognition to see me, turned it to David.

Then I opened the box and handed Deuce three of the five small communication devices that were in it. "In case you guys need to split up." I handed another to Rusty and looked at Jimmy. "If we need to split up, you stay with me. I only have five."

"What about me?" David asked.

"Click on the *Comm* icon on the desktop. That'll open mapping software, and the communications app. It'll show the location of all five earwigs and you can talk to and hear us."

"What's the range?" David asked.

"Unit to unit," I said, "like we did last weekend, only a few miles."

Deuce pointed to the five headphone icons displayed on the left side of the map. "Click each one to activate and connect it via satellite to the laptop. Then our range is unlimited."

"I'm guessing not," David said, giving Deuce a wise grin. "You'll be limited to North America. Maybe the whole western hemisphere. But limited."

"Yeah," I replied, now seeing David as more than just the young man who was dating my daughter. "If you need any tech support, click on the *Soft Jazz* icon. That will connect you straight to a friend of mine named Chyrel. She's a computer whiz, too, and she knows more about you than you do."

He gave me a puzzled look but kept quiet.

I looked around at the others. "It's a big area—twelve hundred square miles—but there are very few people in it and damned few roads. From what Billy and Rusty said, the Blancs know and run everything, so we really can't trust anyone. If that one cop was any indication, we can't even trust the police."

"Where are you going after Goodland?" Tony asked.

"Marco," I replied. "To see a senator."

"I got the tag number," David said. He wrote it on two sticky pad notes from the refrigerator door and handed them to Billy and me. I read it and passed it to Rusty and Jimmy.

"I found out something else." David hesitated when all our eyes turned to him. He gulped. "I don't know if it means anything or not, but I looked for anything else that might have happened about the time Turtle Island was developed and then abandoned."

"What'd you find?" I asked.

"The Flat Tire Killer's last victim disappeared right after that storm you were talking about."

"Flat Tire Killer?" Tony asked. "Who comes up with those names?"

"It says here there was a series of unsolved disappearances of young women," David said.

"Throughout the fifties and early sixties," Billy said, "more than twenty women went missing from around here. Their cars were found abandoned with a flat tire. No bodies were ever recovered, and they were presumed to have been abducted and murdered."

"There's something else," David said. "Since you all mentioned the name Blanc, I added that name to my historical search."

He looked around at the six of us.

"And?" Deuce asked.

"Curtis Roy Blanc disappeared around the same time as the last victim."

CHAPTER TWENTY-EIGHT

It was noon when Willy Quick and Kurt Blanc turned onto the crushed shell driveway in her truck. Quint had picked Willy up well before dawn. Since the asshole from Marathon had blown Quint up, Willy was forced to ride back with her.

He looked over at Kurt's profile as she drove through the overhanging canopy. He didn't trust her. And not just because she was a meth monster.

Had Marley sent her to keep an eye on him? he wondered.

Quint had told all of them that McDermitt's girlfriend was hot, and she had a teenage daughter. Did Marley suspect him?

No, he decided, feeling the single key in his pocket. Marley trusted him completely. The key was to the underground vault out back. The two of them had the only keys to it.

Still, Marley looked to be on the warpath as she came out the front door and stood waiting for them on the porch.

"Pull up to the barn," Willy said. "I'll get the door."

"Hadn't you ought to talk—"

"Security first!" Willy snapped at her. "Ya gotta get that through your skull, Kurt. Without good security, we got nuthin'!"

Kurt drove around to the barn and stopped. Willy got out and opened the doors wide for her to drive through. When she did, he pulled them closed.

Marley came through the side door. "That was a damned expensive boat you lost."

Willy'd been thinking about how she'd react and knew which way to play this scene. His frown didn't convey anger but disappointment.

"Fuck the boat," he said quietly. "I lost two good friends today. Boys I'd known most of my life. They was like brothers."

The big woman stopped her advance just inside the door.

"You sure they're dead?" she asked, almost apologetically.

"That boat had fuckin' machine guns, Mama," Kurt said. "Cops don't use no machine guns."

"Yeah," Willy said, looking down at his feet for a moment. "Zeke and Quint are definitely dead."

When he looked back up at Marley, his eyes were filled with rage and disgust at the fat old cow she'd become, and he turned that hate into his ally.

"I wanna kill him for that," Willy said, raising a massive right fist and shaking it. "I wanna beat him to a pulp, hang him by his balls, and make him watch me beat his friends to death before he dies." Willy grinned evilly. "Maybe even his girlfriend."

Marley seemed genuinely touched by Willy's rare display of emotion, not knowing it was a put on. She quickly recovered. "Did they see either of you?"

"I doubt it," Kurt said. "We never got close enough to see any of their faces."

Marley opened the side door. "Good. Then they don't know who it was they killed either." Her voice softened as he walked past her. "But we do. Don't we, Willy?"

He only nodded. The dumb bitch was a sucker for family ties. It was true that his history with Quint, Bo, and Zeke spanned half a century, but Willy only cared about one person—himself.

Marley followed him across the weed-choked yard. "Where did Bo leave the boat?"

"Back to the marina," Willy replied. "He needed to gas it up."

"Call him and tell him to get away from it. But tell him don't leave the marina."

"They're sure to have turned around, Mama," Kurt said, holding the door to the house open for them. "Or called the cops, or something."

"I don't think so," Marley said. "That guy might not be a cop, but he's sure as hell's a man that doesn't back down. Might be some Miami dealer trying to horn in. Kurt, you get on the phone with the family. Rally everyone here. Tell 'em to bring their guns."

Willy called Bo and told him to hurry and gas up the boat, but to stay close and out of sight.

"Call me the minute the guy in that boat shows up," he growled.

"What makes you think he knows where we keep it?" Bo asked.

"I'm guessing he knows a bit about boats," Willy said. "There aren't a lot of places to get high-octane around here."

"What do I do if I see them?"

"Just keep an eye on them," Willy replied. "And call me. Borrow a boat and follow them if they leave. But don't take the Cigarette."

He ended the call and turned to Marley. She was on the phone with Jubal.

"No?" Her mouth turned up in a nearly toothless smile. "You're sure?"

She listened for a moment, then said goodbye and ended the call.

"There's been no report to either the Coast Guard or the sheriff's office," she said.

"How'd he know that so fast?"

"He put me on fuckin' hold while he checked with dispatch."

Willy knew that Jubal had the sheriff and most of his department in his back pocket. He'd made a legit fortune over on the east coast, selling houses, and came home to turn that money into power. The police dispatchers were high on his list of people to take good care of.

Kurt put down her phone and turned to Marley. "Sue Roy and Braxton are on the way," she said. "They're gonna stop and pick up Jo and Maisey. Jo's gonna get the word out to all the rest of the kids and grands while she waits for them."

An hour later, the barn was full of cars and motorcycles, and there were several 4x4 trucks backed up under the trees that bordered the property. Behind the barn, boats were run up onto the bank.

Willy's phone rang and when he picked it up, he saw that it was Bo. "Everyone shut up," he yelled to the large gathering of the Blanc clan in his and Marley's living room. "It's Bo."

"What's going on?" he asked, after stabbing the speaker button with a thick finger. "Did the boat show up?"

"No boat," Bo said. "But three strangers are out on the dock. A tall guy, a fat guy, and a swamp rat."

Willy pulled up the picture he'd snagged from the internet and sent it to Bo. "I just sent you a picture."

"Hang on." There were fumbling noises as Bo opened the text. "Yeah, that's two of 'em. The tall one and the swamp rat."

"They didn't come by boat?" Willy asked, looking at Marley.

"No, they're in a beastly lookin' four-by-four," Bo replied. "Hang on. They're leaving the dock and heading for their truck."

"Fuck! We're over fifteen miles away. Think you can follow them?"

"Yeah," he replied. "So long as they don't go off road. That thing's a monster."

"Stay on the phone," Willy said, then lowered his, and addressed the gathering. "Everyone out. Get in as few trucks as possible. Whoever's riding shotgun in each one, call me, and I'll patch you in."

The Blanc clan scrambled into action and headed out into the heat of the day. Within minutes, engines were starting, and trucks were pulling out from under trees, with people piling into the beds.

Willy got into the front passenger seat of Kurt's Dodge as Marley got in back with Donnie and Braxton. He put the phone to his ear after patching in the last caller. "You still got 'em, Bo? Everybody else shut the hell up and just listen."

"Yeah," Bo replied. "They're on Goodland Drive, heading out of town."

"Don't follow too close," Willy said. "I'm puttin' you on speaker so Marley and Kurt can hear."

Kurt drove hard through the overhanging foliage and barely slowed when she reached the highway. Someone in the back of the truck slapped at the roof.

"Ease up, Kurt," Marley said. "You gonna spill your cousins out all over the damned road."

She let up a little but continued to accelerate up Tamiami Trail toward the state park. Behind them, three more trucks came pouring out of the driveway.

"He still headin' out of town?" Willy asked.

"Coming up on San Marco, now," Bo replied. "I'm half a mile back and there's a car between us. He's turning north, heading away from Marco."

"Fucker's coming right to me," Kurt muttered.

A moment later, Bo's voice came over the tiny speaker. "Hold on a sec. It looks like he's turning off to the left."

"Oh, no," Marley sighed loudly from the back seat.

"Looks like he's headed to that new construction site," Bo said.

Willy knew they were still a good fifteen minutes from Turtle Island. He also knew the two men working there were still teetering on the edge, no matter what Jubal thought. He'd read it in their eyes.

"Fuck, fuck, fuck!" Willy shouted.

CHAPTER TWENTY-NINE

The boat was there, just as I'd expected. There wasn't anyone aboard. In fact, there didn't seem to be anyone on the whole dock.

"What now?" Rusty asked.

"I didn't think anyone would be here to greet us," I said. "But the fact that the boat returned here speaks a lot about the attitude of these people. They think they're above the law. The Turtle Island development is just a little past where we turned off to get here."

We retraced our steps, heading back to where we'd parked Billy's big, off-road machine. As we walked, I noticed a man over on the next dock rinsing down a boat. He was watching us while he talked on his cell phone. But he was trying awfully hard to look like he wasn't watching.

The truck Billy had given us to use was an early 70s model GMC. At least the body was, which was lifted a couple of inches off the frame. Everything else was modern—from the LED driving lights on the roll bar to the 44-inch mud tires and tall suspension. At six foot three, I had to look up at the door handle. Fortunately, two steps extended down from the door's threshold when it was opened.

"This thing's ridiculous," Rusty said, climbing in next to Jimmy.

"It won't be if we have to leave the road," Jimmy said. "Did you guys see the man watching us?"

"What man?" Rusty asked, looking around quickly.

"Stop looking for him," I said. "You'll tip him off."

"You saw him?"

"Yes," I told him, as I started the truck. "He was pretending to wash down a boat that hadn't been moved in a while."

I backed out and saw the guy in my mirror. He got into a nondescript, gray import.

Driving slowly out of the parking lot, I followed Palm Avenue around to the west side of the island, then turned onto Goodland Drive, headed out of town.

Deuce's voice came over my earwig. "You have a tail?"

"Yeah," I replied. "One guy in a gray sedan, about half a mile back with another car between us."

"Not anymore, dude," Jimmy said, as a red Corvette passed us.

The hum of the big tires on the asphalt reminded me of my own truck, which I hadn't driven in close to a year. I was going slightly under the speed limit if the speedometer was to be believed. Changing tire sizes changed your speedometer reading. In the old days, you had to replace the gear in the speedometer cable. But likely, the old GMC was stuffed with high-tech computer controls and adjusting the ratio was as easy as changing the data in the computer. Everything else about the truck was perfect, so I assumed Billy had done that.

Though the highway was deserted, the gray car behind us didn't speed up or pass us.

After crossing the high bridge over Marco River, I slowed and turned onto a newly paved road that wasn't shown on the truck's sophisticated GPS system. The road became a causeway and at the end was a sign that said there were lots available. The road continued unpaved, straight ahead, but seeing the construction trailer to my left, I turned in.

What I expected to see wasn't there. It was the middle of the week and early in the afternoon. A construction site should have people working. There was only one pickup on the whole island.

I parked next to it and we all got out. I didn't see anyone around.

"Keep your eyes open," I said. "And wait here."

As I started toward the trailer, the gray car drove slowly past the turn off and disappeared beyond the trees. I had no doubt that he'd be pulled over on the side of the road soon.

"Trouble headed your way," Billy said over the comm. "Four trucks loaded with angry whites. Maybe fifteen or sixteen."

"How can you tell they're angry?" I asked.

"Some of them are carrying rifles," Billy replied. "And it ain't deer season. We're gonna turn around."

The trailer door opened and one of the brothers stepped out. It was Ben Woodbury, the younger of the two. He held a gun in his hand but wasn't pointing it at me.

"You can just go back and tell that big ape—"

Recognition registered in his eyes and he suddenly tried to hide the short-barreled revolver behind his leg.

"Tell the big ape what, Mister Woodbury?"

"I thought you were someone else," he said, turning and putting the gun on a table inside the door. "What can I do for you, Officer...what was your name again?"

Though I hadn't pretended to be a cop when the shooting happened, I never told the two brothers I wasn't.

"McDermitt," I said. "Jesse McDermitt. Now, what were you saying about a big ape?"

Ben Woodbury looked at his watch, then out toward the road. "I guess it's safe to tell you now. Dan should be back any time."

"Tell me what?"

"Dan drove over to Miami early this morning. The FBI has an office there. He went there to tell them what we found here."

I took a step closer. "What did you find, Mister Woodbury?"

"A body...um...I mean...a human skull."

Over the next couple of minutes, Ben Woodbury outlined how they'd found the skull, the visits from Kurt Blanc, and another man who came late in the night.

They'd threatened to kill the brothers' families if they didn't keep quiet about the find. At first the brothers had capitulated and kept quiet. They had a lot of money invested in the project and a big police investigation would bankrupt them.

"So, now you've decided to come forward?"

"They gave us money," Ben said. "Blood money. Dan and I decided this morning not to keep it."

"Why would the Blancs be so worried about one skull?" I asked.

"There's a lot more than one," he replied. "The woman told us that decades ago, her grandfather had been a serial killer. They don't want to tarnish the family name. The leader of the family is in the Florida Senate."

"Jubal Blanc?" I asked.

"Yeah, the woman said he was her uncle."

Deuce's voice came over the comm. "I hate to interrupt, and we're hearing everything he's saying, but that convoy just turned off Tamiami Trail onto San Carlos Road."

"That's the only road in or out," Billy added, "without going all the way through Marco."

I looked around the property. The two giant loaders were gone, but there was a smaller one still there.

"Rusty," I yelled, knowing that he too was hearing everything, "grab my sea bag out of the back and you and Jimmy head over there to that loader."

I turned back to Woodbury. "Is that the only gun you have?"

"What's going on?" he asked, as a white pickup turned onto the short causeway. "There's my brother now."

"The Blanc family is just a few minutes behind him," I said. "Get the key to that loader and any guns you have and follow me."

The older brother parked behind Ben's truck and got out. "What's going on here?"

"No time to explain," I said. "The Blancs are coming. Do you have a gun on you?"

He looked at me puzzled, then at Jimmy and Rusty, who were already making their way toward the loader. "Not with me," he said. "There's a handgun in the office and a rifle in the closet."

Just then, Ben came out, carrying a .22 rifle.

"Follow me," I said, and didn't wait for an answer.

I caught up to Rusty, who was carrying the heavy bag, and stopped him for a moment.

"Open it up and pass them around," I said. "Ben, get that loader running. You're taking me and Dan to the other side of the island."

"Where do you want us?" Jimmy asked, taking a Remington .308 from Rusty.

I pointed to where the shooting had taken place several days earlier. "See that high sand berm?"

Rusty nodded, understanding instantly. With me at the far end of the island, he and Jimmy behind the berm, and Deuce and Tony on the bridge, if the Blancs came onto the property, they'd be wide open and vulnerable from three sides.

"Go with Rusty," I told Jimmy. "Stay down until I tell you."

The engine coughed to life on the front end loader, belching black smoke for a moment before it settled to an even idle.

I noticed it had a tall radio antenna. "What kind of radio is in that loader?" I asked Dan.

"CB," he replied.

I looked over at his vehicle. It had a similar antenna. "You have one in your truck?"

"Yeah. Why?"

"Go turn it on," I said. "Turn the volume up all the way and leave the windows open."

He hurried off.

My plan was simple. I wanted the Woodbury brothers as far away as they could be, in case any shooting started. The island was only half a mile long, which was plenty far enough to be safe from most shooters.

But I'm not like most shooters.

I pulled my M40 sniper rifle from the worn sea bag and stepped up onto the first ladder rung on the loader.

Once Dan was hanging on the other side, I told Ben to drive it to the far side of the island and park it facing slightly away from the entrance, with the bucket on the ground.

The ride was bumpy, but the machine had no trouble traversing the island along the beach. Once Ben had it parked where I wanted, I ordered them both to take cover behind the loader's steel bucket.

We didn't have to wait long before the same black Dodge the Blanc woman had been driving turned off the highway. It then turned into the construction site and stopped in a cloud of dust between our trucks and the trailer. More trucks rolled in, parking behind the Dodge. People jumped out with rifles and handguns, all pointed at the trailer.

"Stay down and stay quiet," I said, not just to the two men with me, but to Rusty and Jimmy, as well.

"That's him," Ben said, as a giant of a man got out of the passenger side of the Dodge. "The guy who threatened our kids."

I shouldered my rifle and looked through the Unertl scope. He was bigger than Quint Robbins—if that was possible. He shouted something I couldn't make out, pointing to and directing the others.

"How far out are you, Deuce?" I asked.

Dan Woodbury's head jerked around. "What?"

"We stayed a mile back from them," Deuce replied. "Less than a minute."

"Roger that," I said, looking down at Dan and pointing to my ear. "Stop in the middle of the causeway and block the road. I'm about to open dialogue."

A woman much larger than the Dodge's driver got out of the back, along with the younger man Kurt Blanc had had with her before, and another wiry little man who looked a lot like Kurt Blanc's accomplice.

The big guy appeared to be in charge.

"Billy, do you know of anyone associated with this bunch who's bigger than Quint Robbins?"

"Dark, shaggy hair and beard, both going gray? About our age?"

"Yeah. You know his name?"

"Willy Quick," Billy replied.

Willy Quick? Of course. He'd been a mountain of a kid back in the day, but physically and mentally slow.

I took the mic and stepped down to the ground. The cord wouldn't reach far enough for me to get below the top of the bucket, but I was behind a four-foot-tall tire that was wider than my body. I rested the forestock on the tire and kept my cheek welded to the stock.

"Willy Quick," I said into the mic, without taking my eye off him.

Through my open left eye, I detected a lot of movement. Everyone had been focused on the trailer, not the empty pickups behind them. Willy spun around, pulling a handgun from under his shirt. They were all looking around for the source.

"Willy," I said again, in a jovial tone. "It is you. I haven't seen you in a really long time. This is Jesse McDermitt. Come over to the white Chevy and we can talk."

"I'm in position," Deuce said. "What do you want us to do?"

I could see the massive F550 6x6 sitting on the bridge. It was Billy's off-road recovery vehicle. Instead of dual wheels on a single rear axle, it had two rear axles, with huge forty-four-inch tires all the way around. Like the

GMC, a double step dropped down when you opened the door. But instead of being a two-door short-bed like the GMC, it had a full crew cab with four doors and a twelve-foot flatbed.

The thing effectively blocked both lanes and enough of the shoulders that nobody could get by.

We were outnumbered two-to-one, but they were all sitting in the middle of a clear field of fire from three angles, each with multiple shooters. If we wanted it to be, the killing field before me would be a total massacre.

"On my signal," I said, "you and Tony take out the right rear tire of the two trucks in back."

Deuce had once been a SEAL sniper and Tony was also very proficient with the long gun. And I knew all three of them had one.

"Rusty, you take out the right rear of the truck nearest you, and I'll get the Dodge in front."

"Roger that," Rusty said and repeated it to Jimmy.

I expected Willy to go to the truck, but the older of the women strolled over to it, as if she didn't have a care in the world. I noticed there were a few other women in the group. I moved the reticle to the Dodge's right rear. Willy was still visible as I sighted in on the tire.

"Who the fuck is this?" a woman's voice screeched over the radio in the cab of the loader.

I'd turned the volume all the way up on the loader, too. Willy's head snapped around and he looked right at me.

"Now, gentlemen," I said, as I dropped the mic and squeezed the trigger.

Before I could get my left hand to the forestock, my rifle roared and bucked upward from the tire it had been resting on. I caught it when it came down and saw the Dodge now had a flat tire. I shifted to the other trucks. They were all similarly disabled. Each of the Blancs' four trucks had a flat tire.

I grinned at the irony.

CHAPTER THIRTY

Kim sat the suspect on the bank, hands zip-tied behind his back. When she turned back to the man's airboat, her phone rang.

"There's a call from an FBI agent for you," the dispatcher's voice said when she answered. Besides being coworkers, Melody and her husband were also her and Marty's friends.

"Did he say what it was about?" Kim asked, somewhat puzzled as she put the phone on speaker. "We're kinda busy at the moment."

She and Marty had just stopped an airboat that had been driving erratically through the canals of a neighborhood on Marco Island. It was early afternoon, and the sun was fiercely hot.

"His name's William Binkowski," Melody replied. "Says it's in reference to the shooting you were involved in on Sunday."

They'd stopped the guy by forcing him onto a dry bank, and Marty was searching his boat but stopped when Melody mentioned the shooting.

"Patch him through," Kim said.

There was a series of clicks, then Melody said, "Go ahead, Special Agent Binkowski."

"Officer Phillips?" a voice asked.

"Officer Kim Phillips," she said. "My husband and I work together. What can I do for you?"

"I'll keep this brief," Binkowski said. "I work in the FBI lab in Miami; cold cases. A man named Dan Woodbury told me an interesting story this morning. He claims he found a human skull on his property and knows who the Flat Tire Killer was."

"The Flat Tire Killer?"

"It was a long time ago," he said. "Back in the fifties and sixties. More than twenty women disappeared and were never found. All with the air let out of one of their car's tires. Anyway, Woodbury claims the bodies are buried on a piece of land he's developing. I understand you were involved in a shooting there?"

"The suspects got away," Kim said, now more than a little interested. "One civilian was slightly injured."

Marty had come over beside her and was also listening intently.

"We're on our way there now," Binkowski said. "After listening to Woodbury's story, I believe him. I have three other agents with me and a forensics van. Can you meet us there?"

Kim knew that he could go there without her consent; the FBI was a federal agency. He was merely extending professional courtesy.

"When will you arrive?"

"In less than an hour," he replied. "How close are you?"

Marty grabbed his radio mic and told Melody to send someone right away to take the airboat driver.

"We can be there ahead of you," Kim replied. "We're just a few miles away."

She didn't wait for a reply but ended the call and shoved her phone in her pocket.

"A Marco unit should arrive there any minute," Melody said over Marty's radio.

As if on cue, Kim heard a car stop on the road at the other end of the empty lot they'd forced the airboat onto. A moment later, a uniformed officer appeared through the underbrush.

"Take this man into custody," Marty said. "Operating a motor vessel while under the influence and reckless endangerment. I'll send a tow boat to impound the boat. We just got called away about a shooting."

The two jumped into their twenty-two-foot Proline patrol boat and Marty started the engines.

"What do you think's going on?" he asked as he backed the boat off the bank.

"You heard everything I did," Kim replied. "The Woodbury brothers say they found a skull."

Marty guided the boat back out of the neighborhood and into Roberts Bay at a little over idle speed. Where they were going wasn't far; less than four miles in a straight line, but by water, it was closer to six—and nearly all of it in the endangered manatee zone. There was no need to hurry, though. They could idle over and still beat the feds.

He navigated through another series of canals and cuts while Kim used their tablet to file their arrest report, request for a tow boat, and custody transfer.

Marty turned left into Caxambas Bay, which would eventually take them over to Gullivan Bay and the entrance to Coon Key Pass.

After a few minutes to check over all the facts, Kim sent the files, then pulled her phone out and started a search.

"Here it is," she said. "It says here that from 1953 to 1968, twenty-two women disappeared. The only clues were the women's abandoned cars, each with a flat tire. No other evidence was ever found; no fingerprints on the car, no tracks, nothing. Police assumed they were murdered, though no bodies were ever recovered. The press dubbed the perpetrator the Flat Tire Killer."

Once they reached Gullivan Bay, Marty brought the boat up on plane and headed across it toward Coon Key. The two of them had been all over these waters during the past few years and rarely needed to turn on the chart plotter.

Kim's phone vibrated in her hand. When she looked, she didn't recognize the number, only that it was from Fort Myers.

She put the phone to her ear and moved behind the console to better block the wind. "Officer Phillips, Fish and Wildlife."

"This is David Stone," a man said, then added, "Flo's boyfriend."

Kim was suddenly worried for her half-sister. "What's wrong? Is she okay?"

"This isn't about her," David said. "It's about your dad."

"What's going on?" Kim asked, as Marty slowed the boat, entering the manatee protection zone again.

She put the call on speaker.

"It's a long story," David said. "But him and his friends are about to get ambushed by more than a dozen armed people."

"Where?" Kim asked.

"Turtle Island," he replied. "Where that crazy woman shot at us."

"Are you there with him?"

"No," David replied. "I'm on Marco Island, where they left the boat. He and the others are at the construction site."

"What others?"

"Mister Rainwater," David replied, "and four of your dad's friends, Rusty, Deuce, Tony, and Jimmy. Do you know them?"

"We're just minutes away from there," Kim said, reaching up to the overhead console and switching on the lights. "An FBI agent is meeting us there. Thanks, David. We'll take it from here."

She ended the call, then mentally kicked herself for not asking how David knew Dad was in trouble if they were miles apart.

"A bunch of people are trying to ambush Dad and some of his friends," Kim said.

Marty didn't need any more information. He pushed the throttles forward and the boat leapt up onto plane. Still, he kept the speed low enough that he could probably spot a sea cow on the surface.

Minutes later, they were forced to slow due to heavy boat traffic. That's when they heard the sound of several guns being fired almost at once. It came from the other side of the bridge.

"Gunshots!" Marty yelled, hitting the siren, and mashing down the throttles.

The Proline hurtled forward, nearly swamping a couple of pleasure boats that had music blaring so loud they couldn't hear the siren. Marty swung wide around the north end of Goodland and headed toward the bridge. Beyond it, he could see a bunch of trucks parked by a trailer and a yellow front end loader far across a cleared field. The loader was moving toward the trucks.

As their boat roared under the bridge, Kim saw two men rise from behind a sand dune. She recognized them instantly.

"That's Rusty and Jimmy!"

Marty slowed the boat and pointed past the trailer. "And there's Deuce and Tony!"

A large cluster of people stood between the two groups of their friends as the loader approached from a third direction.

Kim recognized her father on the side of the loader, a rifle slung over his shoulder.

"What the hell's he doing?" Marty asked. "He's not with Homeland Security anymore."

CHAPTER THIRTY-ONE

It was all over in seconds, with no bloodshed. The Blancs knew it; they were caught flatfooted in the open and had no hope of escape. Or they just figured Senator Jubal Blanc would fix everything for them.

With high-powered rifles pointed at them from three different directions, their vehicles disabled, and most of them armed only with handguns, the older woman told everyone to stand down.

Using the CB, I ordered them to put all the guns in the back of the GMC. When they complied, I had Ben fire up the loader. While the others advanced on foot and surrounded the group, we drove across the rutted field.

A boat with blue lights flashing and a blaring siren rushed under the bridge and turned toward where Rusty and Jimmy had hunkered down.

Before we got to the knot of Blancs in front of the trailer, I recognized Kim and Marty in the boat.

"What the hell are you doing, Dad?" Kim demanded, as she strode toward where we held sixteen people at gunpoint. "You're not a federal agent anymore."

"I think you'll want to hear what Dan and Ben have to say, kiddo."

"There's no time for that," Kim said. "The FBI will be here any minute. You can't just go around shooting up people's cars and threatening them."

"He puts down that gun," Willy growled, "and he won't be no threat at all."

Marty held his service revolver on the big man. "He's far more dangerous than you'll ever know, if you're lucky. Now stand there and shut up."

Willy glared at him but said nothing. Billy nudged Kim and cocked his head toward the trailer. The three of us went inside.

"You can't be here when the FBI arrives," Kim said. "Billy, you, of all people, should know better than this."

"We don't have to be," Billy said. "You're here now. We can disappear."

"They could turn onto the causeway any second," Kim said. "That's the only road in or out. You'll have to—"

"Who says we need a road?" Billy suggested with a grin.

Kim thought about it a moment. "Okay. But help us detain everyone first."

In minutes, we'd frisked everyone, found two more guns, a dozen knives, a pair of brass knuckles and a machete. We used flex cuffs that Marty brought up from the boat and had the whole group sitting on the dry, crumbling dirt. Then we put all their weapons in Marty and Kim's boat.

"Go," Kim said. "I don't know how or where but get out of here."

"Follow me," Billy said. "And try to keep up."

With that, the six of us piled into Billy's two off-roaders and he led the way through the dry mud to the northwest side of the island. The going was still sloppy—only the surface of the mud was dry—but the trucks were more than up to the task.

Billy drove right off the island into a shallow tidal creek and followed it for a hundred yards. The wide tires had no trouble in the sandy creek bed. I followed, trying not to give the truck too much gas. The GMC had real all-wheel drive and, judging by the movement of Deuce's truck, his did too.

The big trucks pushed a dam of water in front of them like a barge. The water wasn't deep, but it provided a lot of resistance and spinning the tires in the sandy bottom would sink us.

When he came to another creek, joining the one we were in from the north, Billy turned up it. Tree branches scraped along the roof and sides of the big Ford. This creek appeared to also have a firm sand bottom. Billy told us these trucks weren't made so much for off-road, but deep water. Farther upstream, I knew this creek's bottom would be covered in muck and sawgrass. But I trusted that Billy knew where he was going.

Ten minutes later, a dirt road ran through the narrow creek and Billy turned right, scrambling up the bank and through the brush, as if the truck didn't weigh four tons.

The double ruts of the seldom-used trail led to a better dirt road. Billy turned left and I followed. In minutes, we were on the blacktop and headed south, toward Marco Island.

Billy slowed as we neared the turn onto Turtle Island. Parked behind the Blancs' trucks we could see two gray sedans and a big van with the FBI logo stenciled on the side.

We crossed the bridge onto Marco Island and made our way back to Billy's girlfriend's house.

"I called Kim," David explained when we got back to the house. "I thought you guys needed help."

"It was good that you did," I told him. "We would have been surprised by the Feds and that would have taken a lot of explaining."

"Actually, she said they were already on their way there," David said. "An FBI agent was supposed to meet her there."

"Let's go home," I said. "Hopefully, this is finished."

David stayed in his seat. He closed the laptop and looked up at me.

"That's not all," he said, unplugging the computer. "I also called Chyrel. But by then, everything was about over."

"No harm there," I offered.

"She sent me a message just before you got back, saying that someone named Stockwell had given her a message for you." He picked up a notepad. "I wrote it down word for word. 'Stockwell said that Armstrong wants to see you Saturday. Bring Savannah and David.'"

I looked over at Deuce. He only shrugged.

"What's it mean? Who's Armstrong?"

I mimicked Deuce's shrug, looking down at the rising warrior of the cyber world. "Don't know. But I think you and I are flying to Bimini Saturday morning."

He gazed at me for a moment, maybe trying to figure out if I was pulling his leg. Then he, too, shrugged and continued straightening the table, putting it back the way it was before we arrived.

I turned toward Billy. "Thanks for the assist," I said, extending my hand.

Billy's went past mine and we gripped each other's forearm. "You always deliver an adventure, Kemosabe."

Ten minutes later, we threw off the lines and motored down Big Marco toward the open Gulf. Just as I reached for the throttle, my phone rang. It was Kim. I glanced over at Jimmy, Rusty, and Deuce, then put her on speaker.

"What's up?" I asked.

"Yes, sir," she said. "We're about to wrap up here."

"Kim, it's Dad. Did you mean to call your boss?"

"No, sir. Special Agent William Binkowski is taking over the investigation."

Binkowski? He'd once been an advisor to Deuce's Homeland Security team. I assumed he'd retired by now.

"Put him on," Deuce said.

"Dad?" she whispered.

"It's okay, kiddo, we go back a long way with Bill."

CHAPTER THIRTY-TWO

O ver the course of the next few days, forensics teams worked day and night, along with anthropologists from University of Florida. They scoured every inch of Turtle Island, working in teams all through the hot and humid nights and the blistering hot days.

I brought the Woodbury brothers to my island and Savannah and I told them we'd invest in their development if they adhered to a few of our rules. Once the temporary power pole was no longer needed, and the construction trailer moved off the island, no utilities would be run to it. That puzzled them until I told them the next stipulation. Each home had to be single story, built hurricane proof on stilts like mine, and each on at least one acre, completely off the grid and self-sustainable. One look around my island and they agreed.

They'd already turned over the money Willy Quick had given them, and I wrote a company check on the spot; more than enough to refund all previous investors and finish the project.

With up to three or four feet of new topsoil in some places, the attempt of the brothers to hide evidence using a tiller had been fruitless. Oh, what they'd done would probably have prevented anyone from digging up a bone in their yard, and if they did, it would just be a tiny fragment. But anything deeper than what the eighteen-inch tines of the tiller could reach was left untouched.

Devoid of everything, they brought in a large machine that sifted through the imported dirt a full loader-scoop at a time. The searchers did find bone fragments and bits of clothing in the estimated 30,000 tons of soil that was meticulously sifted for the tiniest clue. But that was only the beginning.

With the imported topsoil relocated, they began to find remnants of the old trailer park—long discarded tools, wire, pipe, aluminum siding, even abandoned kids' toys.

Doc Angelo called on Saturday, while we were in Bimini, to let us know the manatee calf was fine and reunited with her mother.

While showing Savannah around *Ambrosia's* bridge, I asked Jack about Nils Hansen, the captain.

"He's retiring soon," Jack said. "He's gone home for a few weeks, while we're here in Bimini."

"When does he plan to retire?" Savannah asked.

"In one year," Jack said. Then he turned to me. "Will you be ready then?"

I hadn't even talked to Savannah about Jack's plans. Now they seemed a bit inconsequential. I wanted to command this beautiful ship, but I wanted to be with Savannah more.

She looked up at me, puzzled. "Ready for what?"

"Let's get married," I blurted out.

"What?" she exclaimed.

Jack turned, covering his grin, and walked away.

"Let's just do it," I said. "We've talked all around it."

"Well, okay, sure," she replied. "That wasn't the most romantic proposal, but I'll take it. Now, what was Jack talking about you being ready for?"

"Ahem," Jack grunted, returning. "I apologize. I assumed Jesse had already told you. He's going to be *Ambrosia's* new captain."

Savannah looked back up at me and I grinned, looking into her eyes. "Sorry, Jack. Looks like I'm going to be domesticated."

"Oh, no, you're not, buster!" Savannah scolded. "Imagine the adventures we could go on."

When we returned on Sunday, four days after the Blanc clan was arrested, the forensics teams found the graves.

Not as many as the number of women who went missing during the killer's fifteen-year spree, leaving behind the tell-tale flat tire calling card. But they did uncover twenty-two graves and were working to identify the victims.

FBI agents and forensics teams, under the watchful eye of retiring Special Agent in Charge, William Binkowski, dug through the old case files. They estimated that during the time period of 1953 to 1968, the years between Curtis Roy Blanc's discharge from the army and his disappearance and presumptive death, forty-seven women had been reported missing across south Florida after having a flat tire.

Binkowski did retire after the team broke up. I learned from Deuce that even after he retired, he was allowed access to a lab in the federal building in Miami. He'd spent the last several years digging through cold case files every Wednesday, sometimes late into the night, trying to bring closure to cases with few people left alive who needed it.

That was why he happened to be in the building when Dan Woodbury showed up, talking about sixty-year-old murders.

Bill called me on the day they found the graves and asked me to come back up to Goodland. He wouldn't explain why, but he had something to talk to me in person about.

The little island looked a lot different when Savannah and I arrived in The Beast, my 1973 International Travelall. At the far end, piled as big as a four-story condo, was all the soil the Woodbury brothers had brought in from the dredging of Lake Okeechobee.

Otherwise, the island was bare sand, parched by the sun, returned to its original landscape, minus the trees and brush. Most of the activity was out on the southern shoreline, near the west end of the island. Orange cones marked where it was okay to drive and I followed them to where the people were working.

Bill got out of his car when I parked The Beast beside him.

"Bill, this is my fiancée, Savannah," I said. "Savannah, this is very Special Agent-In-Charge Bill Binkowski. He used to work with Deuce's team."

They shook hands and Bill looked up at me, a gleam in his eyes. "Fiancée, huh?"

Savannah smiled. "About time he settled down, wouldn't you say?"

"Yes," Bill agreed with a chuckle. "You're from the Carolinas, right?"

"Born and raised in—"

"No, no. Don't tell me," he said. I'm good at this. As we talk more, I'll tell you exactly where you lived most of your life."

I looked over toward where the front of Bill's car was pointing. He was parked so he could watch everything that was brought out of the burial site. I knew that was what it was, by the demeanor of the people working in the hole.

"So, why'd you want to see me, Bill?" I asked, turning back to the silver-haired sleuth.

"Since Deuce's team broke up, I've been mostly retired," he began. "Truth is, I should have retired a long time ago. Did you know that I'm seventy years old today?"

"No, I didn't," I replied. "Happy birthday."

"Why in the world are you working on your birthday?" Savannah asked.

He winked at her. "The Lowcountry, right? Don't tell me, I'll get it."

"You have a good ear," Savannah said. "Did you study linguistics or is this just a hobby?"

Bill snapped his fingers. "Of course! You're from the home of one of my favorite writers, Pat Conroy. Beaufort, South Carolina. Where The Water is Wide."

She smiled warmly at the old FBI guy. "A very good ear. But which street?"

He laughed, then turned to me. "This is why I never completely retired, Jesse." He waved an arm at what was going on. "This case is what's kept me on the job for nearly forty years."

He opened the door of his car and reached inside. "Take a look at this," he said, handing me a file folder.

After opening the file, I thumbed through the pages and photographs, all old and yellowed. Savannah looked over my shoulder. One photo caught my eye. A picture of a late-40s model sedan with a flat tire.

I went back to the first page in the file, which was a missing person's report that was dated August 31, 1954, exactly sixty-six years ago. The name of the missing person was Emily Binkowski.

I looked at Bill, realizing what it meant.

Savannah's breath caught in her throat.

"Mom just went out to get more ice cream," Bill said flatly, as if he'd recited it a million times. "The store was just a few miles away. She said she'd only be gone a few minutes. My folks had thrown me a big birthday party and we'd run out."

He looked out over the dig. "That was the last time I saw my mother, Jesse. On my fourth birthday, sixty-six years ago, today."

"SAC Binkowski!" someone called from the area of the dig. We all looked toward a young black woman, motioning Bill over. "We've got something."

The three of us started forward, but Bill stopped and turned to Savannah. "Maybe it would be better if you waited here."

Just two days ago, I'd flown David and Savannah over to Bimini to meet with Jack Armstrong. He'd offered David a job once he graduated. During the coming three years, he'd be tutored by Chyrel Koshinski, herself. Jack praised his coolness when handling communications for us down in Belize. He'd also asked Savannah to become a more integral part of our team now that we were to be married. He said he'd based his decision on input from Charity. I learned more about Savannah in that hour-long meeting than I might have been ready for. She and David had both accepted.

347

"It's okay," she said, taking my hand for support, and looking up into my eyes. "It's part of the job description, right?"

We proceeded to where the woman was climbing out of the hole. Below, there were several skeletons lying on the bottom, all turned in different directions and lying in different positions. Workers were carefully removing everything from around them, sifting it through a metal screen.

The woman headed over to a table and we followed her. There, she placed something on the table and carefully began to clean it with a soft brush.

"This was on the fourth body we uncovered," the woman said. The name tag on the front of her white, one-piece jumpsuit identified her as an FBI intern named Deniqua Shaw. "We think she was one of the first victims, because another body was buried over her."

She scraped and used a can of compressed air to blow away decades of dirt and grime, until finally a piece of jewelry began to emerge. Little by little, more detail was revealed as she worked on it.

"It looks like a woman's brooch," she said, blasting away dirt with the air can.

Bill reached into his pocket and pulled out a worn leather wallet. He opened it and thumbed through several photos, each in individual plastic sleeves. I recognized his wife and kids in a couple. Then he flipped to a faded black and white shot of a young, blond-haired woman. He paused a moment, looking at it. She was beautiful in a simple, short-sleeved dress, cinched tight at the waist. On her lapel, she wore a brooch.

Bill pulled the picture out and placed it on the table, next to where the young woman was working. She stopped and picked it up. Then, opening a drawer, she removed a large magnifying glass and looked closer at the picture. She let out a small gasp and turned to look at Bill.

"Who is she?" Deniqua asked softly.

As Bill turned and walked toward the pit, I saw a tear streaming down his cheek.

Deniqua started to go after him, but Savannah touched her arm. "Give him a minute, sweetie. You just found his mama."

THE END

AFTERWORD

The story you just read was based on actual events. The Flat Tire murders happened in Dade County, Florida, in 1975. Five unsolved murders were linked by a common thread—the victims' cars were all found with a flat tire. I fictionalized what happened and moved the events deep into the Everglades and the Ten Thousand Islands area of the wild Southwest Florida coast. I also changed the timeline of the murders, to span fifteen years from 1953 to 1968.

My beta readers tore through the final draft in less than a week, adding a lot of insight about the area and helping me to fix some plot errors. Without these close friends and fans of the series, this story wouldn't have been nearly as good. Thanks Dana Vilhen, Katy McKnight, Jason Hebert, John Trainer, Tom Crisp, Mike Ramsey, Debbie Kocol, Rick Iossi, Glenn Hibbert, Charles Höfbauer, David Parsons, Drew Mutch, Deg Priest, and Alan Fader.

As I write this afterword, this book is just three weeks from being released on August 31. I finished writing it on July 3. During that nearly two month period, a lot of people have had a hand in making this book not just easy to read but presented in an attractive package.

After my beta team, the manuscript went to Marsha Zinberg with The Write Touch editing service. She spent two weeks, combing through every word, sentence, paragraph, and chapter. But she didn't edit this afterword, so any mistakes here are all on me. As always, the rewrite took another week, and I learned a little more about how to actually be a professional writer. Y'all know I lay no claim to that title, hence the week to go over all the corrections and changes.

Then it went to my final proofreader, Donna Rich. Donna has had the last critical eye on all my books since the beginning.

After another rewrite, the manuscript moves on to my audiobook narrator, Nick Sullivan. He always finds a handful of mistakes the others either missed, or more likely, I committed during the rewrites.

From there, the manuscript goes into the hands of interior formatter Colleen Sheehan with Ampersand Book Interiors. She transforms the manuscript into a book that is easy to read.

The final touch comes from cover designer Shayne Rutherford, who makes the outside of the book look every bit as good as what's on the inside.

I would be remiss if I didn't thank my biggest supporters, my wife Greta, our kids, and our grandkids. Without their love, guidance, and support, well, let's see...it's Monday morning as I write this, so I would most likely be leaving the Michelin Tire plant in Lexington, SC, headed for somewhere in the Rocky Mountains with an oversized load of mine truck tires. Thank you all.

Don't miss the next exciting Jesse McDermitt novel, Rising Moon, to be released on December 31. 2020.
https://www.amazon.com/dp/B08FYWL3L4/

If you'd like to receive my newsletter,
please sign up on my website:

WWW.WAYNESTINNETT.COM.

Every two weeks, I'll bring you insights into my private life and writing habits, with updates on what I'm working on, special deals I hear about, and new books by other authors that I'm reading.

The Charity Styles Caribbean Thriller Series

Merciless Charity
Ruthless Charity
Reckless Charity
Enduring Charity
Vigilant Charity

The Jesse McDermitt Caribbean Adventure Series

Fallen Out	*Fallen Hero*
Fallen Palm	*Rising Storm*
Fallen Hunter	*Rising Fury*
Fallen Pride	*Rising Force*
Fallen Mangrove	*Rising Charity*
Fallen King	*Rising Water*
Fallen Honor	*Rising Spirit*
Fallen Tide	*Rising Thunder*
Fallen Angel	*Rising Moon*

THE GASPAR'S REVENGE SHIP'S STORE IS OPEN.

There, you can purchase all kinds of swag related to my books. You can find it at

WWW.GASPARS-REVENGE.COM

Made in the USA
Middletown, DE
24 June 2023

33376548R00203